SEX, LIES,
AND
SNICKERDOODLES

Also by Wendy Delaney

The Working Stiffs Mystery Series

Trudy, Madly, Deeply
Sex, Lies, and Snickerdoodles
There's Something About Marty
You Can't Go Gnome Again
Dogs, Lies, and Alibis
No Wedding For Old Men
Crazy, Stupid, Dead

SEX, LIES, AND SNICKERDOODLES

A WORKING STIFFS MYSTERY

BOOK 2

Wendy Delaney

Sugarbaker Press

Sugarbaker Press
PO Box 3271
Redmond, WA 98073-3271

This is a work of fiction. Names, characters, places, and incidents are a product of the author's imagination. Locales and public names are sometimes used for atmospheric purposes. Any resemblance to actual people, living or dead, or to businesses, companies, events, institutions, or locales is completely coincidental.

Cover by Lewellen Designs

Printed in the United States of America

Sex, Lies, and Snickerdoodles/Wendy Delaney
2nd edition, April 2016

ISBN: 978-0-9969800-3-6

For the other Wendy.
Thanks for the pleasure of your
company on this journey.

Acknowledgments

The expression about it taking a village is certainly true when I think about the path that *Sex, Lies, and Snickerdoodles* took on its road to publication.

First, I must thank the two subject matter experts who supplied this mystery writer essential information so that my story people didn't make unintended blunders: Thank you, Funeral Director Real Robles for sharing your time and expertise to help me get the details right. And huge thanks go to "K." I'm so grateful to have you as my "top cop" advisor for this series.

To Ann Charles, thanks for being there to play the "what if" game with me.

To my husband Jeff, thanks for serving as my "guy stuff" advisor and for understanding why dinner was late, again.

Finally, a boatload of thanks go out to my beta-readers and critiquers: Ann Charles, Jacquie Rogers, Diane Garland, Jody Sherin, Deb Tysick-Hawrylyshyn, Bob Dickerson, Amber Jacobsma, Denise Keef, Wayne Roberts, Brandy Lanfair, Denise Fluhr, Dixie Daniel, Cindy Nelson, Susan Cambra, Barb Harlan, Beth Rosin, Lori Dubiel, Toni Mortensen, Vicki Huskey, Jim Vavra, Betsy Helgesen, and Karen Haverkate. I'm so grateful for your gracious support and invaluable feedback.

Chapter One

I could use one hand to count the number of guys who had seen me naked. For better or worse, that included the cop aiming the Clint Eastwood squint at me from the picnic table at Hot Shots Espresso, a block from the Port Merritt waterfront.

"You're late," Detective Steve Sixkiller said in a clipped tone as I approached.

Our breakfast date wasn't getting off to a good start. "Somehow you seemed happier to see me last night."

"You were naked under a raincoat."

With the mid-morning sun beaming at our backs, I sat on the bench seat next to him and claimed the tall mocha latte he offered me. "Well, there was that."

At least I had known exactly what to wear for a fun Friday evening in with my new sex buddy. I didn't have a clue what to wear to breakfast and had changed my clothes three times because it looked like I was trying too hard to impress one of my oldest friends on our first official date.

This dating stuff had seemed easier back when I was in my twenties and had yet to eat my way through a divorce. The eighteen pounds I'd packed on in the last year caused the girls to strain against the buttons of the linen camp shirt that I finally settled upon. Not that Steve would mind the peepshow if my top button were to launch itself into orbit as long as I didn't take out one of his eyes in the process.

He leaned into me. "Never thought I'd see you do that."

That made two of us. "It was sort of a mood of the moment thing." Something that I'd always wanted to do with my ex and had never worked up the nerve.

He leveled his chocolate brown gaze at me. "You'll have to get into that mood again."

My stomach growled, reminding me of the task at hand for this morning—a normal date, something I had yet to experience with Steve. "Breakfast first."

"Party pooper."

Pushing away from the picnic table, he took my hand and we ambled toward his Ford pickup parked at the corner.

"You know, we could have had breakfast at my place." His chiseled lips curled into an easy smile. "I would have brought it to you in bed…if you'd stayed."

My self-esteem had only recently crawled out of the hole it had been hiding in since my ex won a top chef competition and promptly carved me out of his life. Was I ready for Steve to roll over and see me up close and personal first thing in the morning? And then after breakfast nonchalantly stroll across the street to my grandmother's house in my raincoat and face her parental gaze as I opened the door? Not a chance.

Do you fully understand what you're doing?

Gram had every right to ask the question, especially since I was the one who had spent almost twenty years insisting that Steve and I were just good friends.

As long as Steve and I were strictly *friends with benefits*, the answer to that question was yes.

Or old friends meeting up on a gloriously bright Saturday morning for breakfast—still a yes.

Childhood chums out in public with the intention of spending a lazy summer day together, who would end up in his king-sized bed doing things I'd only dreamed of before? Nope, that was where understanding and I parted ways—pretty much the land where I'd been living ever since the object of my first schoolgirl crush tilted my world by crossing over the friendship line and kissing me senseless two weeks ago.

To avoid raising eyebrows, I had suggested we have breakfast in Port Townsend, a laid-back, artsy community located a convenient thirty-two miles north of the local gossip circuit.

I pushed back the locks of hair that a crisp breeze off Merritt Bay blew into my face. So much for spending a few extra minutes to tame my overgrown brown mop. "I've seen what passes for breakfast at your house. Sorry, I'm not tempted by your poopy peanut butter and spirulina smoothie."

Since this former pastry chef had baked him his favorite bacon and cheese-stuffed croissants last weekend, I didn't think that was half-bad as an evasive answer until Steve shot me a lopsided grin. "Maybe I could tempt you with something else."

Were we still talking about breakfast?

He slipped his arm around my shoulder. "I may not have the culinary school credentials that you do, but I *can* cook, you know."

"I'm sure you do a lot of things well."

Steve stopped next to his sterling gray F150 and looked down at me, his lips so close I could almost taste his coffee. "Charmaine Digby, you have no idea how right you are."

Yes, I did. I was also well aware of Kelsey Donovan emerging from her gift shop on the opposite corner with a cell phone to her ear. And Gloria, the County Clerk who worked downstairs from me at the courthouse, staring at us as she rounded the corner in her Volkswagen Beetle.

Pasting a smile on my face, I raised my cup to Gloria. *Nothing to mention to any of my coworkers in the Prosecutor's office. Just two friends getting coffee. Move along.*

When Gloria disappeared from view I shifted my attention to Kelsey, my lab partner in Mr. Ferris's biology class eighteen years ago. But maybe I didn't need to be concerned about her speed-dialing our mutual friends because Kelsey seemed oblivious to Steve and me as she stared down the length of Bay Street.

"Russell, I'm going to kill you if you don't show up!" she yelled into the phone.

I wasn't aware of Kelsey dating anyone named Russell, but that meant nothing since I was standing next to a guy she didn't know I hadn't been officially dating.

At least I had been standing next to him before Steve

set his cup on the hood of his pickup and jaywalked across the street.

"How're you doing, Kelsey?" he asked in an easy manner as I scampered behind him. It was the same easy manner I'd witnessed in Detective Sixkiller countless times in the three months since I moved back to Port Merritt, Washington. Combine it with the winning smile of a charmer and I'd bet there wasn't a female in my hometown of five thousand and fifty-three residents who wouldn't welcome the former high school football captain into her home with open arms.

Kelsey pursed her mouth. "I'd be doing better if certain men would do what they said they were going to do, when they said they were going to do it!"

Russell was in deep doo-doo.

Kelsey stabbed her sterling silver-adorned index finger in the direction of a colorful sign on the display window of her shop, the Feathered Nest. "Do you see where it says to come and meet local artist, Lance Greenwood, September 7th? As in tonight?"

I sure did. Nice sign. No doubt Kelsey had spent more than a few bucks to have it printed.

"Russell Falco was supposed to be here over an hour ago to install track lighting in the back room and help me set up." She dramatically tossed her head back, her dark blue eyes blinking back tears. "How could he be a no-show when he knew how important tonight was to me?"

According to Lucille, the senior gossip wrangler waitressing at Duke's Cafe, my great-uncle's greasy spoon, Russell Falco had no shortage of ladies vying for his attention. Now that I knew we were talking about *that* Russell, it wouldn't have surprised me if he'd received a more enticing offer.

The summer I was fifteen and filling in as a short-order cook at Duke's, Russell came in after working on his dad's charter boat with his brothers. He was twenty-three, a raven-haired hunk and a half, and a shameless flirt. Despite the fact that we rarely saw him sober, all the waitresses were crazy about him.

"He's trouble with a capital T," Uncle Duke had proclaimed after Russell got his nose broken for sniffing around the wrong woman. Shortly after that, he dropped out of sight. Lucille had said that he fell in with a motorcycle gang and served some prison time in California.

For Russell's and Kelsey's sakes, I hoped that history wasn't repeating itself.

"Do you already have the light fixtures that need to be installed?" Steve asked her.

Kelsey nodded, her fine butterscotch-blond hair spilling over her shoulders. "Everything's inside the shop. The lights, all the hardware, Lance's paintings. Last night, we emptied out the back room to set everything up like a real gallery. All I need now are Russell and his tools."

Given Russell's bad boy reputation and the tension bleeding through Kelsey's brittle smile, I sensed that wasn't the full extent of what she needed from him.

"Russell isn't the only guy around here with tools." Steve turned to me. "Looks like I'm going to owe you brunch instead of breakfast."

Fine with me because either way some crispy bacon

would be in my future. "And you just got a helper to ensure that you make good on that debt."

Two hours later, the Feathered Nest's new track lighting had been installed, and Steve and I were hanging the last of the garish oil paintings Kelsey kept raving about when she wasn't tending to a customer.

I tilted my head at a landscape with red and orange streaks invading muddy violet globs of paint that looked like chocolate raspberry mousse blended with Steve's poopy smoothie. "What do you think this is supposed to be?" I reached for the artist's business card listing the name of the painting as *Olympic Sunset* and sucked in a breath when I read the fifteen hundred dollar asking price.

Steve slid his hammer onto his tool belt. "I call it over-priced crap."

I shushed him but couldn't help but admire the way the tool belt hung low on his hips like a gunslinger's holster. All Steve needed was the black cowboy hat to accompany the steely-eyed glare he was directing toward Lance Greenwood's handiwork.

"Don't you just love what he does with color?" Kelsey gushed from the doorway.

"Yeah," Steve muttered unenthusiastically while I tacked the business card eye level with the artist's Dante's *Inferno* interpretation of the sun setting behind Washington's Olympic mountain range.

She stepped between us and started folding the brown paper wrapper that had covered *Olympic Sunset* a few minutes earlier. "Okay, so it's not your cup of tea, but I'll have you know that he's an up and coming artist, known throughout North America. It's quite an honor to host tonight's event for him."

If the guy was such a big deal in the art world, it was curious that he had agreed to show his work in the tight confines of the Feathered Nest instead of one of the galleries in Port Townsend.

My grandmother had already announced that she wanted to attend tonight's soiree, which translated into me accompanying her as her date for the evening. Personally, I suspected she wanted to see what all the fuss surrounding Lance Greenwood was about. From the gloppy examples of the man's talent hanging on Kelsey's walls, I wondered the same thing.

"I'm sure it is," I said. Clearly, with the way Kelsey was beaming, a prouder hostess couldn't be found.

"It looks like you're about ready for showtime." Steve unhooked his tool belt as he inched toward the door. "And I owe someone breakfast while they're still serving, so Char and I should get going."

Since my stomach had been growling for the last hour, he got no argument from me.

Steve's cell phone rang and he stopped and pulled it from his pocket. "Hey, Captain." His gaze sharpened, then he turned his back to me.

Steve had kidded me about being a human lie detector ever since I participated in a university study as a favor to my former sister-in-law, the clinical psychologist. Even before my perceptive abilities had been documented, he'd made a point of sheltering his face when he didn't want me to read his body language. But since the Port Merritt PD captain was calling his one and only detective on his day off, anyone in the room should have been able to see that something very bad had happened.

"Tell him not to touch anything," he said. "I'll be there in ten."

"What's happened?" I asked the second Steve ended the call, my voice a squeaky blend of breath and apprehension.

He pocketed his cell phone. "Russell Falco has been found."

Chapter Two

It was almost one o'clock when I walked to the end of Dock A at the Port Merritt marina, where a Chimacam County Sheriff's deputy had towed Russell's twin engine fishing boat, a mostly unvarnished wooden hulk named the *Lucky Charm*. Like Russell Falco, whose body had been discovered on a nearby stretch of rocky shoreline, whatever luck the *Lucky Charm* had once possessed had definitely run out.

Since I could honestly say that I had come to the marina on official business as a Special Assistant to the Chimacam County Prosecutor/Coroner, I ducked under the yellow caution tape stretched between two pilings.

Steve glared down at me from the *Lucky Charm*'s stern while a squawking seagull perched on the dock railing sounded no happier about my arrival. "Do I need to remind you what *Do not cross* means?"

I held up a grease-stained Duke's Cafe takeout bag containing a double beef cheeseburger and a side of fries. "I come bearing gifts and news, so you should really be nicer to me."

Steve pointed at the tape. "Stay on the other side. I

don't need anyone suggesting that we contaminated the scene."

Since he was the one wearing latex gloves and blue cotton booties, and my job was typically restricted to interviewing witnesses and delivering subpoenas, I didn't have to guess that *we* meant me—the one who had yet to make it through her thirty-day probation period.

"What do you think?" I asked the one-man CSI team when he stepped onto the pier, the seagull falling silent as if I wasn't the only one interested in Steve's answer.

He snapped off the gloves and dropped them and the cotton booties into the plastic kit slung over his shoulder. "That boat needs a lot of work."

Tell me something I didn't know. "Besides that. Did you find anything?"

Steve bent his six-foot frame under the caution tape. "Not much other than a toolbox, a bag of nails, and some dirty clothes. It looks like he might have picked up some work in addition to helping out at Kelsey's."

"Doesn't that seem a little strange to you?" Finding a toolbox in the back of Russell's beater pickup truck would have made more sense, especially since Kelsey had been expecting him at her shop.

"There's lots of water around here, Chow Mein. And lots of docks in need of repair."

I couldn't help but smile at the nickname he gave me back in the third grade. "I guess." Considering the reason the boat had to be towed to the marina, the handyman equipment still seemed strange.

Steve's attention zeroed in on the bag in my hand. "Is that for me?"

"All yours." With the exception of the few french fries that I'd stolen back in the car.

"Good, I'm starved."

We sat on a concrete bench centered in the patch of grass between Dock B and the parking lot, and I watched him attack the bag.

"I ran into Ben at Duke's." More like I followed Criminal Prosecutor Ben Santiago into the diner, but since I happened to know that he was the deputy coroner on call this weekend, I figured he'd be the one with the most up-to-date information on Russell. I could also count on getting a grilled cheese sandwich compliments of my great-uncle while I was there.

"Yeah?" Steve said with his mouth full. "And?"

"He said it didn't look like Russell had been in the water for very long before he washed up on shore." I left out the part about his flesh not suffering any apparent fish or animal bites since Steve was chowing down on his burger. "Ben wants me to get a statement from Fred Wixey."

"I already talked to Fred. He was walking his dog, saw the body, called it in. Not much else there."

I shrugged. "We need a statement for the coroner's report."

"*We?*"

I was pretty much the low man on the totem pole at the courthouse, where I worked for Prosecutor Frankie Rickard, who also served as the Coroner of Chimacam County. Dairy cows and chickens easily outnumbered the registered voters, who had recently reelected her to a third term, but I was still one of Frankie's badge-carrying deputies and that gave me the right to say *we*.

"Yes, *we*, smart ass. And Ben asked me to call Dr. Zuniga to schedule an autopsy."

Chimacam County operated on a shoestring budget, so it contracted with Dr. Henry Zuniga, a semi-retired forensic pathologist from Seattle, an hour away by ferry.

Steve swallowed. "That's your big news?"

Not entirely. "The autopsy's scheduled for Tuesday."

"You realize it's routine, don't you?"

Uh, no.

It was just the second time that I'd spoken to Dr. Zuniga about an autopsy in my four weeks of working for the county. I might be deputized to interview witnesses and offer my opinion as a deception detection specialist, do background checks, and place calls to forensic pathologists on behalf of the Coroner, but absolutely nothing about an autopsy seemed routine to this former pastry chef.

I sat ramrod straight as I nibbled on a lukewarm french fry. "Of course. I just thought you'd like to know."

He gave me an amused look. "Nice try, rookie."

After Steve finished the last of the fries, he handed me the grease-stained paper sack. "Thanks for lunch," he said, shielding his eyes from the sun as he tracked a fishing boat motoring toward the marina.

"Stay here." He punched some numbers on his cell phone and started walking down the pier.

Two minutes later, I watched Nathan, the youngest of the three Falco brothers, hop over the side railing of the charter boat and tie up to the dock, four rows over from the *Lucky Charm*.

My most vivid memories of the boy who had been two years ahead of me in high school were of him coming into Duke's every Saturday morning to load up on coffee and pastries for their customers when his dad ran the charter business. With Nathan's dark tousled hair and athletic build, he resembled Russell more than the shorter, stockier Andy.

I couldn't hear what the men were saying over the engine noise, so I moved to a plastic lawn chair across from the adjacent slip and caught Nathan's stony-faced glare when Steve hooked a line over a dock cleat.

"We don't need your help," Nathan grumbled as Andy killed the engine.

"Shut up, Nate," Andy said, climbing down from the forty-foot fishing boat's flying bridge.

I didn't need to be able to read their body language to sense the tension rippling like heat waves between the brothers.

After saying their goodbyes to Nathan and Andy, the three middle-aged charter boat customers took turns stepping over the boat railing and onto the dock. The eldest of the three smiled at me as he passed.

"Nice catch," I said, pointing to the plastic bag of silver salmon on ice swinging from his hand.

He grinned at his plastic-wrapped trophy. "Took me all flippin' morning, but I finally caught this bad boy."

I knew that Steve had called Andy almost three hours ago. Since most of the local charter boats trolled the fishing lanes off the south point of Harstone Island—no more than fifteen miles away from the marina—it appeared that Andy and Nathan cared more about guaranteeing their customers' fish stories than their older brother.

I forced a smile at the guy's hollow victory. He was obviously clueless about Russell. "Congratulations."

Steve heard me and shot me a warning glance.

So I wasn't a very good sit and stay girl. He'd known that about me for twenty-six years. However, the second I saw Andy lock his amber eyes on Steve like a nuclear warhead set to launch, I knew to keep quiet with my eyes and ears open.

Andy slowly climbed over the boat railing, his mouth a grim slit surrounded by dark stubble. Pulling at the brim of his red Falco Charters ball cap, shadow cut through his grizzled cheeks. "Where is he?"

"Tolliver's," Steve said.

Tolliver's Funeral Home was the last stop in town for most of Port Merritt's dearly departed. Since the county didn't have money in the budget for a morgue, it was also where Dr. Zuniga would be gutting Russell like that tourist's salmon.

Cursing, Nathan lit a cigarette with a shaky hand.

Ignoring his younger brother, Andy scanned the marina, his gaze landing on the *Lucky Charm*, tied up at the far dock. "Sheriff tow it in around seven?"

Steve nodded. "Yeah."

"Saw it when we were heading out. Thought that was his boat."

"You didn't want to stop and ask why it was being towed in?"

Andy shook his head. "I had customers who paid me to go fishing, not hear about another screw-up of Russ's."

Steve lowered his voice and I couldn't make out what he said. Seconds later, the two Falco brothers boarded their boat.

Thumbing in the direction of the parking lot, Steve closed the distance between us. "Andy wants to see Russell."

Understandable. Sometimes that was part of the grieving process, an opportunity to say goodbye. Or in this case, maybe yell one last time at his brother.

I tried to keep pace with Steve's long strides as we passed by the bench where he ate his lunch.

"They're going to gather up their gear, then I'm meeting them at Tolliver's," he said, surveying the parking lot. "Don't know how long this will take."

The implication couldn't be more clear. Time for me to go.

I had to collect a statement from Fred Wixey so it wasn't like I didn't also have places to go, people to see, but it felt like I was being dismissed.

Steve turned to me when we reached my car. "Maybe I'll see you later."

"If you're lucky."

That earned me a lopsided smile which disappeared the instant that a blue and white Port Merritt Police car pulled up next to his pickup.

"Don't let anyone near Russell's boat," Steve said to Howie Fontaine, a fresh-faced, uniformed officer who barely looked old enough to drive. "I'll be back in an hour."

Howie promptly took his post in front of the caution tape, and Steve pulled out onto Main Street, leaving me alone in the marina parking lot.

As first dates go, this wasn't my best. But I didn't have time to overthink my relationship with Steve. I needed to see a man about a dead body.

Chapter Three

Standing on Fred Wixey's front porch, I read the three laminated signs above the doorbell:

NO SOLICITORS

BEWARE OF DOG

TRESPASSERS WILL BE SHOT ~ SURVIVORS WILL BE SHOT AGAIN

Since I'd known Mr. Wixey for most of my life and I was at his doorstep on official coroner business, I wasn't too worried about the first two signs. The third one made me wish that I had called to let him know I was coming, especially since Barney, a hyperactive fox terrier, was sounding the intruder alert.

The door swung open and Mr. Wixey peered out at me while Barney's toenails clacked on the wooden porch as he danced around me, sniffing my leather sandals.

"Barney, inside." The diminutive Mr. Wixey smiled apologetically, revealing a missing canine tooth, while the fox terrier patrolled the tiny entryway like a furry centurion. "You'd better come inside, too, or he'll never settle down."

On the warmth meter, Fred Wixey's welcome barely registered a blip, but I didn't see a shotgun by the door, so I figured all the bark at the 1940's-era clapboard house was worse than the bite.

"Must be my day for visitors," he said as I followed him to the U-shaped kitchen where a stack of dirty dishes filled the sink and a pan of tomato soup bubbled on the stove.

I was immediately struck by the fact that he had no family pictures on the walls, no homey curtains in the kitchen, and no dining room table in the adjacent room. Instead of feminine touches, faux wood blinds with a few missing slats covered the windows, and the house smelled like an old cigar room, making me suspect that it had been a long time since the never-married septuagenarian had entertained a lady friend here.

With Barney sitting with rapt attention at his feet, Mr. Wixey pointed at a rickety-looking barstool on the other side of the white tile counter. "Have a seat, Charmaine."

I gingerly slid my butt onto the stool where he probably took most of his meals. Guessing that I outweighed Fred Wixey by at least thirty pounds, I prayed that I wouldn't land in a heap on his scuffed hardwood floor.

He turned his back to me to give his soup a stir. "With all the excitement this morning, Barney and I are a little behind on our chow."

"That's why I'm here, Mr. Wixey—"

"About time you called me Fred, don't you think?" he asked, glancing back over his shoulder.

I'd called him Mr. Wixey ever since the day I moved in with my grandparents when I was three. To distract me from my actress mother's hasty departure to the Everglades to co-star in some swamp creature flick,

Gram had taken me to the Big Scoop where Fred Wixey, the owner, introduced me to my first banana split.

Was it any wonder that I'd become a true believer that a big bowl of hot fudge and ice cream could turn a frown upside down? Probably one of the many reasons why I now outweighed my host.

Nope. Thirty-one years after my earliest memory had been burned into my cortex, there was no way I could call him anything but Mr. Wixey.

I smiled and left it at that. "Ben Santiago suggested that I stop by to take your statement."

"I already told Steve everything I saw. Don't know that there's anything else to say."

I pulled out a pen and one of the witness interview forms I carried in my tote bag. "I realize you've talked to Steve—Detective Sixkiller—but would you mind me asking you a few questions while you eat your lunch?"

"No skin off my nose." Mr. Wixey turned off the front burner of the stove. "Fire away."

I skipped the first two questions since I didn't need him to help me fill in the blanks about his name and address. "I understand you called nine-one-one this morning."

He met my gaze as he pulled a glass bowl from a nearby cabinet. "I realize you're new at this, but isn't that why you're here?"

He reminded me of my grandfather the time I'd shown him my report card with the "C-" I got in Physics. *You're better than this, Char.*

I would concede Mr. Wixey the point if it would get him talking. "Yeah, but we need to start somewhere."

He poured his soup into the bowl and pushed it across the counter. "Not that I mind the pretty company, but why don't we skip the stuff you already know."

"That's the problem, Mr. Wixey—"

"Fred." He took the seat next to me, Barney's toenails clickety-clacking behind us. "Go lay down," he told the fox terrier, who click-clacked to the corner and hopped onto a suede dog bed that looked like a giant bagel.

"The Coroner needs to determine the cause of Mr. Falco's death and we aren't necessarily privy to the information you provided to Detective Sixkiller." At least I wasn't. "Sorry if this seems repetitive, but could we start at the beginning?"

Mr. Wixey shrugged and slurped his soup.

I took that as a *yes*.

"What time did you discover Russell Falco?" I asked.

"I didn't. Barney did."

I glanced back at the dog whose ears had perked up at the mention of his name. "And what time was that?"

"Nine-ish."

I wasn't about to submit a report to my boss with a time of *nine-ish*. "Do you think it was before or after nine?"

"Like I told Steve, it was around nine. Barney and me, we left the house around eight forty-five. After that, who knows? I'm retired. Don't wear a watch anymore."

Fine. Nine-ish.

"Where did you find him?" I asked as I made note of the approximate time.

"Ben was there. He saw where I found him," he said, enunciating every word as if I were hard of hearing.

"Don't you people talk to one another?"

"I need the exact location for my report, so—"

"Government bureaucracy. Everyone asking the same questions. Mighty inefficient way to do business if you ask me."

Drawing in a deep breath, I pasted a smile on my face. "I'm sure you're right. But back to the discovery you made around nine. Sorry to ask you this while you're eating, but could you describe what you saw and where you saw it?"

Mr. Wixey dropped his spoon in his bowl. "I served two tours in 'Nam. Saw a buddy's arm blown off. Gave me nightmares for months. Seeing what Barney discovered was nothin' by comparison. Just a dead guy on the strip of rocky beach this side of the boat launch at Cedars Cove."

Andy and Nathan might beg to differ about the "nothin'" aspect of Barney's discovery, but at least we were finally getting somewhere.

"I guess hypothermia set in while the poor bastard was swimming for shore, then the tide washed him up onto those rocks," Mr. Wixey added, picking up his bowl to suck down the last of the soup.

"Why do you say that?" As far as I knew, Fred Wixey had no information about Russell taking a tumble from his boat.

"Well, it didn't look like he walked to shore. And he wasn't wearing shoes. Just socks."

After making a note of Mr. Wixey's observation, I looked up to see him frowning at his empty soup bowl. "What? Did you remember something else?"

"Just occurred to me. Now that I know that the stiff was Russell, he seemed kinda gussied up."

"What do you mean, 'gussied up?'"

"White shirt. You know, the kind with a collar, long sleeves. New-looking blue jeans. Never seen him in anything but a black T-shirt before."

Neither had I. "Did you notice anything else that seemed unusual?"

He turned to me, a twinkle in his watery gray eyes. "You mean aside from him being dead?"

"Yep."

"Nah. That's about it."

"Okay, and then you called the police around..."

"Nine-thirty-ish."

Since Steve's captain called him almost an hour later, it seemed like Russell Falco wasn't a priority for anyone this morning. At least I could verify the time with the nine-one-one dispatcher. "Why not call right away?"

Fred Wixey pulled a small bone-shaped biscuit from his pocket and tossed it to his dog. "Barney hadn't done his business yet. Old guys like us can get a little ornery when we're rushed. The plumbing just ain't what it used to be."

"No cell phone?"

He shook his head.

"No one else on the beach with a cell phone?"

"Nah, it's quiet as a tomb down there." He winked. "Barney likes his privacy, so it's one of his favorite places."

If this wasn't an accident, that might also make that stretch of beach a great place to dump a body.

I eased off the barstool and handed Mr. Wixey one of my cards. "If you think of anything else, please give me a call."

He squinted at my business card, a scowl carving lines into the marionette-like folds under his cheeks. "Leaving so soon, Charmaine Digby, Special Assistant to the Prosecutor/Coroner?" he asked, reading the card. "Me and Barney were about to have some ice cream. You still like strawberry?"

I planted my butt back on the barstool. "Maybe I can stay for a few more minutes."

After making a quick stop at Clark's Pharmacy, I pulled into the marina parking lot, walked to the end of Dock A, and flashed a smile at Howie Fontaine. "I just need to check one more thing for my report."

He stepped between me and the caution tape. "Sorry, ma'am, I can't let you pass."

I pulled on a pair of the latex gloves I'd picked up five minutes earlier at Clark's, snapping one against my wrist like a doctor prepping for surgery. "You can't let the *public* pass. *I* am a deputy coroner here on official business."

"I don't know—"

"The Coroner's waiting and I don't have all day." Because Steve could show up at any moment.

Howie shot a worried glance toward the parking lot as if he were hoping backup would roll in to rescue him from having to make a decision. "Maybe I should call—"

"Officer Fontaine, do you really want to look like a rookie who can't show good judgment?"

While he stared at me as if I'd asked him a trick question, I slipped under the caution tape. "I'll just be a minute."

I stepped down onto one of the two unvarnished bench seats of the *Lucky Charm's* stern. In fact, almost every square inch of surface area appeared to have been stripped of its varnish. Between jobs like the one at Kelsey's shop, it looked like Russell had been keeping busy.

Maybe that accounted for the red and black plastic toolbox I spotted on the floor of the cabin. But it wouldn't explain the circular saw in an open compartment next to that toolbox. I'd seen my grandfather use a similar saw when he built the deck in our backyard. Unless Russell had planned to give up his restoration efforts and make kindling out of the *Lucky Charm*, that saw had no purpose on this boat.

I took a quick inventory of the contents of the toolbox. Files, hammers, screwdrivers, drills, compartments with assorted bits, tacks, and screws, a plastic bag of nails, and not one varnish brush—exactly what I'd expect to see in the toolbox of a handyman.

Lifting one of the bench seats at the galley table I saw two handsaws atop a couple of orange life jackets. Next to the life jackets was a cardboard box filled with dirty rags, sheets of sandpaper, and a dozen assorted brushes, most still wrapped in plastic. I turned to the other bench seat. There I found epoxy tubes neatly stored in a small wooden crate along with several cans of turpentine, linseed oil, resin, and varnish.

Other than the stained rags and several well-used sheets of sandpaper, the bench seats looked more like storage lockers, filled with inventory for a boat restoration project that wouldn't be happening anytime soon.

I agreed with Steve. It appeared that Russell had been working somewhere other than on his boat yesterday.

One thing was certainly evident. Russell was definitely one of those *a place for everything and everything in its place* guys. Except for the black T-shirt that had been tossed over the back of the cracked leather captain's chair.

I leaned over to sniff the shirt. Not unpleasant and most decidedly male. Light flecks resembling sawdust dotted the black cotton. I brushed one of the larger pieces into my palm and held it under the sunlight cascading through the cabin window. It appeared to be a thin sliver of wood.

Running a gloved finger over the surface of the threadbare carpet I came up with several more slivers. Russell had probably taken his shirt off here.

But did that happen in the last twenty-four hours? Not necessarily. For all I knew, the shirt could have been draped over this seat for the past week.

I turned my attention to the apparel I was more interested in—Russell's missing shoes.

If he'd been *gussied up* as Fred Wixey had stated, Russell Falco would have been wearing shoes—most likely the type of shoes a man wouldn't want to get wet. So if he'd jumped into the water to retrieve something that had fallen overboard, he would first have removed his shoes.

That meant I should see a pair of shoes on the stern of the *Lucky Charm*. But I found only a crab trap, a net, four rubber fenders and a few coils of rope.

Or Russell could have taken off his shoes inside the cabin to make himself comfortable. I searched under the captain's seat, under the T-shirt, under the table. No shoes. But I did spot an unzipped black canvas duffle bag opposite the bench seat with the hand saws.

To avoid transferring any wood splinters to the bag, I grabbed a yellow pencil from a compartment next to the table, pulled it open, and saw a pair of shoes – a pair of well-worn Reeboks that hadn't seen white in a long time—not the shoes I had been looking for. Rolled up under the Reeboks was a grimy pair of faded blue jeans dotted with sawdust. The only other thing the duffle contained was a brown leather shaving kit similar to my ex-husband's—what he had brought with him every time he spent the night when we were dating.

So it appeared that Russell might have been working a construction job that he traveled to by boat. Then, instead of going home yesterday to get *gussied up* for a date, he had changed his clothes here. But where were his shoes?

A red feather suspended from a dreamcatcher hanging in the corner grazed my shoulder as I angled around to open the door of the head. Nothing in there but an old towel next to a grungy shower, and a pine air freshener that was probably supposed to mask the outhouse perfume. "Oy." It didn't.

A cursory inspection of the bow revealed nothing other

than a light blue dress shirt hanging next to a denim jacket in a compact closet, and a pillow on top of a rumpled green sleeping bag on the bed.

Since I was no closer to solving the mystery of the missing shoes and I needed to make myself scarce before Steve came back, I stepped off the *Lucky Charm* and nodded to Howie as I ducked under the caution tape. "It's in our mutual best interest that you don't mention that I was here to Detective Sixkiller."

Howie cringed. "You didn't touch nothin', did you?"

"Nope." Hardly anything. "And that needs to be your answer when he asks if anyone got anywhere near this boat. Say it with conviction and he might even believe you."

Since it wouldn't be at all believable if Steve saw me at the marina, I sprinted to my car to beat it to my grandmother's house. While I headed up 5th Street, something niggled at me—the haunting feeling that I'd overlooked something.

But what?

I mentally rewound the day's events, retracing my steps back to the Feathered Nest, where Russell had been a no-show.

When I parked in front of Gram's two-story Victorian, I spotted my cell phone as I reached for my tote bag and a light bulb clicked on in my brain.

Kelsey had said she'd been trying to reach Russell by phone. A man who wouldn't want to miss an opportunity for a job would certainly carry a cell phone, and I didn't see one on the boat.

Since Steve's car wasn't parked in the driveway across

the street I pulled out my phone and selected his number.

After four rings I thought I was going to have to leave a voice message and then he answered with a brusque, "Yeah?"

Apparently my sex buddy wasn't in the mood for pleasantries. "I need some information for my report."

"I'm busy. Can't this wait until later?"

Yes, but that didn't help me now. "Nope. But I'll make this quick. I just need a yes or no to two questions. Did Russell have his cell phone on him?"

Steve blew out a breath. "No."

"Did you find his shoes or phone on the boat and take them as evidence?"

A few silent seconds ticked by.

"Frankie will want to know," I added since Steve was well-aware that my boss would expect him to keep her apprised of the chain of evidence in the case.

"No."

"Then where are they?"

It had to be highly unlikely that Russell Falco would have willingly dived into the cold waters of Merritt Bay wearing his shoes. But it was virtually impossible that he would have hit the water with his phone, at least by choice.

"Someone who didn't search that boat probably shouldn't be asking that question."

Crap. "Uh..."

"I have to go," Steve said before promptly disconnecting.

I may have just been busted for the unauthorized search of Russell's boat, but the non-answer from Mr.

Less Than Forthcoming told me he'd been asking himself the same question.

That was enough for me, especially since I also had to go. In my case, inside my grandmother's house to make a quick pit stop, and then I needed to skedaddle to the courthouse and park myself in front of my computer to write a preliminary report for Russell's file. At least I now had two additional important pieces of information to add to it—a pair of shoes and a cell phone that had both gone missing.

That meant one of two things: Russell Falco had either fallen overboard, couldn't get back onto his boat and had removed his shoes to swim for shore, or his death was no accident.

Chapter Four

It was almost two in the afternoon when I stepped out of the upstairs bathroom and discovered my eighty-year-old grandmother changing my bed linens.

"What are you doing?" I asked.

Gram clutched a celery-green bed sheet to her ample bosom as if I'd caught her in a compromising position. "I..."

I took the sheet from her. "You don't have to do this. Part of the deal with me living here for a few months is that I help you with the chores, not the other way around."

Given the installment plan I was still paying off with the divorce lawyer, maybe more than a few months.

I smoothed the sheet over the double bed. "That means that I don't create work for you, Gram."

She stood at the other side of the bed and tucked in the sheet. "You didn't," she said, avoiding my gaze. "The fresh sheets aren't for you."

Translation: My mother was back in town.

When I was a little kid, sharing a bed with my mother had felt more like a slumber party—something I'd

yearned for. Now that I was thirty-four, I had no intention of partying with Marietta and didn't want to share.
But Gram's implication couldn't be more clear. It was
my duty as a good daughter to temporarily relinquish
my claim on her guest room.

I scanned the room for my mother's monogrammed
Louis Vuitton luggage. No luggage, no hint of jasmine in
the air—nothing to indicate that Hurricane Marietta had
blown into Port Merritt. In fact, aside from the bed everything was exactly as I'd left it, which meant I needed to
scoop up this morning's wardrobe rejects from the floor.
"Where is she?"

"Barry is picking her up at the airport."

Barry Ferris was my mother's man of the moment—
the same Mr. Ferris who had been my biology teacher at
Port Merritt High School. Kind, responsible, over forty—
not at all her usual boy toy type. Everyone could see he
was completely and utterly smitten with Marietta. She'd
told me that he even wanted to marry her, the poor sap.

Their relationship had just entered its fourth week.
Over the course of the last thirty years, this typically
signaled *kiss-off week*, when my mother would kick the
guy out of her Malibu home. Or worse, she'd marry him.

For all our sakes, and especially for Mr. Ferris, I
prayed that she'd let him down easy. And since my
mother would be sleeping in my bed, I hoped she'd do it
soon.

I knew the drill from her last visit, so I cleared some
space for Marietta in my closet and carried a week's
worth of clothes downstairs to my grandfather's study.
There I found a couple of pillows on the hide-a-bed sofa

and Gram's fat, orange tabby cat, Myron, lying on the stack of bed linens she'd left for me.

"Comfy?" I asked him.

Myron cracked open one eye and flicked his striped tail at me as if I were invading his space.

Obviously I wasn't the only one who wasn't in a sharing mood.

"Just don't get too comfy. This is *my* bed for the next few days." Not that I welcomed the notion of sleeping on the lumpy mattress of the *Crippler*, as my grandfather used to call the brown Naugahyde sleeper sofa. But since my next best option would have been the king-sized bed at Steve's house, going a few rounds each night with the Crippler might leave me battered, but it would be much less complicated.

With my mother in town I was all for avoiding complications.

As I draped my clothes over the back of a desk chair, I heard a door bang shut.

My mother had always possessed a talent for making her presence known so I didn't have to guess who had just made her entrance.

"Hell-o-o, anybody home?" she sang out.

I couldn't be home for long if I wanted Frankie to have my preliminary report on Russell Falco first thing in the morning.

With my mother's entrance as my cue, I grabbed my tote and car keys and headed for the kitchen, where she was waiting for me with outstretched arms.

"Chahmaine!" Marietta Moreau exclaimed, gliding toward me in red stilettos that gave her a two-inch advantage over my five foot six.

Leaving Barry Ferris in her jasmine-infused wake, my mother hugged me to her double-D's, then her manicured hands slid over my waistline like I was being frisked. "Honey, ah do believe you've lost a few pounds," the former Mary Jo Digby said in the fresh-from-the plantation accent she'd adopted in her mid-twenties after being cast in a southern-fried version of *Charlie's Angels*.

I'd probably lost three pounds since her visit last month. Unfortunately, every time I stepped into Duke's I found them again.

Like me, with every break-up over the years, starting with my father, the *pasty-faced French bastard*, who we knew better than to refer to by name in her presence, Marietta found comfort in the kitchen. Since she didn't cook, she'd hire someone to bake her favorite chocolate fudge ripple cheesecake while paying a shrink to strengthen her fledgling coping skills.

Unlike me, to keep her hips from spreading, Marietta had tried practically every fad diet that had come out of Beverly Hills. That didn't mean I wanted to avail myself of her weight loss expertise or listen to her false praise about how *fabulous* I looked.

I pulled out of her embrace. "Maybe a couple." Which might be true if I skipped dinner tonight. And fat chance of that happening.

"Ah knew it." Marietta aimed a Botox-treated, wrinkle-resistant frown at the tote bag slung over my shoulder. "You're not leaving, are you? I just got here!"

"I have to go to work for a few hours." I looked past

her and smiled at Barry Ferris. "Do you need any help with the luggage?"

"Actually, I'm not sure that it's coming into the house," he said, his gaze fixed on my mother.

Her cheeks flushed the same shade of crimson as the cigarette pants hugging her long legs. "Don't be silly. Of course the luggage is coming in."

She narrowed her green eyes at Mr. Ferris for a split second. As a kid I'd seen that look plenty of times, usually when she'd fly me down for a movie premiere and I acted like something less than the perfect child in front of a member of the Hollywood press corps.

Mr. Ferris sighed. "Fine."

"Ah don't know what he was thinkin'," Marietta said, fluffing her cropped auburn hair as the door shut behind him.

I did. After two weeks without seeing the woman he thought he loved, he wanted as much time with her as possible. Alone. At his house. If this hadn't been my mother and my former biology teacher, I would have envied the blatant desire in their furtive glances.

Given the fact that Marietta was making a surprise visit during kiss-off week, the less I knew about what anyone in that relationship was thinking, the better for all of us.

"I thought I heard you come in," Gram said with a welcoming smile as she entered the kitchen.

Marietta swept my grandmother into her arms. "Hi, Mama."

I could see Gram's hazel eyes misting over with joy. A split second later, she honed in on my tote bag like a laser.

"Where do you think you're going?" she asked, frowning at me.

"Work." And since Mr. Ferris would be stepping back through the door any minute, spending the next couple of hours as a desk jockey had never held more appeal.

As if reading my mind, Gram pulled away from my mother and looked out the back window at the dark blue Nissan parked in her driveway. "It's Saturday."

"I know, but sometimes people die on the weekends."

"Who died?" Gram and Marietta asked in unison.

"I can't talk about the case." Sort of true, even though this wasn't yet an official coroner's case. But since I didn't know if Russell's mother had been notified, I knew I needed to keep my mouth shut.

Gram pursed her lips. "Will you be back in time for dinner?"

"Maybe." It depended on how fast I could get the report done and whether I'd be setting two extra places for my mother and Mr. Ferris.

"I'm making pork chops and twice-baked potatoes," Gram added as if I needed a little nudge in the decision-making department.

She knew I was a sucker for her cheesy potatoes. "You don't fight fair."

Gram kissed me on the cheek. "I fight to win."

Four hours and one preliminary report later, I was digging into an extra cheesy potato when my grandmother turned the dinner conversation to the art show *date* she and I had scheduled for later that evening.

Marietta smiled at Mr. Ferris. "Doesn't that sound like fun?"

Not to me it didn't. Based on the fake smile Barry Ferris was sporting and the fact that he hadn't had a minute alone with Marietta since they'd stepped through the door, he shared my opinion.

"We should all go together," Gram declared.

Seriously, Gram?

"And go out for dessert after. Maybe to that chocolatier next door to the Feathered Nest." She nodded at me with the confidence of a poker player holding a royal flush. "How's that sound?"

Since Gram had just sweetened the pot with chocolate—my weakness—it sounded like a bribe.

"Fabulous!" Marietta said, her eyes aglow with excitement.

Stone-faced, Mr. Ferris met her gaze. "Yeah, fabulous."

For a split second my mother's smile slipped. She fumbled with her fork, looking as ready to crumble as my first graham cracker crust.

I didn't know what was going on between them, but I wished they would take it somewhere else, where they wouldn't have an audience.

The mantel clock in the living room chimed seven times, breaking the silence as Marietta pushed her plate away, the cheese missing from her potato the only evidence that she hadn't lost her appetite completely.

"We should leave soon," Gram said, chipping away at the tension in the room. "Parking on Bay Street will probably fill up fast."

Marietta bolted from the table like she couldn't get away from Barry Ferris fast enough. "I'll get my purse."

Mr. Ferris met my gaze over the top of his wine glass, his blue eyes hard as granite.

"I'm so glad you could join us tonight, Barry," Gram said like a perfect hostess.

His lips tightened into a smile. "It was my pleasure, Eleanor."

No it wasn't. Not even close.

A half hour later at the Feathered Nest, Gram removed her trifocals and squinted at the thick raspberry-purple brushstrokes Lance Greenwood had used in *Olympic Sunset*. "Hmmm." Frowning, she took a step back as if some distance would make her heart grow fonder of the garish oil painting. "I give up. Where the heck is the sunset?"

"Mama, this is *art*, an *interpretation* of sunset." Marietta's bejeweled hand swept in front of the painting, fanning me with her musky jasmine. "Look at the color, the lines, the texture in this piece."

Gram wrinkled her nose as if she had just sniffed a piece of something else. "Uh-huh." With her glasses back on she scanned the business card I'd tacked to the wall. "Look at the price! For that kind of money, it should dang well look like a sunset!"

My mother clucked her tongue. "Good artwork isn't cheap."

"Neither is some not-so-good artwork," Mr. Ferris said in my ear.

Marietta's eyes tracked the latest love of her life as he headed for the corner wine bar. Touching the base of her throat with her fingertips, she stared down at the parquet floor as if she needed to find a hole she could disappear into.

The throat touch thing was one of my mother's *tells*— a silent alarm that everyone in the family had learned to recognize and largely ignore since it usually accompanied some drama of Marietta's creation that none of us wanted to deal with.

As if sensing I'd been watching her, she gave me a subtle head shake. *Don't ask.*

Fine by me. When it came to the men in her life, we'd had a *don't ask, don't tell* policy ever since she eloped with one of her TV series co-stars at the mid-season break and then divorced him after the guy's character was killed off in the season finale. I'd always assumed she'd had a hand in his demise. The only thing Marietta ever said about it was, "Don't ever get involved with any-one you have to work with."

Probably pretty good advice, but I had to work with Steve, sort of. More accurately, I needed his cooperation whenever the coroner's office conducted a death investi-gation. Just how emotionally involved we were had yet to be determined.

While I watched Marietta saunter over to where the artist, Lance Greenwood, was holding court under a strip of newly installed track lighting, Gram sidled next to me. "I worry about her."

"I wouldn't. Whatever is going on between them will probably blow over." Or blow them apart.

Gram frowned at me. "What are you talking about?"

"The tension at dinner. The nervous glances Mom's been stealing every time she thinks Mr. Ferris isn't looking."

My grandmother's gaze tightened. "You don't know."

The concern etched into the network of fine lines around her eyes filled me with a sinking feeling that we weren't talking about Barry Ferris anymore. "Know what?"

"Your mother is having some *financial difficulties*."

After two very expensive divorces, I knew she'd had a prenup with husband number three. Between the makeup line she had lent her famous face to and the infomercials, I'd assumed she was rebuilding her savings. Undoubtedly not to the level of when she co-starred in a Bond movie spoof thirty years earlier, especially when I could name only one film that she'd appeared in since hitting the big five-oh. Still, if my mother could learn to live on a budget...

And if I could lose thirty pounds and wear my skinny jeans on my next date with Steve, I'd be a happy girl. But as my mother's daughter, I wasn't a big believer in minor miracles. "Define financial difficulty."

"Whatever savings she had is pretty much gone, to the point where she has to sell her house."

Marietta's home in the Malibu hills was her one asset from her mid-twenties that she'd managed to hold onto through each failed marriage. If she could no longer afford to keep it, things were much worse than I had thought.

The spacious, red tile roofed hacienda shrouded in

bougainvillea, where I'd spent the occasional summer as a girl, had to be worth millions. "It'll sell and she'll be fine, right?"

"Sure," Gram said, staring at her daughter like she wanted to believe it herself. "All the repairs are going to be expensive though. On top of everything else it's really bad timing."

Huh? She was losing me. "Repairs to what?"

Gram heaved a sigh. "She doesn't tell you anything, does she?"

We tended to get along better that way. "I guess not."

"Her master bath sprang a leak during her visit last month. The water damage was extensive, so she's here for the next couple of weeks while a work crew's in her house."

I watched Barry hand Marietta a glass of champagne. With the way her eyes sparked in response, I sincerely doubted that the prospect of sharing her home with a few workmen was what had chased my mother eleven hundred miles north. "What did you mean, 'on top of everything else?'"

Blinking, Gram pressed her lips together like she had a secret she dared not tell.

"You might as well spill it. I'll find out eventually." Mainly because Gram had the worst poker face in the world.

"Well..." She glanced back at her daughter. "It appears that your mother borrowed against her house and lost almost everything on some bad investments. When you add in the cost of this last divorce..." Gram slowly shook her head. "Honestly, honey, if it weren't for the remaining equity in that house, your mother would probably have to declare bankruptcy because she's broke."

"What? But she's working—all those infomercials, all the appearances she makes—"

"Are barely keeping her head above water."

Yeowch. "Does Mr. Ferris know?"

"Not yet."

"What's she going to do?"

"Sell her house and soon."

Which meant she was going to have to make some quick decisions about another place to live, increasing the odds of her throwing herself into the willing arms of my former biology teacher.

Criminy, she wasn't about to give him the kiss-off. She'd come to Port Merritt to find out if another wedding could be in her immediate future.

Chapter Five

As Gram and I joined the outer circle of onlookers surrounding Marietta and Lance Greenwood, I realized that I had spent most of my adult life underestimating my mother's acting abilities.

The glamour queen tossing back her head, laughing with Lance Greenwood, was playing tonight's role to perfection. With the jewels adorning her fingers, the Rodeo Drive couture accentuating every curve, and her flawless makeup, my mother looked and sounded the part of Marietta Moreau, *actress*.

Yes, tonight she was delivering quite the devil-may-care performance, because the former Mary Jo Digby had to be heartbroken about having to sell her home of the last twenty-eight years.

She touched the artist's sleeve. "Ah do declare, Mistah Greenwood, you have some snake charmer in you."

With a rakish twinkle in his chestnut brown eyes, the other star attraction of the evening lifted her hand to his lips and kissed it. "And I do believe it takes one to know one. So, Ms. Moreau, do we have a deal?"

My mother's mouth parted, her smile as brittle as

spun sugar. "I..."

Oh, Mom, you don't want to do this. Walk away. Just walk away.

"It's a deal," she said, shaking his hand with all the enthusiasm of a politician during election year.

Gram leaned in. "Mary Jo, what are you doing?"

"Exactly what's expected of me," she whispered, her teeth clenched.

Slowly releasing a deep breath, she got back into Marietta Moreau character. "Mama, you're looking at the proud owner of two Lance Greenwood originals."

"Two," Gram said, her tone dripping with parental disapproval. Unlike my mother, her mother made no effort to hide her misgivings about this *deal*.

Marietta winked at Lance. "I got a little discount for buying two."

Probably because no one else attending this wing-ding appeared to be in a buying mood.

"May I escort you to the register so Kelsey can take care of the rest of the details?" he said, bending slightly at the waist like an officious maître d'.

My mother took the arm he offered her. "Thank you, kind sir."

Kindness had nothing to do with this. He probably wanted her to fork over a credit card and seal this deal before she came to her senses and stopped acting like she had money to burn.

Gram rolled her eyes as we followed Marietta to where Kelsey stood and beamed at Lance Greenwood like he was a rock star.

While my mother pulled some plastic from her wallet,

Lance stepped behind the counter and reached for a pen, brushing Kelsey's fingers.

Incidental contact? From the flicker of a smile playing at the corners of his mouth, I didn't think so.

He wrote a number on a sales ticket. "*Olympic Sunset* and *Port Townsend Twilight* at a special price for this very special lady."

I glanced over my shoulder at Barry Ferris, who was sipping on his wine as he browsed a crowded aisle filled with Native American art.

Clearly, there was a lot my former teacher had yet to learn about my mother, and based on his apparent lack of concern about her decision to become a patroness of Lance Greenwood, the state of her finances needed to be somewhere at the top of the list.

"Two of my favorites from his Pacific Northwest collection," Kelsey said as she snapped up Marietta's credit card. "Obviously yours, too."

While Marietta signed for her purchase, Lance's gaze raked over the hint of Kelsey's décolletage exposed by the V neckline of her beaded vintage dress.

As for Kelsey, she practically glowed with delight, but it looked to me to have everything to do with making a big sale instead of the artist's proximity.

Once her gaze was fixed back on Marietta, Lance fingered the buttons of his tan herringbone blazer and smoothed his necktie.

Lance Greenwood reminded me of the chess club guy in high school, a little nervous and fidgety right before he asked the hottest chick in the room out on a date—which solved the mystery of why tonight's art show was taking place here instead of one of the galleries in Port Townsend. It was to score some face time with Kelsey Donovan.

"You're welcome to pick up the paintings tomorrow, after the show," Kelsey said when she handed Marietta her receipt.

"Ah'm sure that can be arranged." My mother turned to me, leaving no doubt who would be doing the arranging.

Kelsey leaned toward me after Gram herded Marietta and Mr. Ferris toward the door. "Have you heard anything new about what happened to Russell?" she asked, her voice barely a whisper.

I shook my head. "The investigation is just starting."

"It's so sad." Her eyes glistened with tears. "I just saw him last night and..."

Lance wrapped his arm around Kelsey. "Shhhh, you're only going to upset yourself if you dwell on that."

She blew out a breath, the waterworks spilling over her long lashes. "I'm sorry to be so emotional. He was a friend, but this is your night and—"

"And you have every right to be a little emotional." His gaze softened. "Let me get you a drink. I'm sure you could use one."

Kelsey patted his hand. "Thank you. I'd appreciate that."

I watched Lance cross the room to the wine bar. "He likes you."

Looking down at the counter between us, she dabbed at her eyes with a tissue. "He's been very kind. Not at all the temperamental artist type. Really, he couldn't have been more pleasant to do business with the last couple of weeks."

Which sounded to me like the hot chick wasn't interested in mixing business with pleasure.

"Speaking of business," I said. "I know this is a terrible time to ask, but what time did Russell leave last night?"

"Around eight. He would have stayed later to install the lighting, but he said he had somewhere he needed to be."

"He didn't give you any other details?"

"Despite what a lot of people thought about Russell, he could be very discreet."

"So he had a date with someone last night?"

Worrying her lower lip, Kelsey blinked away fresh tears. "He wouldn't have told me. Last year, he and I were..." Her breath hitched. "We had a relationship."

I didn't doubt that she was telling me the truth, but it seemed like their relationship wasn't completely in the past.

"I didn't realize that you two—"

"Hardly anyone knows."

Knows, not knew—what I would have said if I'd been referring to a relationship that had ended last year.

Kelsey reached for another tissue. "Like I said, he was very discreet."

She was certainly the woman to know that about the man, but Russell Falco gussied up for someone after he left her shop. Maybe the last person to see him alive.

After hitting Chocolati, the gourmet chocolate shop,

not only were my fat cells singing a hallelujah chorus from sharing a molten cappuccino with my mother, the synapses in my brain were crackling like a wildfire. Not from the caffeine, but because I couldn't stop thinking about Russell Falco.

Barry Ferris looked like he was going to explode if he didn't get Marietta alone, and Gram needed to get off her feet, so they called it a night after we bought a pound of chocolate silk truffles for the road.

Hey, there was a good reason the Digby women had curves.

A half hour later, since this particular Digby was in need of information as well as a drink, I left my grandmother snoring in front of her television and drove a couple of blocks north of historic Old Town to Eddie's Place, my favorite intel-gathering watering hole.

Eddie Fiske inherited the red brick warehouse shortly after he married Roxanne, my best friend since grade school. They then spent the next three years transforming it into an eight-lane bowling alley and tavern with the best pizza in town.

I scanned the gravel parking lot for Steve's truck. Since it wasn't anywhere in sight and hadn't been parked in his driveway, I assumed he was working late.

Pulling out my cell phone, I checked for messages. Nothing.

Okay, that wasn't the least bit surprising. We'd only had one official date that didn't end as well as I had hoped. Never mind that we'd been sex buddies for the last two weeks. He didn't need to check in and tell me his whereabouts, and I certainly didn't need to tell him what I was doing at Eddie's.

Roxanne smiled at me from behind the bar. "Hey, I thought you were going to that art show tonight," she said over the Guns N' Roses classic blaring through the overhead speakers.

I slid onto my usual barstool and waved at Eddie, who was filling a couple of frosted mugs with one of the local brews he had on tap. "How did you know about that?"

"Steve was here for dinner and said that you had a *date* with your granny." Leaning her elbows on the bar, she lowered her voice. "He also told us about Russell being found at Cedars Cove."

At least he didn't mention the date that he and I'd had in the morning. Rox might be my best friend, but I wasn't ready to tell her about Steve and me. Really, what could I say?

It's nothing serious. At least I didn't think it was.

I'm just using him for sex. Sort of. Which would be like lighting a match to a powder keg since I'd always sworn I wouldn't cross the *friendship line* with Steve.

And since I didn't need it getting back to Steve via his best buddy, Eddie, that I was talking to Rox about us, mum was the word on this subject.

I nodded. "Fred Wixey and his dog found him."

"So he fell off his boat or something?"

"Don't know, but Mr. Wixey said he was gussied up, so I think he had been on a date."

Rox tucked a chunk of chin-length caramel hair behind her ear as she straightened. "Hmmm." Knitting her brows, she poured me a glass of Chablis.

Everything about her body language told me that she had some beans she needed to spill.

"What?" I asked as she set the glass on a bar napkin. "You know something."

"No, I—"

"I saw that look on your face. Don't even try to deny it."

Her gaze tracked a middle-aged couple in matching blue bowling shirts leaving the bar. "I don't know much."

Which was a heck of a lot more than what I knew. I pointed my thumb at the back table they'd just vacated so that we could talk away from Bruce Springsteen blasting our eardrums, and Rox followed me with a black plastic tub.

"Did you see Russell last night?" I asked as she cleared the dishes from the table.

She shook her head. "Earlier in the week. Monday, when I was driving home from work."

I took a sip of wine and waited. Like my grandfather said when he uncorked a bottle of Bordeaux to celebrate my high school graduation, "Some things you need to let breathe."

"It might not mean anything," Rox said, wiping down the table with a dingy white towel.

Considering the fact that Russell's body had been discovered washed up on shore twelve hours earlier, I wasn't about to dismiss anything she might have seen.

Rox set the tub of dirty dishes on the seat between us and slipped into the chair across from me. "It had been a slow night so I left an hour early to get home before dark."

A little quirk of her lips told me that wasn't the whole story. "Before dark, or before something else happened?"

She sighed. "You know, having a friend who's a human lie detector is really annoying sometimes."

"Hey, it's not my fault you weren't telling the whole truth."

"Whatever. So if you must know, Ms. Smarty Pants, I wanted to get home to see the season premiere of my favorite show. Satisfied?"

"Not yet. And...?"

"And I was driving past the old barn on Morton Road when I came around the bend and spotted Russell's pickup parked in front of Joyce Lackey's house."

"Maybe he was doing some work there."

Pete and Joyce Lackey's Cape Cod-style home on the south shore of Merritt Bay had been in a continual state of repair for as long as I could remember, so it didn't seem out of the ordinary that Russell would have been there to lend a hand.

Rox leveled her gaze at me. "At nine-fifteen, when Pete's not home?"

"How do you know he wasn't home?"

"I drive by that house every day. When he's home, that big-assed truck of his is in the driveway."

The blue and white Pete's Plumbing truck with the leaky faucet depicted on each side panel would certainly be tough to miss.

Okay, now her Russell sighting at the Lackey house didn't seem ordinary by any stretch of the imagination, but I'd been burned before by drawing some hasty and very incorrect conclusions. "There could be a reasonable explanation why he was there."

"Who was where?" Steve asked, pulling up a chair.

I could lie and spin him a yarn about his best buddy, Eddie, being somewhere he shouldn't have been, but I knew Steve would call me on the fib the second it left my lips. Instead I opted for full disclosure. "It seems that Russell was at Joyce Lackey's house a little late for business hours."

His gaze hardened. And without an ounce of surprise. Not the reaction I was expecting.

He folded his arms. "You heard this from…"

I sneaked a peek at Rox.

"Me," she said. "I saw his pickup there Monday night."

Steve drew in a breath and slowly released it. "I know I might be asking the impossible, but keep this to yourselves."

"We can be discreet," I said, borrowing the adjective from Kelsey. Although if Joyce had been the latest object of Russell's affection, I didn't consider his decision to park his truck in front of her house a good demonstration of his discretion.

"I won't say a thing." Which in Roxanne-speak meant that it would still be subject to discussion with Eddie and me.

She pushed back her chair. "You really think they were having an affair?"

Steve stared at her for several silent ticks. "You really think I'm going to answer that question?"

"I liked you better earlier." Rox picked up the plastic

tub. "When you weren't playing the role of the strong silent type and actually exchanged some ideas with me."

Steve's expression didn't change.

"Nice to have you back, and as much as I'd like to stay and have more stimulating conversation, I need to get back to work." She shifted the tub of dirty dishes on her hip. "Wanna drink?"

"Got one, thanks." He reached for my wine glass and took a sip.

Once he and I were alone, I leaned closer. "Joyce Lackey and Russell Falco? Seriously?" Since Joyce was going on fifty and was known more for her blue ribbon cookie-baking than her feminine charms, this wasn't the most probable illicit relationship in Port Merritt.

Steve set down the glass. "No comment."

"Well, if you didn't want to talk, what did you come back here for?"

"I saw your car outside in the lot." Standing, he tossed a ten dollar bill onto the table. "You coming?"

"Are you going to tell me why you already knew about the thing between Joyce Lackey and Russell?"

"Good night, Chow Mein."

"Wait a minute!" I followed him to the parking lot, my sandals crunching on the loose gravel. "Good night? That's all you have to say to me?" This had to be the most confusing almost-relationship I'd ever had.

"Yep. Unless you want to come over and not talk about this."

I froze, trying to read him in the shadows created by a street light. The innuendo in his words came through loud and clear, but the angular face with the high cheekbones he had inherited from his Cherokee grandfather revealed nothing except a man who looked like he needed eight hours of uninterrupted shut-eye.

Leaning against his F150, Steve folded his arms. "Do you need an invitation?"

Probably. "Of course not."

He stepped toward me, his eyes dark as onyx. "I'm not quite convinced."

He pressed his lips to mine, giving me another taste of the wine I didn't get to finish.

"Nope, still not convinced." Flattening my C-cups against his chest, he kissed me again, longer, deeper.

I wrapped my arms around him, holding on while he rocked my world.

When we came up for air he glanced down at the unmistakable bulge in his blue jeans. "I think we're done here, don't you?"

Clearly he was a man who could make do on less than eight hours of sleep. "I'm right behind you."

✻

I sat up like a shot on the Crippler when the next door neighbor's car backfired around four. With Myron promptly claiming my vacated pillow, I headed for a long, hot shower with the hope that it would steam out the kinks in my aching back.

It didn't, so I swallowed a couple of aspirin and eased my way back downstairs for a caffeine chaser. Unfortunately, once I spotted my grandmother sitting at the kitchen table in her pink chenille robe, I had a sinking feeling that, instead of relief, more hot water was in my immediate future.

"Morning, Gram." I refilled my cup with the French roast I'd brewed at o' dark thirty and waited for her to say something about tiptoeing into her house well after my old curfew.

Running her hand over her frothy helmet of peach-tinted hair, she squinted at the metal file of index cards she was hunched over. "Chocolate chip walnut or peanut butter?"

Either my grandmother had suddenly turned into a very sound sleeper or she was oblivious to the fact that I'd been spending most of my evenings across the street. And I knew better than to believe that the woman who had raised me had an oblivious bone in her body. "Huh?"

"Maybe butter pecan." She tapped a card. "I won a blue ribbon back in '96 with this recipe. Of course, the competition wasn't as stiff then."

I sat at the table next to her. "What about your snicker-doodles? Those are always a big hit."

Gram's thin lips puckered. "And take third place behind Joyce Lackey and Beverly Carver like I have for the last two years? Nope, I need something different—something that'll wow the judges."

Joyce Lackey was a quilting, gardening, and baking goddess—probably stiff competition in any of the county fair categories she entered. Beverly Carver, on the other hand, was the mother of my childhood nemesis, Heather. Aside from baking some mighty fine chocolate chip cookies for our Girl Scout troop twenty-four years ago, I'd never known Mrs. Carver to be renowned for much of anything in Port Merritt aside from having an affair with the former mayor, a local scandal in the last decade that had cost him the election and his marriage.

I took a sip of coffee. "Then I'd go with the butter pecan. The best I've ever tasted and plenty of wow factor."

Gram's eyes glinted with pride. "You're biased."

"Would I lie to you?"

"I don't know. I imagine that would depend on what we were talking about." She leaned back in her chair and nailed me with her steady gaze. "For example, if we were talking about what's going on between you and Steve."

"Gram—"

"But I know you're not ready to do that yet." She patted me on the hand. "Just know that you can talk to me when you finally are ready."

I'd never talked to my grandmother about sex and didn't intend to start, especially since Steve wasn't just one of her neighbors; he was a friend. "That probably won't be anytime soon."

"That's okay. Just be careful. I don't need both my girls rushing into something they might very well come to regret."

Great. I was being lumped into the same category of poor decision-making as my mother.

"I can honestly say that I'm not rushing into anything." Unlike Barry Ferris and Marietta, Steve and I weren't making any plans for the future. There had been no declarations of love—actually, no declarations of any kind. What we had was more like a time-out from the rules that had governed my relationship with him since the third grade. And the last thing I wanted to do was to rush into anything that could screw up that relationship.

"Good girl. Now then…" Gram pushed away from the table and tightened the belt of her robe. "Are you ready for some breakfast? Maybe some pancakes?"

I wasn't particularly hungry, but since she was in a cooking mood and I wanted to change the topic, I nodded. "Sure."

I leaned against the blue and white tile counter as Gram reached for the aluminum flour canister that had been a fixture in her kitchen since before I was born. "You mentioned Joyce Lackey a minute ago. What do you know about her?"

Gram's hazel eyes hardened behind her silver-framed trifocals. "You want to know about Joyce? She has to be one of the most competitive women I've ever met. You should have seen her pout four years ago, when my snickerdoodles won the blue ribbon. I'm sure that's why she had Pete buy her that new oven."

"Nothing says lovin' like a new oven," I said, fishing for details about Joyce Lackey beyond Snickerdoodle-gate.

"Maybe. More likely he wanted her to stop complaining about the kitchen remodel he's been working on the last five years."

"A five-year remodeling project is a very long time. You'd think he'd get some help to get it completed."

Gram shook her head as she measured flour into a glass bowl. "Based on my experience with Pete Lackey when he came out to replace my hot water heater, he's very capable. He also strikes me as a proud man and that kind of man doesn't ask for help."

So, if Joyce wanted something done around the house in a quicker timeframe, it would make more sense for Russell Falco to be there when Pete wasn't around. Not necessarily late at night, but Russell's presence at the house Monday fit into the realm of possibility.

"Anyway," she said, reaching into the cupboard next to me for the can of baking powder. "He's a hard-working man—keeps to himself a lot and is a little rough around the edges, but he seems like a decent sort. Has to be to be married to Joyce." Gram chuckled. "Oh, did I say that out loud?"

I grinned. "Yep."

"Ah well, just shows that there's someone for every-one."

"Even if it's not a match made in heaven."

"There's a lot of ways to make a relationship work." Gram eyed me over the rim of her glasses. "And not all of them include the bedroom."

Yep. Not one oblivious bone in the woman's body.

She pulled the milk carton from the refrigerator. "But, of course, you already know that."

Yes, I did. Didn't mean I wanted to discuss it on an empty stomach though. Or a full one for that matter.

Marietta pushed open the back door, breaking the silence in the kitchen. "Mah goodness! Either you two are up very early or ah'm home even later than I'd thought."

"Or both," I said under my breath.

My grandmother's gaze shifted to her daughter. "Want some pancakes, honey?"

"No thanks, Mama. I had a late supper." Marietta tucked her left arm behind her back. "And one of the most wonderful nights of my life with *the* most wonderful man."

Uh-oh.

Not only was my mother hiding her ring finger, she'd dropped her Georgia peach accent—an ominous combination that had me holding my breath.

"And you'll never guess what happened!" She dangled an emerald cut diamond ring in front of Gram's nose. "I'm engaged!"

Chapter Six

I could hang around the house and wait with Gram for Marietta to wake up and participate in the *please don't rush into anything* discussion, or I could go on a mocha latte run and pick up Marietta's impulse buys from last night.

It was my no-brainer decision of the weekend.

Ten minutes later, I pulled into a diagonal parking spot in front of the Feathered Nest. Since the sign on the gift shop's front window indicated that it was open for business and the two sedans waiting in the Hot Shots drive-through line were the only other cars on the block, I took this as the perfect opportunity to speak with Kelsey alone.

A tone buzzed, announcing my presence as I stepped into the shop, but Kelsey was nowhere to be seen. I peeked into the room where most every piece of artwork from last evening's show still hung. "Hello?"

When I heard a door shut, I turned to see Kelsey holding two rolls of masking tape along with several sheets of brown paper.

Kelsey's eyes widened, red and puffy as if she'd been

crying. "Char, sorry. I must have been in the storeroom when you came in."

"Are you doing okay?" I didn't need to ask. Her pale face, the slope of her shoulders, and the grim set of her mouth as she tried to smile told me everything I needed to know.

"I'm fine," she said, averting her gaze.

Sure. "Well, it looks like I'm just in time to help you wrap things up from the show."

She shook her head, her ponytail bobbing side to side. "You've already done so much. I wouldn't dream of asking you to spend any more of your weekend here."

I had nowhere else I needed to be and I wanted to find out more about Russell from Kelsey, so I wasn't going to take no for an answer.

"Marietta's keeping Gram company this morning." Which was almost the truth. "So I have nothing but time at my disposal. Let me just run across the street for a coffee. Want anything?" I asked, heading for the door.

"Actually." Kelsey pointed a slim finger at Lance Greenwood standing on the other side of the door with a tall to-go cup in each hand and a white paper sack tucked under his arm.

So much for my perfect opportunity to have Kelsey to myself.

"You look like you could use a little assistance," I said, opening the door for him.

His charmer's smile was a split second late affixing itself to his face, his dark eyes as cool as the breeze blowing in from the bay. It couldn't have been more obvious that he was as happy to see me as I was to see him.

"Thank you so much."

Lance brightened when he looked past me to Kelsey. "Here you are, one cappuccino. And I took the liberty of picking up some scones to go with our coffee." He glanced back at me as he set the coffees and the paper sack on the counter. "If I'd known you'd be joining us... I'm sorry. I know you're Marietta Moreau's daughter, but I don't think we were ever introduced."

I extended my hand. "Charmaine Digby."

He pressed his hand in mine. It felt smooth and warm, much like the persona he was trying to portray.

"Charmaine." His gaze slid over my face as he released his grip. "Yes, I see the resemblance. Remarkable really."

I wasn't wearing any makeup besides strawberry-flavored lip gloss, so this morning, more than most, I knew I bore a closer resemblance to my father, the *pasty-faced bastard*.

I looked at Kelsey. Surely I wasn't the only one in the room who could see through this guy's act.

She shrugged. "You have her eyes. Of course, with a little less makeup this morning."

Heck, if I'd known I was going to have these two staring at me, I would have made more of an effort in front of the mirror.

Lance popped the top of his coffee cup and took a sip. "So, you work for your mother?"

It only felt that way when she was in town. "I work for the county."

"Ah," he said with an air of indifference, making it sound as if my resemblance to Marietta wasn't quite as remarkable as he had thought. "But you're obviously here to pick up her purchase from last night. You have that ready for Charmaine, don't you, Kelsey?"

She pulled out two rectangular parcels from behind the counter. "I wrapped your mother's paintings first, since I knew you'd be coming sometime today."

Lance took the paintings from Kelsey. "Allow me to help you to your car." He nodded toward my ex-husband's Jaguar XJ6, the shiny silver wheels that he'd provided in the divorce settlement to fast-track me out of his life. Of course, the jerk neglected to mention that his oil-sucking Jag would break down before I made it out of California, so make that a fast and *costly* track.

I wasn't quite ready to be escorted to the door. "Thank you. It's not locked."

I turned to Kelsey once Lance stepped out the door. "Maybe three's a crowd and I should go."

"Sorry. He can come on a little strong sometimes, but he wanted to help me clean up after the show. Since it was his show, I couldn't very well say no." She blinked, her dark blue eyes pooling with tears. "And without Russell..."

"It's not a problem. Give me a call later if you want some help," I said, wishing I had parked further away to give myself another uninterrupted thirty seconds with Kelsey. "Before I go, I need to ask you a question about Russell."

Wiping her eyes, she gave me a nod.

"When you were with him Friday night, what was he wearing?"

Her full lips curved into a wistful smile that tugged at

my heart. "What Russ always wore—a black T-shirt and blue jeans. For him, that was his work uniform."

Which exactly matched what I found on his boat. "Did he tell you where else he had been working lately?"

"I don't know, but wherever it was I know he had to get there by boat the last few days."

"Why by boat?"

"Somebody came to the house and slashed the tires of his truck Monday night."

With no desire to head home and do the requisite oohing and ahhing with my mother over her new paintings, or worse, her diamond engagement ring, I hit the road after fortifying myself with a mocha latte. Really, it was the perfect, lazy Sunday morning for a drive. It couldn't have been more perfect because the turn off for the Falco home on Morton Road was just ahead, and I knew that Andy and Nate would be fishing in the channel off Harstone Island.

After I took the left turn and passed the old Hansen farm where my grandmother used to buy her eggs, I slowed, remembering that the Lackeys' house was around the next bend.

A modest gray-blue Cape Cod-style house with white trim, dormer windows, and a beautiful yard bordered by a white picket fence came into view.

The street was deserted, so I parked the Jag at the next turn-out to get a better look.

The flower bed behind the fence, resplendent with cobalt blue flowering sage, red bee balm, tall Shasta daisies, lavender phlox, and white candytufts, intersected with hydrangea bushes in full bloom at each corner.

Joyce Lackey's reputation as a master gardener certainly lived up to its billing, but I was more interested in the back of the house. Specifically, how far away was it from the southern shore of Merritt Bay if Russell Falco had been commuting by boat?

I looked at the fenced yard that abutted the Lackey property. No open invitations to trespass here. I trekked further up the street with the hope that there might be some public access to the water. No such luck, but I did see a friend of my grandmother's pumping her fists as she walked in my direction.

Sylvia Jeppesen, dressed in a maroon jogging suit and white Nikes, wore wrap-around dark glasses and had her short silver locks tucked behind her ears. Her mouth split into a smile almost as bright as her sneakers.

"Fancy seeing you out here," she said, catching her breath.

"It was such a pretty day I thought I'd go for a drive around the bay." Which was true enough but not much of an inducement to draw Sylvia in and get her talking. "Plus, I thought it was time I start looking for a place of my own. Do you know of any houses for rent down here?" Preferably unoccupied.

She pointed down the street. "Well, there is the old Hull house on the other side of that willow tree. It's been for sale for almost a year, so they might be willing to rent it out. You should go down and take a look. It's empty."

I didn't want to appear too eager, so I stayed for a few minutes and chatted with Sylvia about the quilt she was entering in next week's county fair. Then as soon as her Nikes started slapping asphalt, I made a break for the Jag.

Less than a minute later, I parked in front of a dingy vanilla-colored rambler with a for-sale sign pitched by the driveway. In case anyone was watching, I took a flyer from the plastic sleeve attached to the for-sale sign. The listing agent had done an excellent job featuring all the positive attributes of the property, highlighting the thing I was most interested in—the private dock.

The front curtains were closed, so I did what any prospective buyer would do and walked through the weeds threatening to take over the side yard to the back of the house. Just as advertised, the property sloped down to the shore, where a boat dock beckoned me like a siren's call.

Walking the plank and stepping onto the fifteen-foot wooden dock extending over the glistening waves lapping against the pilings, I shielded my eyes from the glare and surveyed the neighborhood to the west.

Unfortunately, a thicket of trees blocked my view of the Lackeys' house three doors over, but I had a clear shot of the rocky shoreline between the water and the vine-covered gazebo standing at the center of their backyard. No dock, but a boater with a dinghy wouldn't need one to access the property.

I knew better than to jump to the conclusion that Joyce Lackey had hired a handyman who was commuting by boat last week and that this had somehow gotten him killed. However, given the sighting of Russell's truck and what Kelsey had told me about someone slashing his tires, I couldn't help but think that Russell had run into some serious trouble between Joyce's house and the Port Merritt dock.

Just as I turned to go back the way I had come, I heard a dog barking.

"May I help you?" asked the familiar-looking ash blonde restraining a growling golden retriever by the collar as she stood at her back door.

Crap.

For over three months I had managed to avoid any encounters with Beverly Carver. As for her daughter, Heather, it seemed to be my destiny to bump into Steve's former girlfriend on a weekly basis. My mother would be quick to channel the therapist who aligns her chakras and inform me that this was the universe telling me to get over Heather, or more specifically, *Steve* and Heather.

Sometimes destiny can be a real bitch. The same could be said for Heather.

It wasn't always that way. She and I had been best buddies until I started showing off in a game of *Truth or Dare* during a slumber party and caught her in a whopper of a lie. She branded me as a freak in front of our sixth-grade class and got us both called to the Vice Principal's office. Mrs. Carver never really warmed up to me after that. And I wasn't any closer to getting over my twenty-four-year history with her daughter than I was to fitting into my skinny jeans.

I waved. "Hi, Mrs. Carver! I didn't know you moved down here." I scanned the raised beds with a riot of color lining the east end of her yard opposite a row of tall sunflowers. "Wow, that's quite the flower garden." Almost as impressive as the Lackeys' front yard.

Much to my relief she stepped onto her redwood deck, leaving her dog whining from the other side of the sliding glass door. She narrowed her eyes, her hands firmly planted on her slim hips. "What are you doing out here?"

Unlike Sylvia, I knew Beverly Carver would never believe that I could afford waterfront property, so I needed to think of something that she could believe. Pronto.

I pulled out my deputy coroner badge from my tote bag and aimed it at her. "I was looking to see what boats were docked at this end of the bay. It might be relevant to one of our cases."

Okay, since Russell's death wasn't an official coroner's case and I had no reason to think that any of her neighbors' boats might be involved in this non-case, this was a reach of epic proportions. I just hoped Heather's mother didn't agree with me.

She heaved a sigh. "I guess you'd better come in then."

I should?

Breathing in her sultry, musky scent, I wedged past the golden retriever sniffing my heels as we entered a carpeted sitting room with a red brick fireplace.

Mrs. Carver took a seat in a rocking chair next to a built-in wood box and pointed in the general direction of a country print love seat. "Sit."

I assumed she was talking to me and not the dog at my feet, but we both immediately sat at her command.

"I figured it was a matter of time until someone

would come knocking at my door." She tilted her head, her full glossy lips drawn into a tight, fake smile. "But I never thought it would be you, Charmaine."

That made two of us because up until five minutes ago, I was more interested in what Joyce Lackey could tell me about Russell Falco. But if one of her neighbors could fill in the blanks about what was going on at the Lackey house, no matter what Heather's mother thought about me, I counted myself as the lucky girl who got to hear all about it.

I reached into my tote bag for my notebook. "What can you tell me about Friday night?"

Crossing her long legs, a shapely calf peeked out from under her khaki capris as she slowly rocked back and forth. "It started out much like the last two Fridays. Russell—"

"Russell Falco?"

She shot me a withering look, the same one that I'd received from Heather on numerous occasions. "Given why you're here, isn't that obvious?"

I forced a chipper smile. "Just wanted to make sure."

"As I was about to say, Russell worked most of the day at Joyce Lackey's house and then—"

"What was he working on?"

"Building her some bookcases, I think. I don't know. We didn't talk much shop when he came over."

Holy cow! This was the woman Russell had been seeing?

I picked up my jaw from the floor and tried to act like I'd heard a more shocking revelation in my four weeks on the job. "You two were dating."

She brushed back a long curl. "I wouldn't exactly call it dating, but yes. We had a relationship."

"An intimate relationship."

I got the look again, and the retriever, as if sensing the growing irritation being directed toward my side of the room, moved to sit alongside the mistress it appeared he'd been sharing with Russell.

"Yeah," she said in a clipped tone.

"How long had you been seeing him?"

She leaned over to scratch the retriever's floppy ear, revealing a couple inches of cleavage that had been hiding beneath her peach slouch sweater. "Four months off and on."

Clearly Kelsey hadn't known about this. Russell could definitely be discreet, which made me wonder whether he had been getting busy with something other than bookshelves over at the Lackey house.

I made a few quick scribbles in my notebook. "Going back to Friday night, did you see Russell consume any alcohol?"

She gave me another weary look. "He didn't drink."

"Ever?"

"Never anything stronger than cola."

Okay. "What was he wearing?"

"White button-down shirt and a nice pair of jeans."

The woman Russell Falco had *gussied up* for had just described the clothes he'd been found in.

"And mocs," she added.

"Mocs?"

"You know, slip-on moccasins."

Which could have easily slipped off in the water. "And

you were with Russell until...?"

"Around one in the morning."

"Did you see him leave?"

She shook her head. "I stayed in bed, but the window was open and I heard his boat start up."

"You didn't hear any other voices? Anyone he may have encountered on his way back to his boat?"

"No, nothing."

Something in the way she pressed her lips together suggested that there was more to this story.

"How about earlier?" I asked, fishing. "Did he have an exchange with any of the neighbors?"

Mrs. Carver folded her arms under her breasts and leveled her gaze at me. "You should probably talk to Pete Lackey about that."

"They had words?"

She nodded.

"What time?"

"A little before nine."

"You heard it yourself?"

"Anyone who was home and had an open window heard Pete standing on the shore yelling obscenities at Russ before he even shut off his engines."

"What else did you hear?" *Any threats?*

"I heard him say, 'Stay away from my wife. Do you hear me?' He shouted it over and over again."

"How did Russell react to that?"

"He'd told me before, it wasn't like that. That it was just a job. I went into my backyard and saw them going back and forth the entire time Russ was making his way over to my place in his dinghy."

"Did either of them make any reference to Russell's tires being slashed earlier in the week?"

"No, I didn't hear anything like that."

"Did Russell ever give you the impression that he thought Pete had something to do with that?"

"The only impression I got was that he didn't want to talk about it."

Dang. Then again, it didn't appear that Beverly Carver had wanted much in the way of conversation from Russell.

"What about Mrs. Lackey?" So far, she'd barely been mentioned. "Where was she during this exchange?"

Mrs. Carver's lips tightened into a flicker of a smirk. "She was standing behind Pete, crying like a baby. Pathetic really."

Her flippant remark about what had to have been a mortifying situation for Joyce Lackey surprised me. "Why do you say that?"

She stopped rocking. "Because Joyce practically threw herself at Russ whenever Pete wasn't around. Baking him cookies, serving him little finger sandwiches in the gazebo. Like he'd be impressed by her second-rate Martha Stewart imitation. Trust me, he wasn't."

"Did he talk to you about Joyce?"

"Not really. But Friday night, he said that it was a good thing that the job over there was close to being done because he didn't need any trouble from Pete."

It looked to me like trouble had come to Russell Falco whether he'd needed it or not.

✳

After I left Beverly Carver's house, I walked back to my car and drove another mile and a half on Morton Road past a sprawling horse farm on the right, and parked in front of a fenced yard of fir trees and grass that hadn't seen a lawnmower for most of the summer. In the gravel driveway was the candy apple red Mustang I'd seen Andy Falco driving around town alongside a dented Chevy pickup listing like a crippled battleship. For an obvious reason, as I soon saw when I stood next to it—it had two very flat right tires.

Maybe this had been meant to be a warning, like a shot across the bow. Based on what Mrs. Carver had told me and the fact that this truck had been seen parked at the Lackey house Monday night, I couldn't help but think that this was the handiwork of a jealous husband. And if that was the case, had he been jealous enough to kill?

I heard an approaching *clip clop* and turned to see a large brown and white face staring at me from behind the fence.

"Don't suppose you saw what happened here Monday night," I asked the horse.

She nickered.

"That's what I thought."

I retraced my steps back to the road. Aside from my new friend and her three pals grazing in the shade of a giant cedar tree, I didn't see another living soul. Nothing but abandoned pasture land across the street, and the neighbor's house to the east was set so far back from the road, chances were slim to none that they would have heard anything.

Whoever had slashed Russell's tires could have been in and out of here in less than two minutes. Easy peasy. Especially for someone who lived down the street.

Probably not so easy to prove that Pete Lackey had anything to do with Russell's death, but that wasn't my job. That would be Steve's job, once this became a coroner's case.

"If this becomes a coroner's case," he said fifteen minutes later when I bumped into him outside of Duke's, "there will be an investigation. In the meantime, there's something I'd like you to do."

There was? My heart beat a jungle rhythm against my rib cage. "What?"

"Stay out of this." Steve turned, walking toward his pickup parked two cars down on Main Street.

"Come on!" I said, hot on his heels. "You and I both know that Pete Lackey had something to do with what happened to Russell."

He grabbed my wrist and pulled me to his chest. "We aren't going to talk about this here."

"Then when can we talk about it? Over dinner maybe?"

His grip eased. "In front of your grandmother and Barry Ferris? Probably not what you had in mind."

Who was including them? "I was thinking about grilling a couple of steaks at your house."

"Nice thought, but your granny already invited me over. And her pot roast trumps steaks."

Yes, it did, but that meant we'd be spending most of the evening together not talking about the Russell Falco case and not touching one another. So far I didn't much care for two out of the three items on tonight's menu.

I watched him climb into the cab of his truck. "You're going to have to talk to me about this sometime."

"Says you."

I leaned against the driver's door. "Really, there's a lot I need to tell you."

Steve's brown eyes sharpened their focus. "It sounds like you've been a busy girl."

"I was just—"

Actually, I wasn't sure what I was doing beyond trying to connect a few dots in my own mind.

"—following up on some inquiries that I made about Russell."

He slowly shook his head, the tic of annoyance at his jawline cancelling out the easy smile on his tan lips. "I said it before, but seeing how you seem to have selective hearing, I'm going to tell you again. Back off. I don't need anyone else getting involved in this mess, least of all you."

"Too bad because I have to ask people questions. It's part of my job."

"Uh-huh."

Okay, we both knew that throwing the job thing at him was a weak move, but I was desperate and Steve hadn't left me much to work with.

He started the engine.

"We still need to talk," I called after him as he pulled out of the parking spot.

Without a sideways glance he accelerated down Main Street.

"You can run but you can't hide. I know where you live." And planned to be over there later tonight whether he was in a chatty mood or not.

I walked back to Duke's, the silver bell over the front door signaling the entrance of a hungry patron, who in this case got a family discount.

Lucille, roaming the diner with a coffee carafe, filled a cup and pushed it at me the second I took a seat at the lemon yellow Formica counter. "What was going on out there?"

"Nothing." I reached for one of the laminated menus stacked behind a stainless steel napkin holder to put a little distance between my mouth and her prying eyes.

Duke's longest-tenured waitress leaned her elbows on the counter in front of me, her platinum bob framing her full cheeks. "You two aren't fighting, are you?"

"Nope." I perused the menu. "How are the patty melts today?"

Snatching the menu out of my hands, Lucille narrowed her light blue eyes at me, the frown lines between her thin brows echoing her displeasure. "The same as they always are. Greasy. Are you really not going to tell me what's up with you and Steve?"

"Nothing's up. And I'll have the patty melt with fries."

It wasn't the healthiest of food choices, but I came from a long line of women who ate in times of crisis. Not that a dead body, two slashed tires, and a best friend who wouldn't take two minutes to let me talk to him necessarily overburdened my coping skills on my usual fifteen hundred calories a day. But when I added my newly engaged mother to the equation, it was as good as sticking a fork into my goal of losing thirty pounds.

Grimacing, Lucille lumbered to the kitchen pass-through window in her squeaky white orthopedic shoes and slipped my lunch order onto the aluminum wheel over the grill. "Patty melt. Fries."

Hector Avocato, Duke's weekend line cook for over ten years, pointed his spatula at me through the window. "You should have a salad, *mi querida*."

Having my friends know about the diet I was supposed to be on was beyond inconvenient, particularly at lunch time. "Fine, no fries. Salad instead."

"I meant instead of the patty melt," he said.

"Not negotiable, Hector."

"Hey, it's your funeral."

Speaking of funerals reminded me of the fact that Hector used to work with Russell's dad, back when the boys were little.

Cradling my coffee cup, I leaned against the kitchen door jamb. "Hector, could I ask you something?"

He tossed a hamburger patty onto the grill. "Shoot."

"When you worked for Falco Charters, did you have much interaction with Mrs. Falco?"

"Sure, back in the day she handled the payroll, paid all the bills." He glanced at me, a melancholy smile at his lips. "Gil and the boys used to call her *the boss*."

I took a sip of the industrial strength sludge in my cup and reached for the milk carton in the refrigerator next to me. "I know things didn't end well between her and Mr. Falco." Which was putting it mildly considering that Mitzi Falco had stabbed her husband in the shoulder and then disappeared after cleaning out his bank account.

Hector's lean cheeks puffed out as he exhaled. "She was a handful, a woman who marched to her own tune."

No kidding.

I filled my cup with enough milk to make it taste like a bad latte. At least it was a marginal improvement over Duke's crude oil brew. "Do you think she knows about Russell?"

Hector nodded. "She knows."

"I hope so." Even though she walked out on him when he was a teenager, he was still her firstborn.

"*Querida*, I saw her on my way into work. She definitely knows."

Criminy, Russell's funeral was going to be standing room only. Not just with all the women he had dated, but because Mitzi Falco was back in town.

Chapter Seven

"I hope you all saved some room for dessert," Gram said as I cleared the dishes from the dining room table.

Marietta ran a hand over her flat stomach. "Oh, Mama, I couldn't eat another bite. Truly."

Sure. She'd barely eaten a thing all day—atypical behavior for a Digby approaching critical mass, in her case because her checking account balance was looking dangerously similar to mine, but she had yet to broach that subject with the fiancé sitting next to her.

Gram passed me her dinner plate. "Pity. I was hoping to get your opinion on the butter pecan cookies I was thinking about entering in the fair."

My mother's lips formed a perfect oval. "Ooooh, mah favorite. Well, maybe just one. Just to offer mah opinion."

"Good. I want you all to pretend that you're on the panel of judges and give me your honest feedback." Gram sighed. "I'm sure the competition is gonna be tougher than ever this year."

I saw an opportunity and jumped in with both my size eights. "Where do you think your stiffest competition will come from? Joyce Lackey or Beverly Carver?"

Picking up Steve's plate, I ignored the *back off* look he gave me.

Gram reached for her wine glass. "Joyce without question. She's won the blue ribbon three years in a row, but they'll both be tough."

I nodded like she was telling me something I didn't already know. "I have it on good authority that Joyce was trying out some recipes on Russell Falco while he did some work at her house last week. You'd better watch out, Gram. She's definitely going for a fourth blue ribbon."

Steve pushed back his chair and leveled his gaze on me as he pulled the stack of plates from my grasp. "Let me help you with those."

My mother sucked in a breath. "Russell, the man who turned up at Cedars Cove yesterday?"

"Guess he won't be serving as one of this year's judges," Mr. Ferris quipped as he refilled his wine glass.

Marietta swatted his arm with the back of her hand. "Let's have a little respect for the dead, if you please."

Gram frowned at me. "Are you sure about Russell working over at the Lackeys'? That really doesn't sound like something Pete would agree to."

Thank you, Gram! "That's what I thought."

Shaking his head, Steve headed for the kitchen.

"Stevie," Gram said, calling out to him. "You know Pete better than the rest of us. Doesn't that seem out of character to you?"

"I really couldn't say, Eleanor. I see people doing crazy things almost every day." He crooked an index finger at me. "Charmaine, you're needed in the kitchen."

To avoid Steve's glare I headed straight to the freezer. "So what sounds good? French vanilla or mocha almond fudge ice cream with the cookies?"

Bracing himself against the refrigerator with one hand, he leaned over me, his breath warm in my ear. "You know what would sound good?"

"Does it involve finger-painting one another with mocha almond fudge?" Because that sounded really good to me.

"Now's not the time to be cute, Char."

I thought it was the perfect time, particularly after he'd been dodging me most of the day. "I can't help it if you think I'm cute."

He reached past me, grabbed the carton of French vanilla, and then slammed the freezer door shut. "You're pushing it, and I want you to stop. Now."

"But I have information that could be important in the investigation into Russell's death, and I need to talk to you about it."

"I told you before, *there is no investigation*. Jeez, there hasn't even been an autopsy."

"But there will be soon, and when the results go to Frankie and she makes this a criminal case, you'll want to speak with Joyce and Pete Lackey. Beverly Carver, too!"

Steve slapped the brick of ice cream onto the tile countertop. "If...*if*...this becomes a criminal case, I'll launch a thorough investigation. In the meantime, I'll take your suggestions under advisement."

"Oh yeah?" I stared into what felt like an impenetrable block of bittersweet chocolate. "Then here's my best advice. You'd better put Beverly at the top of your witness list because she was sleeping with Russell Falco and might be the last person who saw him alive."

Steve's gaze softened as he looked over my shoulder. "There's no proof of that, Eleanor, so I wouldn't repeat anything you heard."

I turned to see Gram's pupils magnified to twice their normal size behind her trifocals.

"Beverly and Russell were lovers?" she asked as she crossed in front of me and pulled out five glass bowls from the cupboard. Her face blanched. "You don't think she had anything to do with his death, do you?"

Steve shook his head. "Char and I were just talking a little shop and one of us was letting her imagination run away with her."

I stuck my tongue out at him.

"Sorry," he said with a disarming smile. "It was the wrong place and time to speculate about what might have happened to Russell."

I pushed him aside to grab the platter of cookies Gram had left on the counter. "Yeah, we'll save our *shop talk* for later."

She shifted her gaze from me to him and back again to me. "Are you two fighting?"

Sort of. "Nope."

"Uh-huh." Gram looked unconvinced. "Whatever you're doing, stop it and bring in that ice cream before it melts."

Steve's lips curled into a satisfied smile the instant she stepped into the dining room. "You heard the woman. Stop it."

"You can be a real jerk sometimes."

"Keep it up, Chow Mein, and there will be no mocha almond fudge for you later during our *shop talk*."

"Maybe I don't want any."

Steve headed for the dining room. "Yeah, you do."

Yeah, I did. Darn it.

✳

The next morning, I staggered up the chipped marble staircase of the Chimacam County Courthouse, my head pounding from a mocha almond fudge hangover.

I stepped onto the gold and black tile of the third floor landing and waved at the sheriff's deputy eyeballing me from his desk opposite the stairs.

The county's human security system acknowledged me with a curt nod. He then shot a glance at the ancient brass clock mounted above the front door, one of the many historical artifacts in the four-story, red brick building that dated back to the late eighteen hundreds.

I was ten minutes late, not because of the hangover. I couldn't zip up the cotton twill slacks I had thought I'd be wearing. Not good since they were supposed to be my fat pants. I had to finally settle on a pair of stretchy black yoga pants and a pink cotton knit tunic I found last summer on the sale rack. I threw on a chunky silver and onyx necklace so that I wouldn't look like I was heading off to my morning exercise class and left the house swearing that I'd atone for all the ice cream and cookies I'd scarfed down in the last twenty-four hours.

Of course, that was before I stopped at Duke's for a

coffee to go and had to sample one of the chocolate chip cookies my great-aunt Alice planned to enter in the county fair.

Really, could I say no to the woman who taught me how to bake my first apple pie? Especially when she thought she had the perfect recipe to beat Joyce Lackey in the drop cookie division?

I'd concede the point that a smarter person would have known when it was time to say *when* and go back on the diet wagon. But then I would have missed out on one of the best chocolate chip cookies I'd ever tasted.

However, all wasn't lost for my atonement plans this Monday. With the sun burning through the morning haze over the bay, it was shaping up to be a warm and clear September day—tailor-made for a walk during my lunch hour. Maybe even meander down to the harbor to see if anyone had seen Russell on his boat Friday night. Yes, that sounded like a great atonement plan to me.

I entered the first door on the right and headed down the threadbare hallway to find out if Frankie had read my preliminary report on Russell.

One of the junior assistant prosecuting attorneys, a skinny twenty-something in a cheap wool suit, slowed as he passed me in the hallway. "We're out of coffee. I just used the last of it."

Like I wasn't already well aware of the pecking order around here. Not only was I being told that he resented having to make a pot of coffee, but I needed to get my ass to the store.

I forced a smile. "I'll take care of it." *And good morning to you too, Brett.*

I mentally added making a coffee run to my to-do list and then stopped outside Frankie's office, where her legal eagle assistant, Patsy Faraday, glanced up from her post. "You're late," she said with her fingers poised over her computer keyboard.

"I know. I had a small emergency this morning." Which stretched the truth, but starting the week by not being able to fit into my fat pants constituted an emergency in my book.

Considering that plus-sized Patsy had also recently forked her way through a divorce, she should have been the one person I could confide in about my fat pants dilemma.

She leaned back in her chair, the little pucker of contempt at the corner of her fleshy mouth serving as a clear reminder that Patsy wouldn't shed a tear if I didn't make it through my thirty-day probation period. I let the sharing moment pass and hoped that she wouldn't rat me out to Frankie.

Patsy's steady gaze went to the mass of loose curls I hadn't bothered to restrain before I left the house. "I see."

I had more important things to worry about this morning than a bad hair day, and the investigation into Russell Falco's death was at the top of the list with Junior's coffee emergency a distant second.

I peeked through the open door of the office she protected like a guard dog and saw Frankie Rickard waving me in with a telephone receiver pressed to her ear.

"I understand, Herb," Frankie said, pointing across her desk at a Georgian high back chair. "I should have more information for you tomorrow afternoon."

She rolled her eyes while I took a seat and tried to act like I couldn't hear Herb raising his voice to the Chimacam County Coroner.

Seconds later, she hung up the phone and finger-combed a wayward auburn-gray lock back into her up-swept hairdo. "The mayor isn't happy about a body washing up on shore. Says it's bad for business."

Frankie leaned back in her chair and tapped the blue file folder on her desk with an unvarnished index finger.

Blue was the color used in the office to distinguish coroner's cases from the criminal cases that would be assigned to Ben Santiago's team. I didn't have to look to know what name I'd see on the folder tab: *Russell Falco*.

She pursed her peony pink mouth, accentuating the puckers surrounding it. "At least it was Fred Wixey and not a tourist who found him. Not that it would make the mayor feel any better when he's promoting next week's county fair."

I had served Mayor Herb Carlton over a dozen bacon cheeseburgers earlier this summer, while I was waitressing at Duke's. He was a glad-hander of the first order, always flashing a toothy grin, constantly trading jabs with Duke followed by a hearty slap to the back. A former president of the Chimacam County Chamber of Commerce, Herb certainly knew his stuff when it came to business, but I suspected his phone call to Frankie had been prompted by the pall that would be cast over his peaceful senior citizen mecca if Russell's cause of death were determined to be anything other than accidental. It would surely be a front page headline in the Port Merritt

Gazette while coming as equally bad news for Herb's political future as a keeper of that peace.

Frankie picked up the blue folder "Are you heading back to your desk?"

My heart leapt with eager anticipation. "Unless you have something else you want me to do." Like an interview with Joyce and Pete Lackey, or pop on down to the harbor and chat with Russell's brothers?

"No, not right now."

Dang.

She handed me the folder. "Would you please take this to Karla?"

Karla Tate had been Frankie's senior legal assistant for over a decade and served as the primary death investigation coordinator for the county coroner's office. After a blue folder was created, it didn't pass *Go* without first hitting Karla's desk, so it came as no surprise that I was being asked to be the delivery girl, especially since it had been my job for the last four weeks to shadow Karla so that I could act as her backup.

Because we'd had only two deaths of a suspicious nature in those four weeks and only one of them had become a coroner's case, I'd heard a lot of "we'll cover this later when we have an actual case."

With Russell's folder in my hot little hands, I had a feeling *later* was right around the corner.

Frankie pushed her wireframe bifocals up the bridge of her nose, tension tugging at the fine lines edging her eyes. "Thanks for putting in a little overtime over the weekend."

I knew she meant the report and not my extracurricular activities, so I nodded and headed for the door.

"Oh, and Char, just a reminder in case you get a call from the newspaper or if anyone at Duke's tries to pump you for information about this—we don't talk about any cases outside of this office." She leveled a gaze at me that was worthy of a headmistress setting the ground rules on the first day of school.

Clearly, Russell's death would be at the top of everyone's minds at Gossip Central today, and she and I both knew I'd be a primary target for Lucille, which meant that I'd better buy my lunch elsewhere if I didn't want to be grilled like a cheese panini. "Yes, ma'am."

Patsy handed me a white envelope as I passed in front of her.

"One of the deputy prosecutors needs this subpoena to be delivered today."

Process server, delivery girl, coffee procurer—each one on the list of my level one assistant responsibilities, but at least it got me out of the office a couple of times a week.

As a bonus, since the address on the envelope looked to be several blocks from the courthouse, I figured it gave me an early opportunity to burn some calories if I hoofed it. "No problem." And I could pick up some coffee on the way back.

After heading down the hall to the break room to make sure the coffee was brewing, I rounded the bend that led to the office bullpen that I shared with five legal assistants.

Karla Tate, a two pack a day smoker with a rheumy cough, who sat between a window partially blocked by tall black file cabinets and an old fax machine, looked up at me over her computer monitor. "Mornin'."

"Morning." I placed Russell's folder in her inbox. "From Frankie."

"I figured that would make its way to me today." Karla's gaze softened behind her horn-rimmed glasses. "Such a shame about Russell. My daughter dated him back in high school. Worried about her the entire time, too."

Her daughter, Maggie, several years ahead of me in school, had been a wild child, heavy into the Seattle grunge scene. Last I'd heard she was married to a Port Townsend dentist and had three kids.

"I'll have to tell her about this," Karla added. "I'm sure she'll want to come to the service."

And no doubt join the many girlfriends there from Russell's past.

Karla opened the folder, scanned the first page of my preliminary report, and a smile creased her face. "Fred found him around *nine-ish*?"

I shrugged. "He doesn't wear a watch."

"I see."

She turned the page. "You confirmed with Steve that no shoes and no cell phone were found on Russell or on the boat, huh?"

"Right." And checked for myself, not that I wanted to admit that little fact to any of my coworkers.

"Okay." Karla closed the file and set it on the edge of her tidy desk. "It looks like we wait for Dr. Zuniga's findings and go from there."

I knew the drill. If the autopsy results supported my

suspicions that Russell Falco's death was no accident, it would become a coroner's case and Steve would proceed with an investigation. In the meantime, everyone waited.

Drill or no drill, waiting wasn't my best thing.

Neither was dealing with an office full of cranky lawyers going through caffeine withdrawal, which I estimated would start in about an hour. So, after I went to my desk and checked for messages, I dashed out the door, subpoena in hand and petty cash in my tote bag for a can of coffee.

After four blocks with the crisp morning breeze at my back, I glanced up 3rd and spotted Steve's police cruiser parked in his usual spot in the Port Merritt PD parking lot. Pretty much as I had expected since I knew he wasn't scheduled to testify in court today.

What I didn't expect to see was the woman exiting the front door of the station – Joyce Lackey, her body shaking with sobs.

"Hi, Joyce. What a small world," I said, trying to keep the mood light as I approached. "My grandmother and I were just talking about you."

She swiped at the tears cascading down her cheeks. "S-sorry…I can't…talk…right now." Her breath hitched as she stumbled toward the parking lot.

Supporting her at the elbow before she crumpled to the sidewalk, I spotted a bench seat across the street in the shade of a tall cedar tree. "Of course you can't. You need to sit down," I said, leading her to the bench.

I gave her a minute to blow her nose and gather herself together. "Would you like some water?" I'd have to run back to the police station to fetch her some and probably arouse Steve's suspicions if she said yes, so it came as a huge relief when Joyce shook her head.

"I'm okay...really." She dabbed at the fresh tears spilling over her sparse lashes. "I just need a minute."

I patted her hand. "Of course. Russell's death must have come as quite a shock," I said, watching for her reaction.

She nodded and blew her nose again.

"Were you close?" As close as Beverly Carver led me to believe?

"We were friends—g-good friends."

That led to a fresh round of tears, and I needed her to focus on the reason she'd come to see Steve today, so I decided to cut to the chase and come clean. "Joyce, I work at the coroner's office, and it would help us understand what happened if you could tell me everything you remember about the last time you saw Russell."

She sat up a little straighter. "I told Steve everything I know."

"I'm sure you did." And there was no way he'd be sharing any of that with me. "But Steve can't launch an investigation until Frankie sends him the case, so if you could..."

Joyce's puffy eyes widened as she turned to me. "But he's the police."

"And his hands are tied until after the—"

I didn't want to upset Joyce further and mention Russell's autopsy scheduled for tomorrow.

"—preliminary investigation by the Coroner."

"Oh. I-I guess that makes sense." She wiped her eyes with the soggy tissue.

I pulled my notebook and pen from my tote. "Maybe we could start with what Russell was doing at your house Friday."

She took a deep breath and slowly released it. "He was building me a new pantry along with a bookshelf for all my cookbooks."

"What was he wearing?"

"A black T-shirt, jeans, sneakers—pretty much what he always wore when he was working."

She'd just described the clothes I found on Russell's boat and provided ample reason for the wood shavings on his shirt.

Okay, so he'd worked at Joyce's house Friday and then headed back over to help Kelsey for a few hours before cleaning up for his date with Beverly Carver.

Busy guy. "Did he seem troubled? Anything bothering him?"

"Everything was fine. Russell was putting the finishing touches on the pantry. I was baking cookies." She smiled while her azure eyes glistened with more waterworks. "Chocolate chip—his favorite."

Uh-oh. Aunt Alice might be in for some stiff competition if Joyce decided to enter those cookies in the fair.

"It was just the two of you there?" I asked, hoping to gain a sense of their relationship.

"For most of the afternoon." Staring blankly at the street, she opened her mouth and then clamped it shut.

Since she had just censored herself, I guessed at the reason. "Until your husband came home?"

Squeezing her eyes shut, she nodded, tears streaking down her cheeks.

"Where were you when your husband came into the house?"

"The pantry."

"And where was Russell?"

"The pantry," Joyce choked out, her voice mainly air as she sat very still, like she wanted to make herself invisible.

Not the behavior of a woman with nothing to hide.

"Then what happened?"

"Pete... my husband walked in on us and jumped to some ridiculous conclusions." Pressing her thin lips together, she slowly shifted her gaze to me. "Completely ridiculous. Really."

"Uh-huh." Now she was digging a deeper hole for herself by omitting the most important part of her story: what she was doing in the pantry with Russell Falco.

I jotted down some notes. "Had Russell been working at your house long?"

"Almost three weeks."

"Three weeks for a pantry and a bookshelf?" My grandfather had built Gram's pantry in less than a week.

Joyce stiffened. "We also talked about other projects I wanted done."

Could she be any more vague? "Like what?"

She narrowed her puffy eyes at me for a fraction of a second, making it abundantly clear that she didn't like the question. Tough. I didn't like her evasive answers.

"Like a walk-in closet. I've always wanted one and Pete's been so busy lately. Anyway, I thought Russell might be interested in the job."

That discussion would account for one hour, tops.

"Did Pete know that you were talking to Russell about these projects?"

"Not at first, but it became obvious. You know, once the construction started."

Pete didn't impress me as a man who liked surprises. "And how did he respond to the news?"

"He wasn't happy about it."

"About the work being done or about Russell being the one doing the work?"

"Both."

"So when your husband came home Friday and caught you in the pantry with Russell..."

"We weren't doing anything but talking." She searched my eyes like it was important that I believe her. "Really."

But I really couldn't, not after what Beverly Carver had told me.

Joyce blinked away a fresh tear. "But he went ballistic, yelling at Russell. Calling him all sorts of nasty names while telling him to get out of his house." Hanging her head, she dabbed at her leaky nose. "It was horrible."

I didn't doubt the truth of this part of her story. "What time was this?"

"Around four."

Giving Russell plenty of time to gather his things, pilot his boat back to the marina, and then work at Kelsey's for a few hours.

"I understand Russell came back later that evening."

Joyce's lips trembled as her eyes pooled. "By b-boat. He'd been having car trouble all week."

Since that trouble consisted of two slashed tires, that was a monumental understatement.

"And your husband and he exchanged words."

"It wasn't an exchange. Pete was spewing all sorts of obscenities, telling Russell to stay away from me."

Pretty much what I'd expected to hear given what Beverly Carver had told me yesterday.

Joyce's shoulders slumped. "But...it wasn't...me...he came...to see," she said between sobs.

She obviously knew that Beverly wasn't just her cookie-baking competition.

I passed Joyce a fresh tissue from the mini-pack I kept in my tote—something Karla had recommended I carry whenever I went out into the field to interview victims' loved ones.

I waited for a moment while Joyce blew her nose and mopped up her face. "Is there anything else you'd like to tell me about that night?" *Or about your relationship with Russell Falco?*

Staring down at her scuffed sneakers, she shook her head until her shoulder-length hair shrouded her round face like a copper veil.

"Do you need a ride home? Should I call your husband—"

"No!"

"Really," I gently prodded, sitting on the edge of the bench seat. "You probably shouldn't drive."

"You don't understand. He killed Russell. I know he did."

I leaned closer, my pulse pounding in my ears. "Who?"

"Pete."

Chapter Eight

"I ran into Joyce outside," I said without knocking on the open door of the Port Merritt Police Department's Investigation Division.

The sole member of that department glanced up over his computer monitor at me. The set of his jaw told me that he wasn't happy to see me.

I shut Steve's door with more force than necessary to let him know that I didn't care.

"Hello to you, too," he said, clicking on his keyboard.

"If Joyce told you what she just told me, why are you still sitting here?"

"I'm paid to sit here." His eyes tracked me as I came around to the edge of his desk. "It's called work. You should head back to your office and try it."

"Cute. What about Pete Lackey?"

"What about him?"

I inched closer, trying to get a better angle on his monitor to see if what he was working on had anything to do with Joyce Lackey.

Steve pointed at the hardback chair facing his metal desk. "If you're staying, sit over there."

"Fine." I scooted the chair closer as I took a seat. "Don't you think you should question him?"

"Don't you think we should get through the autopsy and have a cause of death before we start jumping to conclusions about what could have been an unfortunate accident?"

I hated the way he said *we* when he meant me.

"So you're not buying Joyce's story about how angry Pete was that Russell seemed to be sniffing around his wife?"

Steve leaned back in his squeaky black vinyl chair, giving me a clear view of his face. "I didn't say that."

True enough, but he was skilled at not saying much, particularly when I was around.

If I wanted a glimpse of the cards he was holding so close to the vest, I knew I needed to up the ante. "What if I told you there was a witness to the heated exchange Pete Lackey had with Russell, when he came back later that night?"

Steve's laugh lines tightened. "And what if I reminded you that this is not a coroner's case and that you should stick to doing the job that you were actually hired to do?"

"It's not a coroner's case *yet*."

He stared across his desk at me. "Since the autopsy's scheduled for tomorrow, nothing's going to happen today, no matter how much some people may want it to."

I folded my arms, meeting his stare with equal measure. "Does that mean that you still don't want to hear about my chat with Beverly Carver?" *Because you really need to.*

Lowering his gaze, Steve shook his head, his lips drawn into a grimace he didn't bother to disguise.

"What's with the face? I was just talking to her."

"Are you going to tell me that you just *happened* to run into her?"

"Uh...sort of."

"Stay out of this, Char. The Lackeys and their neighbors don't need you poking around in their private business."

"I'm just trying to—"

"I don't care what you're trying to do. Until this is an official case, you're done. Got it?"

Narrowing my eyes at him, I pushed out of my chair. "Got it." But I wasn't even close to being done. "I take it that you won't be making any inquiries about how Russell Falco's truck ended up with two slashed tires?" I asked, watching closely for a reaction.

"Nothing to inquire about seeing as how that incident was never reported."

Steve had been clever by wrapping up his response in a ribbon of truth, but that didn't make me buy what he was selling, especially since Russell's body was found at Cedars Cove five days later.

"You know I don't believe you."

He shrugged a shoulder, focusing on his monitor. "Have a nice day, Chow Mein."

Ten minutes later, I was in line at the Red Apple Market with a three-pound can of coffee in my hands when I spotted Pete Lackey in the deli section.

Since I was supposed to be avoiding Duke's at lunchtime, this seemed like the perfect opportunity for me to pick up a tuna salad on whole wheat as well as some side dish conversation with Pete.

I stood next to him in front of a refrigerated case of pre-made sandwiches and looked at the plastic containers of doughnuts, potato salad, and fried chicken bundled in his arms. "I don't know that I'm in the mood for a sandwich. How's the chicken?"

Pete squinted at me, carving creases into his leathery skin. "Huh?"

I pointed at the six-piece box of chicken he was holding.

"Oh, don't know. First time I'm trying it." He picked up a roast beef sandwich then added a bag of chips to his pile.

"You're either very hungry or you're buying for a crowd," I said with an easy smile.

"No crowd. Just me." He started to walk away.

I needed to stop him since I hadn't found out anything other than it looked like his wife wouldn't be doing much cooking for him today. "I ran into Joyce earlier this morning—"

"Where?"

By the way he whipped around and stared at me, I knew that I couldn't have surprised him more if I'd lassoed him around the ankles. I also saw something else etched into every line of his face—worry.

Since Joyce had given me the clear impression that she was afraid to be alone with the man, I opted for a generic answer. "Near Old Town." True enough with the police department located three blocks away from the touristy section of town marked by its Victorian-era construction and wooden sidewalks.

"She seemed upset," I added.

Storm clouds brewed in Pete's bloodshot eyes while his heavy brow furrowed, making him look as sympathetic as my ex-husband had when I'd told him I'd gotten rear-ended the one and only time during our marriage that he had let me drive his precious Jaguar.

I'm just fine, dear. Nothing was hurt that can't be fixed. Thanks for caring.

Pressing his thin lips together, Pete averted his gaze. "Yeah."

Clearly, Joyce wasn't the only one who was upset.

"Everything okay?" I didn't need to be able to read his craggy face to answer my own question.

"Sure," he grunted as he turned his back to me.

I watched Pete make his way to the checkout line as if all the energy had been sapped out of him. Given what I'd heard about the guy from Joyce and Beverly, I'd practically expected hail and brimstone to rain from his eyes. Of course, he could have used it all on Russell Falco.

After hightailing it back to the office to make coffee, I did an hour of filing for Patsy, sat in on an interview with a reluctant witness for one of the assistant prosecutors, and then remembered about the subpoena still burning a hole in my tote.

Based on the address I figured I could kill two birds with one stone: slap the subpoena on the civil engineer who'd be called to testify for the prosecution later in the month, and avoid Gossip Central at Duke's by eating my sandwich at Broward Park on the way back.

As I made the left turn out of the Prosecutor's office and crossed the checkerboard tile floor to the third floor landing, I saw Steve coming up the stairs. "What brings you here?"

"A meeting." He gave me a long look. "And where are you off to? Doesn't Frankie have any actual work for you to do here?"

I pulled out the envelope with the subpoena and aimed the county seal at his nose. "I'll have you know that I'm working." But I was more interested in why he was here than in trading jabs. "Who are you meeting with?" *And was it about Russell?*

Steve shook his head. "Stand down, Deputy. It has nothing to do with Russell Falco."

True. That meant he had probably come to see Ben about a criminal case that would soon be going to trial. "Did I ask?"

He grinned. "You didn't have to."

I hated that he could read me that easily.

Leaning toward me, Steve sniffed the base of my neck.

My temperature rising by the second, I scanned the rest of the third floor. Fortunately, the only person in sight was the sheriff's deputy, eyeing us intently from his post. "What are you doing?"

"You smell good," he whispered in my ear. "Not like mocha almond fudge anymore but still good enough to eat."

Oh, my.

Heat radiated from his body. "Next time you want to do some finger-painting I pick the flavor. Something without nuts." He winked. "Seems kind of redundant."

My, oh, my!

I needed to hit the street and deliver the subpoena before I melted into a puddle of mocha almond fudge, so I pushed him away with an index finger to the chest. "We will definitely continue this conversation later."

"Speaking of later," he called after me as I dashed down the stairs.

I turned, trying to play it cool but feeling as giddy as a thirteen-year-old on her first date.

"Want to go to Eddie's for pizza?"

Instead of joining Marietta and Gram for dinner and hearing all about my mother's wedding plans? "Heck, yeah."

"I'll pick you up around six."

"I may have to run an errand after work. I'll meet you there."

Just two friends sharing a pizza like we had dozens of times since high school. Nothing there to resemble grist for the rumor mill—as long as he didn't order any ice cream for dessert.

Almost twenty minutes later, after a short uphill hike to an engineering firm located in a strip mall a block from Broward Park, I served the subpoena on a less than pleased civil engineer.

On the way back I spotted a vacant picnic table in the

shade of a huge Douglas fir tree—a perfect spot to eat my lunch. Just as I sat down and pulled my tuna sandwich from my tote, I saw Andy Falco climb out of his pickup and walk over to a park bench where a woman with short black hair sat. The woman, who looked like she outweighed Andy by close to fifty pounds, stood and embraced him.

I sucked in a breath. I hadn't seen her in over twenty years, but there was no mistaking that the woman was Mitzi Falco.

The last thing I needed was for Andy to think I was spying on him, especially since he'd seen me hanging around the marina Saturday, so I dropped my sandwich back in my tote and stepped away from the table. Unfortunately a preschooler squealing after a ball he'd rolled in Andy's direction caused him to look over and lock gazes with me.

It didn't take five seconds before I had an irate Andy Falco in my face. "What do you think you're doing? Are you following me or something?"

I showed him my sandwich. "I was just stopping for lunch. If I'd known you and your mother were here—"

"Sorry. I thought..." He raked a hand through his shaggy dark hair. "Never mind. Just don't say anything about seeing me here, okay? I don't need this getting back to Nate."

I looked behind him at the five feet two inches of pissed-off mother marching toward my table.

She swatted Andy's arm. "Need what getting back to Nate? That you're seeing your mother? If he has a problem with that, he needs to get over it."

Andy squeezed his eyes shut and uttered a few choice expletives. "This is exactly what I was trying to avoid."

Inching closer to the picnic table, Mitzi pulled on a pair of black, rhinestone-edged glasses and gave me a once-over. "I know you."

I pasted a smile on my face. "Hello, Mrs. Falco."

She folded her glasses and dropped them into her oversized purse, a diamond wedding band sparkling on her ring finger. "It's Mrs. Walther now."

Okay, she appeared to have moved on after leaving Gil Falco and the boys to fend for themselves.

I didn't have to guess what had brought her to town. "I'm sorry for your loss." With little else I could say, I fished a business card from my tote and handed it to her. "If there's anything I can do while you're here, don't hesitate to let me know."

"Charmaine Digby," she said, reading my card. "Yeah, I remember you from Duke's." She flicked the card at me. "And what exactly do you think you can do? Bring my boy back?"

"I'm sure there will be a coroner's investigation after the..." I couldn't bring myself to say *autopsy* to Russell's mother, and I immediately regretted opening my big mouth.

Tears pooled in her dark eyes as the cords in her neck tightened. "There'd better be. I want some answers!"

Looking as tentative as a man embracing a porcupine, Andy draped his arm over his mother's shoulder. "Let's go."

Mitzi shrugged him off. "Russ was a good swimmer. That needs to be included in that investigation," she said punctuating her statement by stabbing a stubby index finger two feet from my nose. "My boy could swim like a fish."

Andy blew out a weary breath. "He could drink like a fish, too."

"Andrew!" She looked up at him, teardrops spilling onto her cheeks. "Why am I the only one in this family who's shedding a tear over your brother?"

"Maybe because you weren't around for all his screw-ups and all the times I had to bail him out of jail. He was a drunk who couldn't hold down a job. Heck, Dad even had to fire him…twice!"

Mitzi straightened, her chin jutted out like she wanted to ram it into the chest of her second-born. "Russell was not a drunk. He was in recovery and had been sober for three years."

"How would you know?" Andy smirked. "It's not like you've been around to check up on us."

"Because I'm a recovering alcoholic and he was my sponsor."

Holy crap. That had to mean that Mitzi Falco Walther lived nearby, and from Andy's wide-eyed stare, this revelation came as news to him.

Pulling a tissue from her purse, Mitzi wiped her eyes. "Thank you for meeting me here." She sniffed, her head held high. "I thought you might want to talk to the police with me, but I can see that I'm wasting your time."

I watched Mitzi bolt past Andy. As she climbed into a white sedan and sped away, I looked up and saw that he had the same grim expression on his face as my ex had when he handed my divorce attorney the keys to the Jag.

I felt like I needed to say something to cut through the tension Mitzi had left in her wake. "Sorry to intrude on you and your mom. I'm sure you had a lot to talk about and my being here didn't help."

"Doesn't matter. It's been a long time since I had anything to say to her," he said and turned to leave.

"Andy," I called after him.

The lack of focus in his eyes as he looked back at me told me he was emotionally spent, but at least I had his attention.

"Do you think Russell was drinking again?"

"I don't know. I hardly saw the guy."

"He'd been living at the house with you, right?"

"Off and on for the last few months." Andy pressed his lips together. "I can't really tell you too much."

True, but that seemed like a deliberate choice.

He glanced over at the little boy with the ball. "Russ spent a lot of time on his boat."

I handed Andy the business card his mother had thrown back in my face. "If you find any bottles or cans in his room, will you let me know? It could be important to our investigation."

He stared down at the card. "There's definitely going to be an investigation?"

"Of course." One way or another.

He slowly nodded his head. The way he was drawing back his unshaven upper lip as he slipped my card into his shirt pocket gave me the distinct impression that this didn't come as good news.

Sitting down again to eat my tuna sandwich, I watched Andy walk back to his truck. Clearly, he was a man caught in the middle of twenty years of family drama between his mother and his brothers. But what I'd just witnessed had raised my antennae because I'd seen a man with something to hide.

Six hours later, I arrived at Eddie's. Since Steve's pickup wasn't in the parking lot and Rox was behind the high luster oak bar, I walked past a speaker reverberating with the Doobie Brothers rocking out *China Grove* and slid my butt onto my usual barstool.

"Hey, you'll never guess who I saw today," Rox said, placing a white bar napkin in front of me.

"Mitzi Falco."

"Wow, you're good." She held up two bottles. "Chablis or chardonnay?"

I pointed at the bottle of chardonnay. "I'm not *that* good. I ran into her during my lunch break." I didn't want to mention anything about Andy being there. Port Merritt's gossip circuit was probably already heating up about Mitzi being back in town and I had no desire to throw another log on that fire.

"Didn't really have a chance to say much more than hello." Which was almost true. "Any idea where she's living these days?"

After delivering my wine, Rox rested her elbows on the bar. "I only saw her for a minute at the Red Apple, but a few months back someone mentioned something about her living in Bremerton."

Bremerton was also home to a naval base, almost an hour away to the south. The largest town on the peninsula, Bremerton could have served as the perfect location for a woman who wanted to start a new life without being too far away from her old one.

I sipped my drink while Rox refilled a pitcher for the middle-aged guys in matching bowling shirts congregated in front of a flat screen TV.

When she returned to my end of the bar, I tried to pick up where we left off. "Bremerton, huh? I guess I never thought she'd be living that close."

"I think that's a recent development. There were rumors earlier this year that she married someone who works for the shipyard."

"Did you hear anything about the boys attending the wedding?"

"Andy and Nate were loyal to their dad right to the end," Rox said. "As far as I know, they haven't talked to Mitzi in years. They definitely didn't have the relationship with their mom that Russell had."

"Really. Why do you say that?"

"Back in the day Mitzi used to be quite the drinker."

No kidding. Today was one of the rare times I had seen her sober.

"The Falcos lived across the street from Tawny Renner. Remember her from junior high?"

Not really, but I nodded to keep Rox talking.

"Tawny had a huge crush on Russell—"

Who didn't?

"—and she thought he was all kinds of wonderful to drive his mom home and take care of her when she'd had one too many."

"He was probably the only one of the boys old enough

SEX, LIES, AND SNICKERDOODLES | 109

to drive," I said.

"Yeah, but I'd always thought that it was more than that. You know, how some kids take after one of their parents more than the other one?"

"Yep." Russell had certainly followed in his mother's footsteps when it came to racking up a bar tab.

Based on what Mitzi had said today about Russell acting as a sponsor to support her through her recovery process, it sounded like they had both turned over a new leaf. At least until Russell's efforts had been cut short last Saturday.

Rox's gaze shifted to the door. "Hey, Steve. The usual?"

"Sure," Steve eyed my wine glass as he sat down next to me.

I picked up the glass by the stem, holding it out of his reach. "Contrary to what you might think, this is *not* your usual."

"You're right, because only a girl would drink wine with pizza."

I looked up at Rox as she set a foamy glass of beer in front of Steve. "I think I was just insulted."

"I know you were," she said, winking at him on her way to the tap to refill another pitcher.

"Then again, there's no pizza in front of me. There could have been had you been on time." After I took a sip from my glass, I smiled sweetly.

"Sorry." Reaching past me, he snagged a laminated menu from a rack at the end of the bar. "So what sounds good?"

I knew what I wanted more than anything else. "How about some conversation?"

Staring intently at the menu, he loudly exhaled. "Here we go."

"Okay, I'll start. I saw Mitzi Falco today." I watched his face for a reaction. "Oh, excuse me. Mitzi... What's her new married name?"

He angled his head toward me. "Is that supposed to be my cue?"

"Walther as you and I both know because she came to see you today."

"Do you have my office staked out or something?"

"No, but it's not a bad idea."

"Did you kids decide what you want?" Rox asked, her pencil poised over her order ticket.

Steve ordered his favorite three-meat supreme pizza without asking for my input, so I took that as a clue that I wasn't going to get much of anything that I wanted tonight. Then, as soon as Rox headed for the kitchen with our order, he picked up his beer and spun on his barstool to face me. "We're not having this conversation here."

He started walking toward a table in the back, and I grabbed my wine glass and followed him.

Leaning back in his chair, he stretched out his long legs under the table and folded his arms. "Okay, so you saw Mrs. Walther today."

"And Andy... at Broward Park."

Steve's eyes narrowed, carving a crease between his eyebrows.

"Don't give me the stern eyebrow look."

Staring at me, his expression didn't change.

"And don't assume that I wasn't working because I

was."

"Did I say anything?"

I waggled my finger at his brow. "Yes."

Steve shook his head, but I saw a flicker of an uptick at the corner of his lips so I knew he wasn't totally annoyed.

"And you were at the park...why?"

"I stopped there for lunch after delivering a subpoena. That's when I saw Andy and his mother."

He leaned toward me. "Since her oldest son just died, I wouldn't make too much about her being in town."

"Did she mention that Russell had been three years sober? Or the fact that he was a good swimmer?"

Steve shrugged a shoulder—his usual non-answer.

"Unless he recently fell off the wagon, I don't think alcohol had anything to do with his death."

"As I seem to have to remind you, there will be an autopsy and we'll find out soon enough." He reached for his beer.

"I know, but don't you think it's strange that Andy portrays Russell as this major screw-up, and his mother credits him for being her AA sponsor?"

"Family dynamics can be complicated, Chow Mein. Relationships can be complicated. You of all people should know that."

"Yeah." I should and I did, but were we talking about me and my mother, or the new *friends with benefits* phase in Steve's and my relationship?

I didn't need him to read anything into the apprehension that had to be etching a path across my face, so I stared into the depths of my wineglass.

"You're awfully quiet all of a sudden," he said, tapping my foot with his. "Was that enough conversation for you?"

"For now. If I want to talk some more, I know where to find you."

His eyes darkened. "You can also find me if you don't want to talk."

If he was trying to improve my mood he knew exactly what to say.

"I could even pick up some ice cream on the way home. You know, if you save room for dessert."

Yep, exactly what to say.

I drained my wineglass and scurried into the kitchen to ask Rox to make that a pizza to go.

Chapter Nine

"Are you going to stare at that menu all day or are you going to order somethin'?" Lucille asked, squeaking by me in her orthopedic shoes.

Ninety-year-old Stanley, one of Duke's more senior regulars, sat next to me at his usual barstool. He stirred another sugar into his decaf. "Yeah. What's up with you? Off your feed?"

Yes, because I'd kicked off my lunch hour with a drive-by of Tolliver's Funeral Home, where I had a sighting of Dr. Zuniga's canopied truck. The forensic pathologist's igloo on wheels parked in Tolliver's lot meant only one thing—Russell Falco's autopsy was underway.

I might be the kind of deputy coroner who never got any closer to dead bodies than their blue file folders, but I'd heard enough grisly details from Karla to know what was happening four blocks away, and my stomach was churning.

Of course, last night's wine, greasy pizza, and ice cream had given me three more reasons to pop another antacid and search the menu for something unlikely to make a sudden reappearance on my leather sandals.

"I'm fine," I said, tucking the roll of antacids back in my tote.

Lucille's eyes raked over me as she topped off Stanley's coffee cup. "You sure? Cause you don't look so good."

Stanley pointed his thumb at me. "She's eating antacids."

I glared at Stanley for ratting me out.

He pushed his thick horn-rimmed glasses back up his bulbous nose. "What? You are."

Lucille's gaze softened. "Aw, hon. Are you hung over?"

I handed the laminated menu to her. "I'm not hung over, and I'll have two eggs scrambled."

She pursed her lips. "You're hung over all right."

"I'm not hung over!" I said, raising my voice, and then I looked past Lucille and caught a scowl from my great-uncle Duke.

Darrell "Duke" Duquette, a twenty-year Navy veteran sporting a silver crew-cut, pointed his stainless steel spatula at me through the cut-out window above his grill. "You're hung over? I swear, girl, you're trying to get yourself fired from that new job of yours."

Stifling a sigh, I slid off my stool to avoid exchanging barbs with the man from twelve feet away.

After I pushed open the swinging kitchen door I almost ran into my great-aunt Alice. She stuck her nose in my face and sniffed me.

Not quite as appealing as when Steve had done it, especially since he hadn't been frowning at me like a disapproving school marm.

"You smell minty." She cupped my face with her hands and peered into my eyes. "A little bloodshot, but lately that's normal."

Swell. My new normal.

Smiling, Alice patted my cheek. "Hello, sweetie." Her gaze slanted toward her husband of fifty-two years. "Get off the girl's case."

Duke pulled an order ticket from the aluminum wheel over the grill and waved it at me. "What's this then?"

Alice snatched my lunch order ticket from his hand and sucked in air as she read it. "Eggs! Oh, honey, are you pregnant?"

"No!" I could say that unequivocally having woken up this morning with some pre-menstrual bloat to accompany my queasy stomach. But beyond that, I didn't need any pregnancy speculation out of one of the three people who knew that I'd been seeing Steve. "Sheesh, you two, can't a girl order a couple of eggs? I could just be back on my diet."

Duke rolled his eyes and then cracked two eggs onto the grill. "Sure."

Okay, since I was eating cookies in this kitchen yesterday, that was a stretch even though it should have been true.

"Everything's fine," I said, trying to ignore the image in my head of Russell being filleted by Dr. Zuniga.

Alice arched an eyebrow. "I seriously doubt that. Your mom is still in town, isn't she?"

I nodded. At least we weren't talking about me anymore.

"Is she still planning to marry Barry?"

"Who knows?" I hadn't given up hope for kiss-off week to work its magic, for both their sakes.

My great-aunt clucked her tongue. "I wish that girl would stop making these rash decisions."

Me, too.

"She just got divorced," Alice added.

Me, too—a month after my mother.

Alice opened the refrigerator I was standing next to and pulled out a pound of butter. "There's no reason to rush into a new relationship. Anyone with an ounce of sense would know that now's the time to take things slow."

I thought about Steve and me. Had I rushed into something? Maybe not a real relationship, but a sex buddy fling I had no business thinking about? Day and night. "Maybe."

"There's no maybe about it." Alice headed back toward her butcher block worktable in the middle of the kitchen.

Given the fact that I didn't have a crumb of prior experience with casual sex, truer words had never been spoken.

Duke plated my scrambled eggs. "Okay, what gives? You don't show up for lunch yesterday and today you're green around the gills."

I took the plate from him and grabbed a fork from a drawer behind me. "Russell's autopsy is today, probably going on right now."

"Jeez! Sorry I asked. You don't have to…you know… actually *see* anything, do you?"

I shook my head. "My job ended with calling the doctor who's doing the…you know." I didn't want to say the word one more time today. I didn't think Duke had the stomach for it any more than I did.

His eyes tracked Lucille as she tacked another lunch order to the wheel in front of him. "Poor bastard."

"What do you know about Russell since he came back to town?"

"Nothin' much. Came in to eat once or twice a week. Flirted with all the girls, but that was nothin' new."

I speared a mouthful of egg with my fork. "Since you're so interested in people who are hung over..."

Throwing a couple of hamburger patties onto the grill, he shot me a dirty look.

"Did Russell ever look like he'd been drinking?"

Duke shook his head. "I think he'd put those days behind him."

Mitzi would certainly agree.

Leaning against the counter behind the grill, he turned to me as I chewed. "Or am I wrong about that? Was he drinking that night?"

"I don't know." But according to Beverly Carver and the lack of bottles and cans on his boat, I believed the answer to that question was *no*.

I downed the last bit of egg and set my plate in the plastic tub of dirty dishes by the sink. "Thanks for lunch."

I headed for the door and stopped when a couple in their early sixties pushed it open. I didn't recognize the woman at first, but the man with the thick head of salt and pepper hair I'd have known anywhere. "Dr. Zuniga."

Dr. Henry Zuniga's friendly face crinkled into a roadmap of fine lines. "We meet again, Charmaine Digby. You know my wife, Madelyn."

"Of course. Nice to see you again." I'd only met Dr. Zuniga and his surgical assistant wife once before, after an autopsy last month. Since it was obvious why they had come back to Port Merritt, I hoped my "nice to see you" remark didn't sound weird.

She nodded pleasantly. "I've always heard Duke's has the best burgers in town and thought we'd grab some lunch since we have over an hour before the two-thirty ferry."

"Someone's hungry," Dr. Zuniga said with a wink.

I didn't want to think about how she'd been working up an appetite, but at the same time, since they'd completed the autopsy this was an opportunity I couldn't pass up.

"I don't want to keep you from your lunch, but I wonder if I could speak with you for a moment." Or five.

He smiled at his wife. "Why don't you get us a table. I'll be along in a minute."

Madelyn Zuniga directed her steady gaze at me. "No problem," she said, but I got the message. *Whatever you have to say, make it fast.*

Dr. Zuniga held the door for me and we stepped outside into the warm September sunshine.

"I've been assisting on the Russell Falco death investigation. There appears to be some circumstantial evidence to suggest that he could be a victim of—" I hesitated to say murder, especially if the doctor was going to tell me that it looked like Russell may have fallen off his boat and drowned in a drunken stupor. "—possible foul play."

Dr. Zuniga knit his thick brows. "Really. I didn't see anything to support that. The head contusion could have happened when Mr. Falco fell overboard."

"So you didn't see anything that looked particularly suspicious?"

"A little bruising below his right eye—from the color I'd estimate someone landed a pretty good punch five to seven days ago."

Russell had been in a fight? Something that had escalated into his tires being slashed? This tidbit of news made me wish I'd taken a good look at Pete's hands for cuts and bruises.

"Other than that," Dr. Zuniga continued, "nothing that wasn't typical with an accidental drowning. Frankie will get my report tomorrow, but that's how I'm calling it."

Then this wouldn't become a coroner's case and I'd soon be transferring the contents of Russell's blue folder into a manila one.

Before that file joined me in the nether regions of the third floor to spend the rest of its days tucked away and forgotten in a metal filing cabinet, I needed to ask one more question. "Dr. Zuniga, was Russell Falco intoxicated at the time of his death?"

"His blood and urine is headed to the state crime lab. Frankie should have the results in six weeks, maybe longer. Depends on how backed up they are."

Six weeks. Criminy! All the cop shows on TV would have that answer by the time they got back from the next commercial break.

Dr. Zuniga smiled as if he could read my mind. "Patience is a virtue, Charmaine."

"Right." So was forgiveness, and I knew I'd never forgive myself if I simply filed that folder once Frankie signed off on the death certificate. Not with everything Joyce and Beverly had told me about Friday night.

"Thank you, Doctor," I said, shaking the hand he offered. Thanks for a few morsels of information that didn't tell me much.

After hightailing it back to the courthouse I promptly filled Karla in on what I'd learned.

"Okay, then," she announced the second I paused to take a breath. "It looks like we'll be able to release the body to the family, but beyond that, we'll sit tight until we get the final report from the crime lab."

Sitting tight required patience and as Dr. Zuniga would attest, I was fresh out. "What about in the meantime?"

Karla squinted at me. "What about it? You said it yourself—accidental drowning."

"Russell Falco's tires got slashed on Monday, close to the same time he got punched in the face, and then the guy drowns less than a week later. You don't find that a little suspicious?"

She shrugged a shoulder. "If Dr. Zuniga didn't find anything to point to this being anything other than an accidental death, it doesn't matter who was having a beef with him or what I think."

"Even if Pete Lackey made threats against him?"

Karla leaned back in her desk chair, her gaze fixed on mine. "Is this gossip you picked up from Lucille or do you know this for a fact?"

Neither, but one of the women who was there Friday night certainly believed that her husband offed her would-be lover.

"Joyce practically admitted it to me yesterday morning."

"*Practically* isn't a word Frankie has much use for."

"Then maybe I should interview Joyce to see if she'd be willing to give me a few more details."

Karla shifted her focus back to her computer monitor. "Find out what she knows and send me your report before noon tomorrow. I don't want Frankie signing off on that death certificate if we have a witness that heard threats made against Russell."

Neither did I.

After making a fresh pot of coffee, I pulled the Jag out of the parking lot and headed south on Main. Since I wanted to speak with Joyce alone, I took a right on 5th Street to drive by Pete's Plumbing with the hope of seeing his blue and white truck. To my relief it was parked right outside his front door. Unfortunately, Joyce and Pete were standing by the Toyota sedan parked next to it.

What the heck? When I saw him at the deli counter yesterday, Pete Lackey was acting like a guy whose wife had left him. And now the wife who told me that she knew he had killed Russell was paying him a little visit?

This made no sense unless she was up to something. What that might be I didn't have a clue, but I sure needed to discover one so I turned into the parking lot of a CPA's office on the opposite corner. Crawling out of the Jag, I sought cover behind a sour-smelling garbage bin and

122 | WENDY DELANEY

watched Joyce hand her husband a plastic-wrapped plate.

Pete pulled back the plastic, picked up what looked like a cookie and consumed it in two bites.

A minute later, after giving her husband a peck on the lips, Joyce got into the Toyota and drove away while Pete headed into his plumbing supply store carrying the plate of cookies.

What?

A woman who was afraid that her husband had murdered her handyman/boyfriend wouldn't bake him cookies, and she certainly wouldn't go out of her way to deliver them to his office. Unless she had a very good reason like needing to experiment with a new recipe— one that included some fast-acting, husband-be-gone secret ingredient.

Since Joyce obviously wasn't home, I decided to question the other member of the Lackey household. The sooner the better if there was a chance I could be right about what was in those cookies.

I grabbed my tote from the passenger seat and headed across the street.

Pete was sitting at a cluttered desk next to a street-facing window when I walked in. He frowned at me for a split second before saying, "May I help you?"

"I hope so."

He pushed back his chair and stepped up to the service counter.

I smiled across the counter at him. "Small world, huh? Who knew yesterday that we'd be chatting again today?"

"Uh-huh."

I pointed at the plate of cookies near the cash register. "Those look good. Did Joyce make them?"

He nodded and pushed the plate toward me. "Help yourself."

I had no appetite for anything that might have come from Joyce's kitchen. Although on the offhand chance there really could be a lethal dose of something other than artery-clogging butter in the cookies, I'd be stupid to not take one as evidence.

"Maybe one for later." I pulled a strip of clingy plastic wrap from the plate and rolled it around the chocolate thumbprint cookie.

I tucked the cookie into a side pocket of my tote and then showed him my deputy coroner badge. "We're investigating the death of Russell Falco. May I have a few moments of your time?"

"I have nothing to add to what I already told the detective."

So Steve had already talked to him. What else was new? "This is for the coroner's report."

"Come on back," Pete grumbled.

He sat at his desk and I took a seat in the creaky vinyl chair he'd pulled over from another desk.

Since the computer monitor at that desk was displaying a screen saver of family photos, I looked around for a dad-type. "I don't want to take somebody's chair if they need it." With any luck, he'd be just a scream away in the back room if I needed him.

"He's out on a call."

Swell.

"If you don't mind, I've got a business to run so…"

"Of course." I pulled out my notebook and moved the chair a little closer to his desk to get a better angle on him. "I understand you had some words with Russell Falco Friday night around nine."

Tight-lipped, he glanced out the window. "You could call it that," Pete said in a calm tone at odds with every muscle in his face.

"What happened?"

"He didn't seem to get the message earlier that I didn't like him hanging around my wife, so I gave him a reminder."

"What do you mean by *reminder*?"

Pete leaned toward me, gripping the armrests of his chair. "I told him plain and simple," he said, dialing up the volume, "to stay away from her."

True. Plus he was confirming what Beverly Carver had already told me. I made a note for my report.

"Then what happened?"

"Nothing much. I said my piece and he left."

"What about later that evening? Did you see Mr. Falco?"

"He knew better than to come back."

"So you didn't see him around one in the morning?"

Pete jutted his chin at me. "I was in bed."

Maybe he had been, but he reminded me of a seventeen-year-old Steve at his dad's funeral—fueled by anger and defiance to mask the pain he didn't want anyone to see.

"All night?"

"All night."

I didn't believe him any more than I believed Steve every time I heard him say, "I'm okay."

"And where was Mrs. Lackey around one in the morning?"

"Right next to me."

Another lie.

"All night?"

"Yes!" Pete Lackey bit out through clenched teeth.

Sure.

He stood, his hands balled into fists as he stared down at me. "And now I need to get back to work."

"Of course." I stood and rolled the chair back to the desk behind me. "Just one more thing. May I see your hands?"

"What?"

"I need to see your hands," I said, trying to do my best impression of Criminal Prosecutor Ben Santiago. After having observed him interview hostile witnesses at least a dozen times over the last month, I knew I had to appear firm, uncompromising. "Front and back please."

Okay, I added the *please* since I figured good manners couldn't hurt my cause, especially when there was no judge in the room to compel this irate husband's cooperation.

Huffing his displeasure, Pete sounded like a venting pressure cooker as he held out his hands.

Not the cleanest pair of hands I'd ever seen, but I didn't notice any cuts or bruises to indicate that he'd been in a fight. "Turn them over please."

Without wavering he provided me a palms up view.

I pointed at a thin inch-long slice on his right index

finger that looked to be in the process of healing. "How'd you get that?"

"Box cutter."

I didn't have any reason to doubt him so I decided to try a more direct approach. "Did you throw a punch at Russell Falco in the last week?"

"Nope." His lips stretched into a humorless smile—the first one I'd seen on his craggy face. "Not that I didn't want to."

True again.

"I understand. Then would you know anything about Mr. Falco's tires being slashed?"

Pete shook his head. "All I can tell you is that it wasn't me."

I believed him. Heck, if he didn't slash Russell's tires, who did?

"Are we done?"

"Yes, thank you. I appreciate you taking the time to…"

Turning his back to me, he walked to the door and opened it.

Clearly he'd wanted me out of his place of business since the moment I'd arrived. Since I'd just treated him like a suspect, it was understandable that he'd dispense with the social niceties, but that didn't mean that I should do the same. The odds were probably pretty good that I'd be speaking with him again once Russell Falco's death investigation became official.

I pulled out a business card from my tote and extended it to him. "If you think of anything else that might be useful to our investigation…"

Without another word he shut the door in my face.

So much for the niceties. At least Pete Lackey had been cooperative enough for me to learn that his name wasn't the only one on Russell Falco's enemy list.

Now to find out what I could glean from the missus.

Chapter Ten

"Charmaine, what a surprise," Joyce Lackey said as I gazed up at her from her front porch. A stiff smile finally registered on her face, making her look as pleased to see me as her husband had been thirty minutes earlier.

"I'm sorry for the imposition, but I was going over my notes from yesterday and had a couple more questions."

She blinked. "Questions?"

To avoid another door slam I tried to channel my inner Emily Post and appeal to Joyce's need to maintain appearances. "Would now be a good time?"

After a moment of hesitation her features visibly relaxed and she waved me in as if she had turned her good hostess switch on. "Of course. Do come in."

Joyce shut the door behind me and I followed her into a compact kitchen with robin's egg blue walls and white appliances.

"Please," she said, pointing to a hardback oak chair at the table set for two with gingham placemats in the same blue as the kitchen curtains.

She picked up a white enamel tea kettle from the stove. "Would you like some tea?"

Not particularly, but since she didn't wait for my response and started filling the kettle, I figured that I should just go with the flow. "Sure, thanks."

I pulled out my notebook and a pen and then set my tote on the floor, a couple of feet away from a six-foot-tall oak bookshelf filled with cookbooks on the bottom two shelves and romance novels at the top. "Nice. Is this the new bookshelf?"

Joyce nodded, her eyes glittering with tears. "Russell finished it Thursday."

And she didn't waste any time putting it to good use.

Since she'd be busy in the kitchen for the next few minutes, I pushed out of my chair and took the opportunity to check out the walk-in pantry adjacent to the kitchen.

Two white wire racks had been filled with glass jars of fruit and preserves, I assumed from the apple and plum trees I saw bordering her flower garden. Cans of soup had been sorted alphabetically on one shelf while sacks of flour and a tall tin of baking powder dominated another. Condiments of every variety lined one shelf. Bars of baking chocolate, a small bag of coconut, a commercial size jar of peanut butter, and plastic canisters filled with walnuts, almonds, and pecans lined another. It was like she'd cleaned out the Red Apple Market of a few of its aisles and set up her own home store.

"Wow!" I turned to face Joyce when I realized she was standing behind me. "This has to be the most well-stocked pantry I've ever seen."

She beamed and reached past me to turn a small jar of Jamaican ginger so that the label faced front. "I do love having what I need right at hand."

Did that also apply to the men in her life? With her husband working such long hours, had she been enjoying having an abundance of Falco charm in her pantry?

"Russell certainly did good work," I said to steer our conversation the direction I wanted to go.

Her eyes glistened like melting ice. "Yes…he did."

Once again I saw genuine sadness, but my mother had always looked sad at the end of every summer vacation I spent with her. It never meant she wasn't itching to jump into her next role and get on with her life. In Joyce's case, since she had been willing to accuse her husband of murder, I wondered if that meant a life without Pete.

The kettle whistled, demanding her attention, and I followed Joyce into her kitchen. I noticed that there was no evidence of her baking those thumbprint cookies, no baking sheets or mixing bowls in her polished aluminum sink—not even a lingering scent of chocolate. Instead, her spotless kitchen smelled lemony, like she'd wiped it down with disinfecting cleanser.

And I thought Steve was a neat freak. This chick made him look like a slacker.

The white cabinets appeared to have been recently painted. "I like the white with the blue and yellow gingham. It creates a very clean and homey look," I said, assuming that had been her kitchen decor goal.

Her lips curled with satisfaction while she filled a rose-patterned, bone china teapot. "I hope to replace all the cabinets next year, but in the meantime a fresh coat of paint helps brighten things up in here."

She angled a glance at me as she set two cups with

saucers on a wooden serving tray. "But I don't think you came here to talk remodeling projects."

"No, I didn't."

With a solemn nod, she gestured to the table. "Please. Sit."

I returned to my seat and Joyce joined me at the table with the serving tray.

Placing a cup and saucer in front of me with a shaky hand, she smiled apologetically. "You'll have to excuse me. I've been a little rattled ever since... Well, I'm sure you understand since you haven't exactly seen me at my best."

I knew she was referring to yesterday's conversation across the street from the police station, but less than an hour ago she had looked as if she didn't have a care in the world.

"I know it's been a difficult time," I said as she filled my cup.

"The worst of my life." She set down the teapot and offered me a small white plate with four perfect little thumbprints. "Cookie? I baked them this morning."

I didn't want to tell her that I had stowed one in my tote bag as possible evidence in case her husband started foaming at the mouth.

"No, thanks. Dieting." The diet I was supposed to be on provided me an easy excuse to avoid eating anything that didn't have great appeal, like arsenic. "They look delicious though."

That earned me another prideful smile which seemed at odds with the flood of raw emotion I'd witnessed in yesterday's broken version of Joyce Lackey. Same with the scene with her husband. Either she used the comfort of everyday rituals to compartmentalize her emotions or Joyce was an Oscar-worthy actress.

Fortunately, I was pretty darned good at telling when people were acting.

I took a sip of tea. "I appreciate you speaking with me yesterday. That was very helpful to our investigation."

She reached for her teacup. "Whatever I can do to help. You said you had more questions?"

"The Coroner is trying to put together a timeline for Friday. Since you were one of the last people to see Russell I thought you could help me assign times to the events of that night."

A frown creased her brow as she stared across the table at me. "I hate even thinking about it."

"I know, but I think we owe this to Russell, don't you?"

She blinked back tears. "Of course we do."

Okay, that fit the emotional response I had expected to see.

Pushing my cup aside, I flipped to a clean page in my notebook. "You told me yesterday that Russell returned later in the evening. What time would you say that was?"

"Probably around nine. Maybe a little earlier."

Which matched her husband's statement.

"Then your husband said a few things to Russell."

Nodding, she gazed into her teacup and swiped at the tear trickling down her cheek.

"What time did Russell leave?" If what Pete had told me about her sleeping next to him was true, she shouldn't know.

"Leave?"

"Yes, did you see him return to his boat several hours later?"

"No," she said, blotting her eyes with her napkin.

"What about the sound of his boat as Russell started the engines? On a quiet night I imagine that could make a lot of noise."

Joyce met my gaze with a determined set to her jaw. "I didn't see or hear anything."

Since I'd heard pitches from used car salesmen that sounded more convincing, I didn't have to look at her to be certain she was lying.

I jotted a note to let her think I was taking her statement seriously. "Where were you around one Saturday morning?"

"In bed. My husband gets up at six every morning so we don't keep night owl hours."

"You and Pete were both in bed at that time."

"Yes."

"Together."

Her eyes narrowed for a fraction of a second. "Of course."

If my husband had spewed obscenities at my would-be lover and embarrassed me in front of my neighbors, sleep would be an impossibility—almost as impossible as lying next to a fuming husband.

"Does your bedroom face the bay or the street?" I asked.

"The bay."

I glanced behind her at the gingham curtains fluttering from the breeze coming through the open kitchen window. "It would have been a warm evening that night. You probably get a nice breeze through your bedroom window."

She sharpened her gaze. "It's rare that we don't get a breeze."

If she had been awake—and I couldn't believe that she wasn't—she would have heard Russell start his twin diesels through that open window.

I smiled to diffuse some of the tension between us and then flipped back two pages in my notebook. "I'm sorry, Joyce, but I'm having a hard time understanding something. Yesterday you said, 'He killed Russell. I know he did.' If you believe that, how could you two just go to bed that night like nothing happened?"

Cringing, she gave her head a little shake. "I...I was upset and had taken a sedative. I probably said a lot of things I shouldn't have."

Most of which I believed a heck of a lot more than anything I'd heard in the last ten minutes.

The banana yellow telephone mounted on the kitchen wall rang and she sprang up from her seat faster than Marietta expecting a call from her agent.

Joyce had her back to me while she answered, but by her yes and no answers, the subject under discussion wasn't tough to figure out.

"I'll be right there." She hung up the phone and turned to me. "You'll have to excuse me. Pete has to go out on a call and needs me to come to the shop."

More like he needed her to stop talking to me.

I dropped my notebook and pen into my tote and pushed back from the table. "No problem. I appreciate your time. Just one last thing so that I get it right in my report. Do you still believe that your husband killed Russell Falco?"

She looked like a life-sized bobblehead doll as she shook her head for several seconds. "He was just angry and was being protective of me. Really, he's a very good man. He just has a bit of a temper."

I didn't hear a *no* and everything about Joyce's body language made it appear that she wasn't entirely sure what her husband was capable of.

She teared up again. "I truly regret what I said yesterday. If there's any way you could just forget that…"

Forget that she thought her husband killed Russell? I may have been an investigator in training, but no one needed to instruct me to include that part of her statement in my report.

After I thanked her for her time, Joyce ushered me out the front door and marched straight for her car.

Since I knew she'd lied about being needed at the shop, I took my time walking to the Jag and waved goodbye to her as she backed out of her driveway. Then, once she rounded the bend on Morton, I put the car in gear and followed her back to town.

I had to head that way anyway to go back to the office, but I was happy to make a side trip if it would reveal more information about the Lackeys' involvement in Russell Falco's death.

Five minutes later, Joyce hung a left on 5th Street, toward Pete's Plumbing. I took the next left on 4th, then left again on B Street and pulled into my favorite CPA's parking lot.

Okay, I'd freely admit I didn't know what I had expected to see. Some sign of panic that a flunky from the coroner's office was asking questions? Not likely to be a sign visible to my eyes, especially while they were behind a closed door and I was crouched in my car across the street.

Just when I heard Steve's voice in my head telling me that all this cloak and dagger stuff was a stupid, amateur move on my part, a tearful Joyce slammed the door behind her and climbed back into her sedan.

I watched her peel away and decided that I might as well stick around to get a sense of Pete's next move since he seemed to be the one calling the shots for this couple.

After forty minutes of waiting for a next move that was looking less and less likely to happen, I rummaged through my tote to see if I had anything in there to eat aside from Joyce's plastic-wrapped cookie.

Nothing. Not even a breath mint. *Dang.* If I was going to do more stakeouts on this job I needed to pack some snacks.

Just as I was about to pop an antacid to see if it would appease my growling tummy, I noticed Pete's blue and white truck backing out of the parking lot.

I waited until he turned right on Main and then eased the Jag out to follow him behind a full-sized pickup. I didn't know if Pete Lackey knew what kind of car I drove, but if he looked in his rearview mirror, I figured that the pickup afforded me a pretty good shield.

After two blocks, Pete parked in front of the Red Apple.

So much for my shield.

I parked on the side street, where I could see his truck, and waited.

Fifteen minutes later, he came out carrying two plastic bags. His wife gave him a shopping list to pick up a few things that she needed to complete her pantry? Given that door slam, it seemed unlikely.

I started my car and waited for his truck to merge back onto Main before I pulled out.

Hanging back ten car lengths, I slowed, figuring he'd turn left on Morton, but when Pete didn't make the turn to head home and drove another mile before turning right on 42nd Street, I thought he must be making a late afternoon service call at one of the many houses perched on the bluff overlooking Merritt Bay.

Creeping up the hill so that he wouldn't see me in his rearview mirror, I rounded the turn onto Bay Vista Road and scanned the tree-lined residential street. No blue and white truck.

Great. My cloak and dagger skills obviously left a lot to be desired, but how hard could a one-ton truck with a leaky faucet be to find?

As I discovered when I spotted the Pete's Plumbing truck in the driveway of a large two-story home at the corner of Bay Vista and Abalone Place, not that hard.

I pulled up behind a row of mailboxes in front of the house two doors down and felt like a chump. Nothing about this remotely resembled a next move. More likely he was simply responding to a call to clear a clogged drain.

Since my bladder wanted me to drain the cup of tea I'd consumed an hour earlier, I headed back to the courthouse with no more proof of the Lackeys' involvement in Russell Falco's death than I'd had yesterday.

All I had was an accusation that rang true as a bell.

He killed Russell. I know he did.

And despite all the mixed signals, everything that I'd witnessed today appeared to support Joyce's original statement.

After spending the next two hours preparing a report that included today's interviews and all my observations—minus any mention of following Pete and Joyce through town—I studied the timeline I had drawn on a legal pad. The Lackeys and Beverly Carver all agreed that Russell arrived in his boat around nine Friday night. After that, Pete and Joyce admitted to nothing that wouldn't provide an alibi for one another, and Beverly was the only one to say that she heard Russell start his boat around one in the morning.

I had no smoking gun—nothing but yesterday's emotionally charged statement fingering Pete, made by the woman who kept hiding behind the Martha Stewart mask. Now that Joyce was backpedaling and seemed willing to cook up any palatable kind of fiction to protect her husband, I could only assume that she was either an unwitting accomplice or Pete had reminded his wife of everything she had to lose if she continued to point that accusatory finger at him.

Either way I smelled a rat.

Since Dr. Zuniga had pronounced Russell's death as accidental, and there was nothing in my report other than a distraught wife recanting the accusation she had made against her less than truthful husband, this case would go nowhere if I didn't come up with a rat trap.

I headed home to make a strong pot of French roast because it looked like it was going to be a long night.

Thirty minutes later, with a thermos filled with enough coffee to keep me fueled for the next few hours, I changed my clothes and grabbed my grandfather's binoculars from the desk in the study.

"Gram, I need to borrow your car." Mine was low on gas and I didn't want to take the chance on one of the Lackeys recognizing it.

My grandmother looked up from the cheese slices she was layering in a casserole dish. "Where are you going?"

"I have some work I need to do."

She eyed the black jeans and navy sweater tunic I was wearing. "You look like you're dressed for some kind of stakeout."

"Nothing that exciting." At least nothing that I was willing to admit to.

"What's going on?" my mother asked, coming in from the living room, a fashion magazine in one hand and her reading glasses in the other. "Did I hear *stakeout*?"

Good grief. "I just need to see a witness about a case I'm working on." Sort of true.

Marietta aimed a wrinkle-resistant frown at me. "Seems a little late to be interviewing witnesses. Plus, that's not exactly your usual deputy coroner attire."

She had me there. "I..." Shoot, I couldn't think of a

believable lie, especially with the binoculars in my hand. "I'm just going to follow up on something a witness told me."

My grandmother's eyes narrowed. "I don't like the sound of that one bit. Look at you. You're dressed like a Mata Hari."

I doubted that Mata Hari ever wore black denim. "There's nothing to worry about," I said, grabbing Gram's car keys from a hook by the back door. "I'll be just fine."

"Yes, you will because I'm coming with you." Marietta tossed her magazine and glasses onto the kitchen table. "Just give me three minutes."

"No, Mom!" I called after her. "That's really not necessary. Besides, don't you have a date later tonight with Barry?"

"He has some sort of teacher's meeting tonight," she said as she dashed up the stairs. "Three minutes. Five tops."

"Swell."

"Yeah," my grandmother grumbled. "I *was* making dinner."

"I'm sure we'll be hungry when we get back. Just keep it warm for a couple of hours."

I glanced at the page she had her cookbook open to and recognized the tomato sauce stains. She'd made this lasagna recipe so many times over the years that she probably didn't need to read the directions.

But this didn't look like her usual lasagna.

"Where's the mozzarella?" I didn't see any ricotta either.

Gram shrugged. "I didn't have any, so I thought I'd try this fat-free American instead."

This was one of the many reasons my Italian ex-husband would insist on doing all the cooking over the rare occasions that he'd grace my family with his presence.

I made a mental note to pick up a couple of deli sandwiches at the Red Apple.

Heaving a dramatic sigh, my grandmother pulled another slice of cheese from the pack. "When it's all dried up in the oven after you get home from gallivanting around, I'm sure you won't even notice the difference."

I smiled at her. "Nice guilt trip."

She winked. "I tried my best."

"Okay, I'm ready," Marietta said, strolling into the kitchen wearing the designer version of my black jeans and tunic sweater, only hers were three sizes smaller and ten times the price. "Bye, Mama. Don't wait up."

Gram frowned at me. "You think you're going to be out that late?"

I shook my head. We'd better not be.

"You just never know about surveillance." Marietta slung her tote bag over her shoulder. "Take mah show for example—"

Here we go.

"—the girls and I would often be out until all hours. Really, most every episode we'd have to get ourselves out of some sort of pickle."

"Very comforting," Gram muttered.

It was too late for damage control, but I had to try. "We won't be getting into any pickles."

"I packed my Taser just in case," my mother said, patting her tote.

Gram rolled her eyes. "Heaven help us."

The last thing I wanted to see tonight was Marietta in a shooter's stance, so amen to that.

I kissed my grandmother on the cheek. "We'll be fine."

"If you're not home by ten I'm going to send Steve out to look for you." She arched her eyebrows. "And where did you say you were going?"

And have her telling Steve that we were going to be hanging out at the Lackeys' house tonight? Not happening.

"Out," I said, opening the back door.

Gram groaned as if I'd popped her bubble and she was slowly deflating. "Be careful!"

"Ma'am, we'll do our very best," Marietta said with an exaggerated Southern drawl even for her.

I glared at her. It was bad enough that she wanted to ride shotgun on my stakeout. Now she was treating this like a revival of her old show? "Seriously?"

She gave my arm a playful slap. "Come on! That was my signature line. I said it every episode."

"I know." I'd sat glued to the television every Wednesday at nine o'clock. Didn't mean I wanted to enjoy any reruns of it tonight.

I tossed the thermos and binoculars next to the plaid stadium blanket Gram kept in the back seat and climbed behind the wheel of her Honda Pilot SUV.

Fastening her seatbelt, Marietta turned to me. "Are we going to stop for some sandwiches or something? Your grandmother is making lasagna with some funky-looking orange cheese."

I shifted into reverse. "I'm way ahead of you."

Chapter Eleven

"Are you going to eat this?" Marietta asked, interrupting my thoughts while I stared at the Lackeys' driveway where one blue and white plumber's truck was nowhere to be seen.

I looked over to see her delicately holding the second of the two dill pickles that had been included with our deli sandwiches like it was one of Joyce's teacups, extended pinkie and all.

I wanted nothing to do with any pickles tonight. "It's all yours."

"Ah do love a good pickle. Very low carb and a good thing to have when you're on a diet."

I listened to her crunching, which was a lot better than listening to my mother dish out some not-so-subtle diet advice, and wished I'd bought a big bag of chips to keep her mouth busy for the next hour.

I also wished Pete Lackey would come home. How could I see if the Lackeys appeared to be spending something resembling a normal evening together if they weren't physically together?

Marietta pointed the pickle toward the house two

doors down from where I'd parked. "Who lives there again?"

"A couple I interviewed earlier today."

"Well, if you interviewed them already, what are you spying on them for?"

"I'm not spying. I just want to observe their behavior."

"Sounds like spying to me. So does this have something to do with Russell Falco?"

She was asking questions I didn't want to answer, especially if she was going to go home and spill the beans to Gram, who would promptly sic Steve on me if she didn't like what she heard.

"That's not the only case I'm working on." Skimpy on details but infused with possibility—typically the best kind of lie to tell to my mother.

I glanced over to see if she'd bought it and stared as Marietta wrapped her collagen-injected lips around the pickle and sucked on it.

Her eyes widened when she met my gaze. "What? It was dripping."

Good thing none of the guys who'd had my mother's poster up in their junior high lockers were around because this R-rated scene was the stuff wet dreams were made of.

"Uh-huh."

She tossed the rest of the pickle in the plastic shopping bag. "Chahmaine Digby, you have a filthy mind."

"Hey, you were the one rehearsing for the remake of *Deep Throat*."

Dabbing her napkin at her lips, she sat up straight like the Southern belle the general public assumed her to be. "Ah would never do anything so distasteful."

"Unless the right director came calling and it was an art film guaranteed to win at the Cannes Film Festival. Oh, and you got top billing."

"Well, now you're talking," she said without a trace of an accent, flipping down the mirrored visor to reapply her lipstick.

No doubt a film like that would be the best thing that had happened to Marietta's career in the last thirty years. And when her bank balance needed it most.

I wrestled with the idea of saying anything about her finances because I wasn't supposed to know about the dire straits she was in. The safest course for me was to circumvent her money problems. "Mom, I realize that professional opportunities aren't what they once were, but like you always say, you never know what's around the corner."

Judging by the way her mouth flatlined, it looked like she saw only something big and scary around the corner.

"I'm sure that if you take the next several months and make good decisions, you'll create your own good luck." I was probably regurgitating some fortune cookie wisdom my mother had picked up somewhere, but since she'd been dishing this crap out to me for most of my life, I hoped she'd be open to taking it for a change.

She smacked her lips. "Right."

"Really, there's no reason to rush anything right now. What did you used to always tell me? You can't rush luck."

Marietta shifted her gaze from her reflection in the visor mirror to me, the fine lines at the corners of her eyes tightening with tension. "If you're saying what I think you're saying, I don't feel that I'm rushing into anything."

"I'm sure that's true." Actually, I didn't believe her for a second, but calling my mother on a lie was as healthy for our relationship as her trying to give me a makeover. "But you just got divorced. It's okay to slow things down a bit and think about what you really want."

She dropped her lipstick into a side pocket of her tote. "I could say the same to you."

This was so not the direction I wanted this conversation to take. "I—"

"Don't think I haven't noticed all the late nights you've been spending with Steve."

"We're just good friends."

Marietta pursed her freshly painted raspberry red mouth as she fluffed her hair in the mirror. "Uh-huh, and the next time my phone rings it'll be my agent calling about that top billing."

"I... we..." Criminy! I couldn't think of anything that wouldn't end up with me digging myself a deeper hole.

She patted my knee. "Relax, sugar. I'll trust you to make good decisions for yourself if you'll trust me to do the same."

Since I knew that she couldn't afford to purchase the two Lance Greenwood paintings that she'd been trying to talk Gram into hanging in the living room, my mother was asking me to take a big leap of faith. "Fine," I ground out between clenched molars.

After several uncomfortable beats of silence, Marietta settled back in her seat. "Not that I haven't been enjoying having a heart-to-heart with my daughter, but there doesn't appear to be a lot to see here."

She was absolutely right. Without Pete there was nothing to see.

I pulled out my cell phone and glanced at the time. Sixteen minutes after seven—over three hours since I left him at the house on Bay Vista. If he wasn't still replacing some pipes there, I wanted to know where the heck he went.

"Are we leaving?" Marietta asked when I started the Honda.

"We're going to check out another location."

"Could we stop at the Dairy Queen?"

I tightened my grip on the steering wheel as we rounded the bend on Morton. "We don't have time for ice cream."

"I need to use the bathroom fairly soon."

"We'll be there in a few minutes. If the guy already left, I'll take you home. Deal?"

"Deal."

Five minutes later, I spotted the Pete's Plumbing truck right where I'd seen it last. I pulled up across the street from the row of mailboxes I'd parked behind earlier, where I could get a good look at the front of the house. The curtains were drawn so there wasn't much to see here either, but at least I'd located Pete.

"So what's the plan?" Marietta asked.

I didn't have a plan. "We wait for a few minutes and see if he comes out." I reached for the thermos. "Want some coffee?"

"I already need to go to the bathroom, so no."

Twenty minutes later, with no movement on the street except a bulldog on a leash held by an elderly man with a cane, my mother turned to me. "I really need to go."

"I need to stay. Can't you hold it a little while longer?"

Her shoulders slumped. "I swear, if I sit and stare at that leaky faucet for one more minute I'm going to spring a leak!" She opened her car door.

"Where are you going?"

"Surely someone around here will recognize me and will be happy to have the bragging rights that I used their bathroom."

"Just don't knock on that door," I said, pointing across the street. "In fact, go several doors down." I'd been in the same room when one of Marietta's more ardent fans started screaming at the top of her lungs. If there was going to be any sudden noise, I didn't want it to spook Pete Lackey.

"Fine."

From my rearview mirror I watched her rounded hips swivel with every step she took in her platform sandals. My hips should look so good at her age.

Heck, I wished they looked as good now.

She walked up the driveway of the third house behind me and disappeared for a minute.

Then she was back on the sidewalk and heading to the next house. Must have been a no-go since she promptly crossed the street and walked up to a house with a for-sale sign out front. That's when I lost sight of her. It's also when Pete Lackey stepped out of the front door of the house I'd been watching for the last half hour, opened the back of his truck and climbed inside.

Seconds later, he came out, dragging a large cardboard box.

I grabbed the binoculars from the back seat to read the print on the box. Dialing in the focus I could make out the words, *Shower Wall Kit.*

He was replacing a shower? Not just the pipes to the shower? Seemed like something beyond what a plumber would do.

The octogenarian with the bulldog walked by again, obscuring my view. I lowered the binoculars and noticed he was peering into the car.

I gave him a little wave. *Yes, you caught me spying on a possible killer. Move on.*

The old dude frowned at me but continued on his walk.

Good. I didn't want any members of the Bay Vista Neighborhood Watch to think I was casing their houses, which was bound to happen any moment if I didn't move my grandmother's car out of their sight.

It was going on eight o'clock and starting to get dark. It had also been almost ten minutes since I'd last seen my mother.

How long could it take for her to charm her way into someone's home and pee?

Before I moved the car I needed to find her or I'd never hear the end of it, and I couldn't very well do that without arousing suspicion until the dog-walker wasn't around to watch. So I waited for the guy to disappear from view before I slowly backed the car up and parked in front of the for-sale sign.

Since this house was the last place I had spotted

Marietta, I walked up the driveway to take a look around. I climbed several steps and tried the front door. Locked.

I felt like I was playing a game of hide and go seek with my mother, and with Pete Lackey working three doors down this was no time for games.

Looking up the street to make sure his truck was still there, I wandered into the side yard. "Mom?"

Nothing.

There was no way she'd be squatting behind any of the rhododendrons in the landscaping, so I walked around to the small deck at the rear of the house and immediately noticed that the sliding glass door wasn't shut tight.

I pulled it open. "Mom?"

No answer.

Was it considered breaking and entering if the door wasn't locked? I hoped to never find out.

I tiptoed into what looked like a breakfast nook to the left the kitchen. When I rounded the corner and entered a short hallway that led to the living room, I caught a whiff of Marietta's signature scent. It got stronger as I stood at the foot of the stairway. "Mom?"

"I'm up here in the bathroom."

"What are you doing? I thought you were going to use your Marietta Moreau magic on one of the neighbors."

"No one would answer their doorbell. Fortunately, someone forgot to lock the back door because I *really* had to go."

"Well, hurry up. We need to get out of here and move the car."

"Honey, I'm going as fast as I can, but I've been a little backed up if you know what I mean."

Swell.

"I also have a bit of a problem."

"Now what?"

"There's no toilet paper in here. How can they show a house without toilet paper in the bathrooms?"

"The realtor probably didn't expect any non-prospective home buyers to be taking a poop in there today."

"Then they should have locked all the doors!"

"I have a pack of tissues in my bag. I left it in the car. I'll get it."

"Hurry. It's dark and creepy in here. It reminds me of those slasher movies I used to make, where the psycho always lived in the abandoned house."

Which most everyone at my school flocked to every Halloween. "Now you're creeping me out," I said, grateful for the street lamp across the way that was bathing the living room in soft light.

"Just sit tight and I'll be right back." Then we needed to get out of here.

I sprinted out the sliding glass door and came around to the front of the house, where I saw the elderly dog-walker on a cell phone.

"Yeah, she's right in front of me," he said, pointing his cane at me. "Do you want me to make a citizen's arrest?"

What?

"Okay. I'll keep an eye on her until you get here. 4155 Bay Vista." He held his phone out at arm's length and squinted at it. "Dang buttons. They put 'em too close together."

"Would you like me to help you, sir?" I figured it wouldn't hurt to try to lighten the mood before any members of Port Merritt's finest showed up with their lights flashing.

He stabbed his cane in my direction. "Don't move. The police are on their way."

I held up my hands while he tucked his phone into the breast pocket of his flannel shirt. "Okay. I was just trying to help. I'll just get my bag out of the car."

"I said don't move."

"Really, Mr...."

"Brubaker."

"Mr. Brubaker, this looks worse than it is. My mother was going door-to-door because she needed..." I couldn't think of a way to state her dilemma so that he could see we weren't criminals without telling him the unvarnished truth. "Because nature called, and now she's in that house, out of toilet paper, and really needs some tissues."

He narrowed his beady eyes at me. "You must think I was born yesterday. She's probably in there stealing light fixtures and anything else you two can sell on the black market."

Given my mother's fear of bad publicity, his story might be preferable to a report about her getting arrested for breaking into a house to take a dump.

I glanced down the street. At least Pete Lackey's truck still sat in the driveway. But if he came out of that house and saw me talking to the police, he'd probably think I was on to him.

I needed to get out of here and didn't have a second to lose.

"Listen, I'm not a thief. Neither is my mother." Pasting my most innocent smile on my face, I took two steps toward the passenger side door. "In fact, do you know who Marietta Moreau is?"

"You want me to believe that's Marietta Moreau in there?" He came around the back of the car as I opened the door and pulled out the pack of tissues from my tote.

If she could play her star card, so could I. "Stay right here and you can meet her in a minute."

"Don't try anything funny in there!" he yelled at my backside as I ran toward the house.

The only thing I wanted to do was to get my mother's hiney off the toilet, hop into Gram's car, and clear out before Steve or one of his buddies pulled up.

"Mom," I called to her as I huffed and puffed my way up the stairs. "We've got trouble. A neighbor saw us in here and called the cops."

She stared at me wide-eyed as I handed her the tissue pack. "Oh, dear."

I retreated to the hallway to give her some privacy. "I told him who you were and that you were just using the bathroom—"

"What?" She groaned. "If he sells his story to a scandal rag, I'll be a laughing stock."

"Then you'd better be your most charming self in the next few minutes and hope that he doesn't know how to use the camera on his cell phone."

After a few less than genteel curse words, I heard the toilet flush, then water running in the sink.

Come on, come on, come on.

Two seconds later, I rushed down the stairs with my mother hot on my heels.

"Do you think I should have wiped the faucet down to remove my fingerprints?" she asked as I closed the sliding glass door behind her.

"I already told the guy who you were, so it's a little late for that."

She groaned again and I turned to face her. "You're the one who wanted to give one of the neighbors bragging rights, so go do your thing. I'll be right behind you."

Marietta fluffed her hair, licked her lips and took a deep breath. "I guess it's showtime."

She swiveled her hips as she crossed the lawn. "Oh, mah goodness," she said in her best Georgia peach drawl. "I can only imagine what you must be thinkin' of me, but when a girl's gotta go, a girl's gotta go."

"Oh, pahdon me. Where are mah manners?" She extended her hand to the man staring at her, slack-jawed. "Marietta Moreau."

"Arnold Brubaker."

"Well, Arnold, it's mah great pleasure to make your acquaintance." She waved in my direction. "Of course you've met mah daughtah."

I didn't have any more time for social pleasantries and stepped around the front of the car to the driver's door. "Mama, we should get you home. Those directions for the photo shoot were obviously wrong."

She blinked. "Oh, uh, most definitely wrong. I'll have to scold my agent for sendin' us on this wild goose chase. Although it was very nice to meet you, Arnold."

He beamed. "The pleasure was all mine, Miss Moreau."

Since he was no longer brandishing his cane like an ancient pirate, I seized the opportunity to slide in behind the wheel to make our getaway as soon as my mother's butt made contact with the passenger seat.

Arnold opened her car door for her.

"Ah hope you won't mention mah embarrassin' predicament to anyone." She pressed her palm in his. "Ah'm sure you can understand my need for privacy."

"Madam, I do indeed."

Marietta smiled with satisfaction at me as she climbed into the car.

Yes, you done good.

"Well, that was a crisis averted," she said, waving back at Arnold as we pulled away.

"Not entirely."

"Why? I thought I played that perfectly."

"You did."

"Then what's your problem?"

It was driving up the hill in an unmarked cop car.

Chapter Twelve

"Are you sure I can't tempt you with some lasagna, Stevie?" Gram asked, hovering in the living room like a traffic helicopter over a ten-car pile-up. Clucking her tongue, she glared at my mother and me, sitting side by side on the sofa. "I have plenty, especially since certain members of my family decided they'd rather dine out before they got started on their crime spree."

Steve sat quietly, looking no more threatening than a bungling Barney Fife of Mayberry.

I knew better.

"No, thanks, Eleanor," he said. "I already ate."

"Well, I'll just wrap some up and you can take it home with you." Gram smiled sweetly at him. "After your inter-rogation."

Marietta heaved a sigh. "Mama, don't be so dramatic. Steve even said that Mr. Brubaker regretted calling the police."

Heading for the kitchen, Gram glanced back over her shoulder. "Doesn't change the fact that you broke into a house."

"Technically, we didn't break in," Marietta called after

158 | WENDY DELANEY

Gram, then turned her focus to the detective doing the slow burn in the overstuffed easy chair to our left. "Did we, hon?"

If my mother was looking for an ally anywhere in the vicinity of the living room, she was wasting her time.

Steve leveled his gaze at her. "Technically, what you did is called *criminal trespass.*"

"Criminal! That door was unlocked. The owner should thank us for discovering the careless oversight by the last realtor who showed that house." She flicked a gold-bangled wrist to punctuate her argument. "In fact, that person should be reported. Just think about the damage that could have been done."

Way to deflect, Mom.

The tic above Steve's jawline beat in time with the seconds of stony silence between us. "The real estate agent has been informed about the *oversight* and doesn't want to take the incident any further."

"Thank God," Marietta muttered under her breath.

Obviously this was one time that she didn't want her name to appear in the weekly Port Merritt *Gazette.*

Focusing on me, Steve folded his arms. "Want to tell me what you were doing tonight on Bay Vista?"

Absolutely not.

"Oh, look at the time!" Standing, my mother inched toward the stairway. "Barry will be here any minute and I haven't begun to get ready. If you don't have any other questions for me, kind sir, I wonder if..."

I had no doubt that Steve could see through her flimsy excuse to make a hasty exit stage right, but we all knew that her portion of tonight's *interrogation* had come to a conclusion while mine had just begun.

He waved her away and waited for her bedroom door to click shut before he hit me between the eyes with an angry glare. "Well?"

"I was there on coroner business."

"With your mother and a pair of binoculars?"

Okay, he had me there. "It was unofficial."

"Yeah. Arnold Brubaker told me he called because he thought you two were casing the Lackeys' house."

The Lackeys' house? "Arnold Brubaker probably thinks anyone who gets lost in his neighborhood is up to no good."

"Since he seems to have me on speed-dial after his house was broken into last year, probably. But it looks like he can recognize a couple of trespassers when he sees them."

I forced a smile. "I was trying to get my mother out of that house so we could go home."

"I don't care."

He didn't? Then I wished he'd climb off his cop soapbox and stop acting like he wanted to slap a pair of handcuffs on me, and not in a fun way.

He leaned closer. "My concern is that you're exceeding the authority that your little deputy coroner badge grants you."

I didn't like his tone. "My little badge, as you put it, gives me the authority to interview witnesses, including the Lackeys. And if you'd seen the two of them together earlier, you'd want to know—"

"I'd want to know why the Coroner's assistant, who's been on the job for a month, thinks it's a good idea to harass someone when she doesn't like something she thinks she sees."

Now I really didn't like his tone. "I wasn't harassing anyone."

"If Pete Lackey knew that those binoculars had been pointed at him, I doubt he'd agree."

"I know what I saw."

"So I've heard before, but Frankie didn't hire you to spy on people."

"I—"

"And if you're not careful, not only will you put yourself and possibly your mother at risk, you'll lose your job."

That sounded like a threat. "Are you telling me that you'd complain to Frankie about me?"

"Chow Mein, I won't have to. Someone like Arnold Brubaker will file a complaint about you, then that will get back to Frankie. You know how news travels in this town."

Yes, I did. That's why, whenever I needed to dig up dirt on someone, I headed straight to Duke's to get the scoop from Lucille.

Pushing out of his chair, he patted me on the head. "Be good and leave Pete Lackey alone."

Given how today went, Steve was asking for the impossible.

I followed him to the front door. "There's something going on between him and Joyce."

"There should be. They're married."

"No, it's like they're hiding something." *Like how Pete killed Russell.*

"Uh-huh. More likely, they didn't like you nosing around, asking a bunch of questions."

He reached for the doorknob and I wedged my body in front of it, the brass knob poking me in the small of my back. "Even more likely, Joyce is now trying to convince me that the sedative she took yesterday was what did the talking when she told me that her husband killed Russell."

Blowing out a breath, Steve shook his head.

"Don't shake your head at me. Her exact words were, 'he killed Russell.' Not 'I think my husband might have been involved in the death of my boyfriend.' Don't you think some questions need to be asked?"

"Shhhh." Steve opened the door, grabbed me by my upper arm and escorted me outside to my grandmother's porch. "If this turns into a coroner's case, I'll be the one asking the questions, not you."

"Fine." All the better that the person who was doing the questioning had a gun and a pair of handcuffs to take Pete Lackey into custody.

The door swung open and Gram handed Steve a casserole dish. "You almost left without your lasagna. You'll probably want to add some tomato sauce before reheating it." She angled a glare my way. "Since I didn't know when *certain people* would be home, I probably kept it in the oven longer than I should have."

He smiled like the good Boy Scout he used to be. "I'll do that. Thanks, Eleanor."

When the door clicked shut behind her, I lifted the lid and surveyed the overcooked landscape that looked more like desiccated liver than lasagna. "Oy. Like two hours too long."

Steve frowned. "What are the orange globs?"

"Fat-free American. She was out of mozzarella." I replaced the lid. "If you like your pasta really well-done and your cheese not so cheesy, it might be okay."

"Thanks for the heads up." His dark eyes looked like pools of molten chocolate as they held my gaze. "Now take off your food critic hat and do something for me."

Since I felt crampy and bloated, I hoped my sex buddy wasn't going to suggest anything that required an application of ice cream. "What?"

"Promise me that you'll stop skulking around Pete Lackey."

I raised my right hand. "I promise. If you'll tell me about the Lackey house on Bay Vista."

"Contrary to what you might think there's not much to tell. The guy's mother died last spring and he's fixing up the house. Probably getting it ready to sell."

"Oh." A man who couldn't finish a remodeling project on his own house was the one in charge of fixing up his mother's? It didn't seem like the best plan, but what did I know? Maybe it was the cheapest plan.

"Yep, that spy act of yours was on a guy remodeling his mother's bathroom." Steve gave me a thumbs up as he stepped off the porch. "Nice work, rookie."

Eight hours later, Duke glanced at the clock mounted above a vintage red and white Coca Cola sign when his kitchen door banged shut behind me. "Don't you sleep anymore?"

Since my menstrual cramps had my lower back tied up in a knot, the probability that I could get four hours of uninterrupted z's was as likely as me giving up my mocha lattes. "I'm just getting an early start to my day."

My great-aunt Alice scowled at me on her way to the oven, where the heavenly aroma of pie was venting. "That's not what the dark circles under your eyes are saying."

Okay, so the concealer Marietta swore by in her info-commercials wasn't quite the miracle worker she'd cracked it up to be.

"As long as I was up early," I said, not bothering to deny the obvious, "I thought I'd pick up some dough-nuts."

Standing by the stainless steel fryer sizzling with doughy confections bobbing in their oil bath, Duke arched an eyebrow. "Sweetening the pot, huh? You must want something."

I did want something—a conversation with Andy Falco, the one man Russell might have confided in if he were having problems with someone in town.

"Yep, and I'm going to treat him to the best sugar-laden breakfast in town."

Duke smirked as he transferred a dozen old fash-ioneds to a cooling rack. "*You'll* treat him?"

"Yes, it's my treat." I waved a few dollar bills at him before I slipped them into the cash register. "Happy?" I asked as I walked back with a cup of coffee.

"You gonna pay for that coffee, too?"

"You can put it on my tab."

He blew out a breath. "That's what I thought."

Setting down my cup, I donned a pair of plastic gloves and dipped a couple of cooled bars into a pan of maple glaze. "Let me ask you something."

Duke joined me at the glazing table next to a stack of six racks full of cooling pastry. "What's up?"

"You said yesterday that Russell Falco ate here a couple times a week."

He twisted an apple fritter into sugary glaze. "Yeah?"

"Why do you want to know where Russell ate?" Alice asked as she crossed the kitchen to join us. She sucked in a sharp breath. "You don't think he was poisoned."

"No! Nothing like that. I was just wondering if you ever saw him with anyone."

"Seems like he always came in alone and sat at the counter," Duke said.

"Ever known him to have angry words with anyone?"

He looked at his wife, who shook her head. "Not that we ever saw."

"Any rumors of trouble with anyone in town?" I aimed my question at Alice since she typically had her ear to the ground here at Gossip Central.

"We heard about Pete Lackey going ballistic Friday night, but other than that, no."

After I boxed up a dozen assorted doughnuts, I drove to the marina to ask Andy Falco the same question.

Andy handed the white pastry box to his younger brother. "Pass this around and offer the guys a cup of coffee. I'll be back in a few minutes."

Wordlessly, Nate glared down at me from the boat railing, making it crystal clear that he resented me arriving at the same time as the three men who had booked this morning's charter. Too bad. If an official investigation was going to be launched into their brother's death, I needed some answers and I needed to get them before the surviving Falco brothers disappeared for the next five hours.

"I appreciate you making the time to see me." I said, following Andy to the end of the pier, the brisk morning breeze whipping my hair into my face and ruffling the pages of my notebook.

He tugged at his red Falco Charters cap, lowering the bill over his furrowed brow. "Let's make this quick. I have customers waiting."

"No problem." If he wanted quick and to the point, he'd get it. "I understand two of Russell's tires were slashed Monday night."

Andy's thin lips flattened, his body rigid like he was bracing himself for something stronger than the gusts at his back. "Yeah."

"Any thoughts on who did it? Was he having trouble with anyone?"

A wry smile tugged at Andy's mouth. "When wasn't he experiencing some sort of trouble?"

With what I knew about their family history, I figured he was entitled to some sarcasm. As long as he showed me honest emotion as I tried to peel back the covers of his brother's final days, I was okay with the delivery. "Over the last week or two did Russell mention anything specific?"

"No."

"Did you see your brother argue with anyone?"

Andy stared down the length of the pier like he was

considering his options.

"Anything you can tell me could help us in our investigation." Yes, I was laying it on a little thick since my job was simply to provide a preliminary report, but I'd practically promised him that there would be an investigation into his brother's death and I didn't want it getting back to his mother that I wasn't trying to deliver.

His eyes narrowed. "I'm not aware that he got into it with anyone else."

Anyone else?

"What were the two of you *discussing*?"

Andy fingered a greenish-yellow bruise on his right knuckle. "I came home Tuesday night and my new truck was missing. Turned out Russ took it. When he pulled into the driveway three hours later, he said he'd had someplace he needed to be, and with two flat tires he seemed to think he could just grab my keys... No, let me rephrase that. He didn't think. Just like all the other times he didn't think something through, and let's just say that after months of him not doing a frickin' thing to help out, I'd had enough."

Understandable given the brothers' history. "Did he say where he needed to be?"

"Nope."

"Did you ask?"

"Didn't have to. I knew where he'd been spending his time last week."

So he knew about Beverly Carver. "Russell told you?"

Andy's chin jutted out, his lower lip tight with something that, in my experience, looked a lot like contempt. "I saw him a couple of times, hanging around at Kelsey's shop."

Not what I'd expected to hear, but clearly he didn't like his older brother spending time with Kelsey. Based on the long looks Andy had given her the few times I'd seen them at Duke's, Andy's reaction wasn't unreasonable.

I captured his exact words in my notebook. "I know he was doing some work there to get ready for the art show Saturday."

"I didn't see much work goin' on," Andy muttered, his amber eyes dark in the shadow cutting his face in two under the bill of his cap.

"I assume you mentioned that when Russell came back home with your truck." I pointed at his bruised knuckle. "Maybe did more than just talk about it?"

He shrugged. "Russ wasn't in a listening mood, and I guess I was done talking."

"So you gave him the black eye?"

Blowing out a deep breath, Andy nodded.

Holy crap! I'd expected that Russell's brother could provide some insight about the events of early last week, but it never occurred to me that he'd be the one who had landed that punch. That explained why he had given me such evasive answers in the park Monday. He didn't want any fingers pointing at him.

I had no trouble accepting Russell's black eye as a result of an isolated incident between brothers, but it didn't help me get any closer to solving the mystery of who slashed his tires.

I circled back to the primary reason I'd come to talk to Andy. "Was it you or Russell who first saw that someone had slashed two of his tires?"

"Me. I noticed it Tuesday morning when I was leaving for work. Since my Mustang and truck were parked next to his Chevy, I checked all three vehicles for damage."

"And?"

"Looked like they only hit his truck, so I went back in and rousted Russ out of bed so that he could see the situation for himself."

"What'd he say?"

"Not much."

"He didn't give you the impression that he knew who might have done it?"

Andy shook his head. "He just seemed generally pissed about it."

"Any weird phone calls or emails a couple days before or after?"

"Nothing that I knew anything about."

Nate whistled from the stern of their charter boat and Andy glanced down at his watch. "I need to get going."

"One last thing. Actually, could Nate join us for a minute?"

"He doesn't live at the house and won't know anything to help you."

I didn't doubt the truth in what I had just heard, but I needed to find out for myself. "It will just take a moment."

Andy uttered an obscenity and waved his younger brother over.

"What now?" Nate asked seconds later, lighting a cigarette as he closed the distance between us.

"A quick question for the two of you." I smiled with the hope that it would deflect some of the defiance radiating from him. Since he made no effort to stand where the wind wouldn't blow his cigarette smoke into my face, I stepped to the side and dropped the smile. "Last week, did Russell say or do anything to indicate who slashed his tires, anything about any trouble he was having with someone around here?"

Nate took a drag on his cigarette. "Not to me. I didn't see him all week. Not until…you know…Saturday."

True. I turned to Andy. "How about you? Anything else you can tell me?"

"After what Russ pulled, I kicked him out of the house and didn't see him again until Saturday at Tolliver's."

My questions asked and answered, the two brothers headed back toward their boat, leaving me no closer to solving the mystery of who killed Russell than when I arrived.

Chapter Thirteen

After walking three blocks to Hot Shots Espresso, I sat at the picnic table facing the Feathered Nest and sipped a mocha latte while I waited for Kelsey to open up shop.

The sun had yet to rise above the eastern shore of Merritt Bay, so I had plenty of time to review my notes and come to the same conclusion that I'd come to yesterday and the day before that. Nothing anyone had told me trumped Joyce Lackey's statement that her husband had killed Russell Falco.

Since the Lackeys lived less than five minutes away from the Falco house, and Pete could have caught Russell making his house call Monday night, I wouldn't have been at all surprised to find out that he had taken a knife to Russell's tires as a prelude to Friday's tirade of warnings to stay away from Joyce.

At least I wouldn't have been surprised if Pete hadn't convinced me that he didn't have anything to do with it.

So if Pete didn't do it, who did? And why wouldn't Russell have reported what happened to the police? From what Andy had said, it certainly seemed as if his brother had been upset and angry. If that had been the case, the natural thing to do would have been to call the police. Trying to put myself in Russell's head, I'd only want to avoid the police if I didn't want to be hassled about something. As far as I knew there were no open warrants for Russell. That led me to the more likely conclusion—he knew the responsible party and wanted to handle the situation himself.

One person he might have talked to about that situation was opening her door across the street.

I waved to Kelsey as I approached. "Good morning!"

She smiled, a courteous pleasantry devoid of warmth. "You're here early."

She wasn't giving me the stink eye that I'd received from Nate an hour earlier, but that didn't mean she was any happier to see me. "Yep, I stopped for a latte and hoped that I could pick your brain about something you mentioned Sunday."

The electronic buzzer sounded as we stepped inside her shop. "About Russell," she said on a heavy sigh.

No one wanted to talk to me about Russell Falco this morning. Tough. I had a very loud clock ticking over my head and I wasn't leaving without some answers.

I followed Kelsey to the mahogany counter where she stowed her shoulder bag below the cash register. She motioned to one of the two wooden stools behind the counter and I took a seat. "Specifically, I need to know if he told you about any problems he was having with anyone last week."

Several silent seconds ticked by, a little furrow above her delicate brows the only indication that she'd heard me.

"You mentioned Sunday that Russell told you that someone slashed his tires," I added as a nudge to get her talking.

She sucked in a breath while her eyes pooled with tears. "You think someone killed him—that the two things are connected."

"I don't know what to think. That's why I'm asking questions."

Nodding, Kelsey blotted her eyes with a tissue.

I gave her a moment to collect herself and then tried again. "What exactly did Russell say when he told you about what happened last Monday night?"

She cleared her throat. "Tuesday, he stopped by a few minutes before I closed at six, and after I showed him what I had in mind for Saturday night, he said that he'd do his best to arrive on time. I asked him what he meant and that's when he told me about someone slashing his tires."

"Did he act upset, like he knew who did it?"

"No, not at all. In fact, he minimized it, acted like it wasn't a big deal. I think he didn't want me to worry about him."

"Okay, did Russell say anything else about it? Anything that might give you the impression that he was having a problem with someone?"

She shook her head, her hair sweeping her shoulder blades. "He had that black eye, but he said that was from some mishap at a job site."

No big surprise that he'd invent a story to cover for the dust-up with Andy.

"Really, despite appearances, the only impression he

gave me was of a man who'd made peace with his past and was...happy. His work kept him busy—so busy that we had to do a couple of late nights last week."

Blinking back tears while worrying her lips suggested that she didn't want to divulge how they filled their time during those late nights.

Kelsey as good as confirmed Andy's statement. These weren't work meetings.

"But things seemed to be going well for Russ," she added, dabbing her eyes. "Really, it seemed like he wasn't going to let some vandal get him down."

"Why did you say *vandal*?"

"I just assumed...the casual way he acted when he mentioned it. Who else would have done such a thing?"

That's what I wanted to know.

I considered my limited options as I hoofed it back to the marina and slid behind the steering wheel of my car. I could head straight to the courthouse to get an early start on my final report and admit that I had a whole lot of nothing, or I could drive back to Duke's for a free cup of coffee.

Since a certain unmarked police cruiser was parked outside Duke's front door, bad coffee accompanied by a side of conversation would be mighty tasty at any price.

I met Steve's gaze as I stepped behind the counter and reached for the two glass coffee carafes, leaded and unleaded, steaming side by side on their warmers.

"Good morning," I said to Stanley, who was sitting next to Steve.

Stanley had a morning ritual that consisted of reading every regional newspaper he could get his arthritic fingers on and slurping well-sugared decaf while he perused each page. No matter the weather, his ritual included wearing a plaid flannel shirt with every button fastened. Today was no exception.

I lifted up a corner of the Bremerton paper he had his nose buried in to give him a refill.

Steve pushed his empty cup toward me while he watched my show of draining the caffeinated dregs of the other pot into a paper to-go cup.

I smiled as sweet as the packet of sugar Stanley was dumping into his decaf. "Sorry. I'll make some fresh for you."

I emptied one of the premeasured packets into a filter and started the brew cycle, figuring this would buy me ten minutes of his time.

Stanley chuckled. "If I didn't know better I'd say she did that on purpose."

A corner of Steve's mouth twitched into a curl of amusement as he pulled a couple of dollar bills from his wallet. "Yeah, seems a little premeditated."

Since I was being that transparent, I leaned on the counter with the intention of coming clean. "As a matter of fact—"

"Too bad I can't wait for that coffee," he said, heading for the door.

What? I grabbed my cup and caught up with him in front of his Crown Victoria. "I have a problem and need your help."

His gaze was wary.

I raised my to-go cup. "I'll share."

"That's not much of a bribe."

"I know. It's all I've got this morning."

He opened the passenger door. "Get in."

Seconds later, Steve turned to me from the driver's seat. "What's up?"

"Dr. Zuniga is going to tell Frankie that Russell Falco died from accidental drowning, and I haven't been able to come up with anything to convince her otherwise."

He took a sip of my coffee. "That's awful."

"I know, and I'm running out of time and ideas. I still think that the person who slashed Russell's tires had something to do with his death, but no one who was close to him knows anything about that and Russell appeared to be acting like someone who wanted to handle the situation himself. That makes me think it was done by someone he knew. Pete Lackey denied it and didn't give me any reason not to believe him, but he's certainly had motive and—"

"I meant the coffee," he said, handing it back to me.

"Oh."

Three Gray Ladies, members of a Senior Center exercise group that proudly wore matching sweatshirts with their first names stitched on the front like 50's-era Mouseketeers, peered in through Steve's windshield as they walked down the sidewalk. With the way news travelled around here, I had every faith that they'd have some strong opinions about the Pete, Russell, and Joyce pseudo-love triangle—probably just one of the many subjects up for discussion during this morning's coffee klatch with Gossip Central's ringleader, Lucille.

Steve waved like his usual charming self and the three ladies smiled and waved back as if this were another typical late summer morning in Port Merritt. Except there was nothing about this morning that felt typical to me.

His smile disappeared the second they stepped inside Duke's. "So what do you want from me? You've got Zuniga's verdict—accidental drowning."

"What if he's wrong?"

"I got the impression that you don't have anything to counter your forensic expert's opinion."

"Pete and Joyce Lackey appear to be covering for one another and—"

"But you just said you believed him."

"When he told me that he didn't have anything to do with slashing Russell's tires, yes. But they're hiding something. They both lied to me when I asked them questions about the night Russell died."

Steve angled his head to face me. "Chow Mein, it should be obvious to you by now—everyone's hiding something."

Was he referring to me? To the fact that I hadn't wanted to go public about our relationship?

With awareness clawing at me that being seen together in his car could bring some unwelcome inquiries, I searched the length of the street. "I know but—"

"Just don't read too much into what you think you see." He leaned toward me, angling past the computer monitor separating us.

His elbow grazed my breasts, my heartbeat quickening until I realized the contact was accidental.

"I've got a meeting in a few minutes," he said, opening my door.

I took his less than subtle cue and stepped out of his car, but I couldn't let Steve leave without asking the question that had been preying on my mind the last three days. "Do you think there's a connection between Russell's apparent drowning and his tires being slashed?"

"Sounds like you talked to everyone that I would have talked to and they didn't have much to say."

That was an evasive answer if ever I'd heard one. "Nothing useful."

"Maybe that should tell you something."

It did tell me something—that I had yet to speak with the right person.

I went back into Duke's, dumped the foul contents of my to-go cup, and refilled it from the fresh pot I'd just brewed. With Stanley watching my every move, I took the seat that Steve had vacated five minutes earlier.

"Did ya get what you were after?" Stanley asked as Lucille squeaked her way to the pass-through window to pick up a breakfast order, her gaze fixed on me.

Dumping a couple of creamers into my coffee, I was well aware that Stanley wasn't the only one interested in my answer. "Not yet."

I waited for Lucille to deliver three hubcap-sized plates heaped with eggs, bacon, and hash browns to the regulars at table seven. Then, like I'd anticipated, she hovered in front of me like a mosquito as she topped off my coffee.

"Is there some news about Russell?" Without waiting

for an answer she cringed. "The autopsy results came back and the doc found something you want Steve to investigate."

"No, nothing like that." Although I almost wish he had. I glanced over at the Gray Ladies, who were watching us intently. To avoid their prying eyes, I grabbed my coffee and nodded to Lucille to follow me into the kitchen.

Pushing the door open, I was immediately nailed by my great-uncle Duke's scowl.

He pointed his spatula at me. "Just because you're not on the clock yet doesn't mean that everyone else around here isn't."

Lucille planted her feet in front of him and her hands on her rounded hips. "I've worked for you for thirty-six years. If I want to take a five-minute break—trust me, I'm good for the time!"

He grunted. "Your order is going to be up in a couple of minutes."

"And I'm sure I'll hear you just fine from over here when it is," Lucille said, walking toward the fryer.

Duke glowered at me.

Sorry. "I'll make it fast."

"Whatcha got?" Lucille said the instant I turned my back to Duke.

"Not much. No one close to Russell has had much to say about his death or who they think slashed his tires."

"Honey, you're not talking to the right people."

I inched closer, lowering my voice. "What do you know?"

Lucille smiled conspiratorially. "Most of our regulars have daughters, and it seems like Russell knew almost every one of those girls."

"Yeah?" So did I. I may have been a few years behind them in school, but I'd probably served them dozens of burgers and fries growing up. I stared at her, failing to see her point.

She heaved a sigh. "Knew as in *knew*! Sheesh, read your Bible now and again."

Oh, that kind of *knew*. "Are you suggesting that I look up his old girlfriends? That one of them was carrying some sort of grudge?"

That earned me another sigh accompanied by a roll of her baby blues. "From fifteen or twenty years ago? Hardly. But Russell Falco was a hound dog, and a hound dog doesn't change his spots."

She was mixing her metaphors, but the truth of her words made me shiver despite the heat of the oven ten feet behind me.

"Order up!" Duke announced.

"Be there in a sec." Lucille grabbed my wrist, pulling me closer. "Mark my words, a woman did this."

"Slashed his tires?" With Pete Lackey as my semi-prime suspect, I hadn't considered the possibility that a pissed-off former girlfriend could have sent Russell an impassioned message about how she felt about him throwing her over for Beverly Carver.

"And killed him. Did you see *Fatal Attraction*?"

"That movie with Glenn Close?"

Lucille nodded. "I think he messed with the wrong woman and then moved on. Doesn't mean that she moved on quite so easily."

Not a completely outlandish idea being floated by

Duke's resident conspiracy theorist, especially when I considered the fact that Russell never contacted the police to report the damage to his truck—almost like he'd known who did it and Mr. Discretion hadn't wanted to damage her reputation. That could have been his fatal mistake, allowing the situation to escalate into a deadly *Fatal Attraction* re-enactment.

Usually, Lucille's theories had as much substance as puff pastry and I could walk away from them without a second thought. Not only did this one fit into the realm of possibility, given everything I'd learned in the last week, it could even make perfect sense.

If only I could make it make sense in the next four and a half hours, when my report was due on Karla's desk.

Eleven minutes later, I was parked in front of the home belonging to the woman who had most recently played the love interest role in this deadly drama with Russell Falco: Beverly Carver.

I knew that she wouldn't be thrilled to see me on her doorstep before eight in the morning or anytime for that matter. But if Russell messed with the wrong woman, odds were high that it happened some time during his off and on, four-month relationship with Mrs. Carver. Less likely was the probability that he'd kiss and tell, but I had to ask.

I rang her doorbell and heard nothing but barking. After waiting a few seconds, I knocked. More barking.

The last I'd been told, Heather's mother didn't work,

having made a small fortune from the sale of the mini-mart chain her husband had left her. Since she no longer had a job to dash off to and she didn't strike me as being any more likely to work up a sweat on a morning jog than my mother, I walked around to the side of the house to peek through the window and see if Mrs. Carver's car was still parked in the garage.

Wedging myself between two beefy tomato plants, I peered into what looked to be a well-organized and car-free garage.

"Crap." Not only was I going to be late for work, I'd be arriving with little to add to my report beyond how Russell connected with his brother's fist to get that black eye.

"Hey! What do you think you're doing over there?" demanded a gravelly female voice behind me.

My heart pounding, I turned to see gray-haired Angela Doolittle, an old mahjong buddy of my grandmother's, aiming the nozzle of a garden hose at me.

"Hi, Mrs. Doolittle. It's Charmaine." I figured she might douse me if I made any sudden movement, so I planted my feet and pulled out my badge. "I had a couple of questions for Mrs. Carver, but she doesn't seem to be home."

The diminutive eighty-year-old with the oversized eyeglasses squinted at my badge and then lowered the hose. "Oh, that's all right then." She brightened as I approached the low boxwood hedge separating us. "Charmaine, I didn't recognize you at first," she said, her gaze landing on my waistline.

"It's been a while." Probably at least ten years and

double that many pounds.

"I thought you might be another peeping Tom."

"Another?"

"We had someone lurking outside a window a couple weeks back. If that's the right term for it." She frowned, puckering her already pucker-lined lips. "Can you call a woman a peeping Tom?"

I was willing to call her anything Mrs. Doolittle wanted if it would keep her talking. "I think so. You said you saw this woman a couple of weeks ago?"

"When I went outside to retrieve a pair of garden shears I'd forgotten to put away. I was right over there, by the amber queen when I saw her," Mrs. Doolittle said, pointing at a rose bush in full golden bloom bordering the property line she shared with Beverly Carver.

"Where?"

She dropped the hose. Motioning for me to follow her, she came to a stop a couple of feet behind her yellow rose bush. "I was here, about to reach for my shears when I saw her there, standing at Beverly's bedroom window."

"What time was this?"

"It was just before the eleven o'clock news so maybe around ten-fifty."

"And you're sure it was a woman."

"My eyes aren't that bad. I know a woman when I see one."

"Can you describe her?"

She puckered her mouth again—the same *how honest should I be* expression my great-aunt Alice used to make when critiquing my pie crust. "Well...other than being fairly curvy, not really. I only saw her from the back." She looked over at Mrs. Carver's house as if she were replaying the scene. "Honestly, it was just for a second... and it was really dark."

All that may have been true, but I could tell that she was holding something back.

Since this was the only lead I had that might support Lucille's *Fatal Attraction* theory, I needed Mrs. Doolittle to fight through her hesitation and give me a description I could use.

"Curvy like me?" I asked, turning so she could get a good look.

She pressed her thin lips together. "Sort of but shorter." She wrinkled her nose in a little wince as if the truth were causing her pain. "More like..."

Come on. Say it.

"I'd have to say..."

Yes, you have to say it.

"She looked more like Joyce from next door."

Holy cannoli!

"Not that I'm saying it was her. It happened so fast."

Not so fast on the backpedaling. "But it looked like her."

Mrs. Doolittle lowered her gaze and nodded.

"Would it be fair to say that you thought it was Joyce when you first saw her?"

"I'm afraid so," she said, her shoulders slumped in resignation.

"Did you tell anyone about this?"

"I mentioned it to Beverly the next morning, but I didn't name names. Just said that her peeping Tom was a woman."

"What did Mrs. Carver say when you told her that she and her *guest* had an audience?"

"Not much. She made a face and said, 'Pathetic, really pathetic.' I didn't think that much about her reaction at the time." Angela Doolittle glanced back at the yard next door. "But after all the commotion last Friday and that ugly scene between Pete and that Falco boy... Well, let's just say that Beverly probably had a good idea who it was."

And would probably join me in casting Joyce Lackey as the obsessed jilted lover in our local production of *Fatal Attraction*.

Did that mean that Joyce was Russell's killer? Nope, but all the signals I kept getting from the Lackeys screamed that they had something to hide—something big.

Mrs. Doolittle wiped her hands on her baggy polyester slacks. "Such a horrible night. I've never heard such language come out of Pete. Joyce either. Usually she's so quiet, but let me tell you—that woman can slam a door!"

"Could you make out what they were saying?"

She shook her head, her glasses slipping down the bridge of her nose. "Just a few words here and there after he followed her into the house. Not that I was trying to eavesdrop, mind you, but their windows were open and Pete was so angry that he wasn't exactly whispering. I felt like I should sort of keep tabs on things and sat on my patio for a while, until things calmed down."

Not even close to the blissful domestic scene that the Lackeys had painted for me. "And what time was that?"

"Let's see, it got really quiet after that door slam. I guess that's when I saw Pete heading for the gazebo. I didn't want him thinking I'd been spying on them, so I went back inside and watched the news. So eleven-fifteen maybe."

"And things stayed pretty quiet? No more door slams?"

She shrugged. "I must've fallen asleep in my chair. But no. I didn't hear anything else until one-thirty, when I let Sammy out to do his business—"

I looked back at the basset hound staring at us from Mrs. Doolittle's dining room window.

"—and heard Pete starting his boat."

My breath caught in my throat. "Pete Lackey has a boat?"

She angled a little frown at me. "He's had a boat for years."

I did a quick scan of the Lackeys' backyard. Same as the other two times I'd been here, there was no boat in sight. "Where's he keep it?"

"On a trailer in his garage—just like where my Wayne kept it before I sold it to Pete four summers ago to get it out of my garage."

"And you're sure it was Pete starting this boat?"

"Charmaine, I heard Wayne come and go in that old wooden boat for most of our marriage. I know the sound of that engine."

I imagined that Joyce Lackey would recognize it, too. After she heard the news and put two and two together, it was what brought her to the police station that morning.

He killed Russell. I know he did.

Now I had less than four hours to convince Frankie of that same conclusion before she signed off on Russell Falco's death certificate.

Chapter Fourteen

"Well, ladies," Frankie said, looking up from the report on her desk. "I don't see that there's anything here that warrants any more of this office's resources."

I turned to Karla sitting in the chair next to me. She shook her head as if to give me a silent warning to keep my mouth shut.

The heck with that. "What about the boat? Pete Lackey was on the water around the same time as Russell!"

Frankie met my gaze. "The police already questioned him about that. Doesn't appear to be much there other than a pissed-off husband."

The police? I clenched my hands into fists, wishing I could get them on the detective who had done the questioning.

"COD will remain *Undetermined* pending the toxicology results from the lab." She tucked my twelve-page report into Russell's blue folder and handed it to me for filing.

"That's it?" I had slashed tires, a peeping Tom, flimsy alibis, and a witness who placed Pete Lackey on the water around the same time as Russell Falco, but I was being told that our next move was to circle our wagons and maintain an *Undetermined* holding pattern for the next six weeks.

"That's it. Now we wait and see if anything else develops in that time." Frankie smiled. "But don't be discouraged. Your report made for very interesting reading."

Interesting reading! My boss might as well have said "good girl" and patted me on the head.

Sealing my lips so I wouldn't say something I'd regret, I followed Karla to the door.

"Charmaine," Frankie said, stopping me in my tracks. "One more thing before I forget."

I couldn't imagine that she could have anything else to say to me unless Steve had been right when he predicted that someone would register a complaint about me.

Reluctantly, I turned to face the music.

"Congratulations on making it through your first thirty days. You're no longer on probation." She gave me a little nod. "Keep up the good work."

I stared into Rox's big brown eyes when she tossed a coaster in front of me an hour later. "What have you got back there that would be immediately mood-altering?"

Rox leaned against the bar. "Having a bad day?"

I nodded. Despite hearing that I'd get to keep my job a while longer, everything about today had left me feeling powerless and ineffectual. Add in the fact that Steve had already interviewed Pete Lackey only to dismiss him as a suspect and I was reminded of when my ex informed me he was going to be on TV in a top chef competition. No discussion beforehand, no *oh by the way, they loved me in the audition*, no nothing—just a little bomb of a surprise he dropped on me, a precursor to him announcing that he wanted a divorce. Not that Steve owed me full disclosure, but he could have given me a hint when I talked to him this morning.

"Would a chocolate martini make you feel better?"

It would go straight to my hips with no guarantee of a side trip to my happy place and I didn't much care. "Wouldn't make me feel any worse."

As she reached for the vodka and a silver shaker, I closed my eyes and tried to lose myself in my favorite feel good Hootie and the Blowfish song blasting through the speaker above my head.

I heard the barstool next to me scrape the hardwood floor.

"Fair warning. She's in a bad mood," Rox said.

I shot Steve a sidelong glance. "Yeah, you've been warned."

He propped his elbows on the bar. "Very considerate. Are you here to eat, drink, or meditate?"

"Possibly all of the above. We'll see how my evening develops. What about you?" *Have anything you want to tell me?* "What brings you here?"

"Saw your car in the lot on my way back from a call."

Rox delivered my drink in a long-stemmed martini glass. "Madam's cocktail made with love and something eighty proof which should make you feel better very soon." She pointed to Steve. "Want a beer?"

"Iced tea. Not off-duty yet." He picked up my glass

and sniffed it. "What is it?"

"A chocolate martini," Rox and I said in unison.

He pushed it toward me. "A chick drink."

I painted a happy smile on my face as I reached for my glass. "Call it whatever you want. Just know that I'm not sharing."

Rox delivered his iced tea and then looked back over her shoulder as she left to fill a pitcher for a trio of bowlers. "Be nice."

"When am I not nice?" he protested as he scooped up both of our drinks and headed toward the far corner of the bar.

I slid off my stool and trotted after him. "Hey! Can't a girl sit quietly and enjoy her drink around here?"

He set our drinks on a table for two and then pulled out a chair for me. "Have a seat so that you can let that enjoyment begin."

I sat and stared across the table at him. "Why do I have the feeling that's going to be an impossibility?"

He stretched out his long legs, crossing them at the ankle. "I'm not stopping you. Have at it. Then when you're ready, talk to me."

We locked gazes as I sipped my drink and felt like a death row inmate who had just been served her last meal—in my case, a liquefied eighty proof candy bar. "Stop looking at me like you're waiting for my confession."

His dark eyes sparked with amusement. "Do you have something you'd like to confess?"

"Nope. But I'd like to know why you never mentioned that Pete Lackey had a boat or that you talked to him about being on the water the night Russell Falco died."

He reached for his iced tea. "I've told you before. It's not my job to keep you informed."

"But you informed my boss—"

"As a professional courtesy."

"But I didn't rate that same courtesy."

"Sorry, Chow Mein," he said without looking the least bit sorry.

Exasperating man. "Try to pretend that I do, if you ever want to have fun with ice cream again."

"Are you threatening an officer of the law?"

"Yes, and if you intend to have another dinner at my grandmother's house, you'll help me understand this one thing. If a witness heard Pete leaving in his boat around one-thirty, why wouldn't it be reasonable to think that he might have had something to do with Russell's death?"

"You might think that—"

Yes, I would and still did.

"—if you hadn't talked to the teenagers joyriding in their dad's boat that night. They had him to answer to when they got back to the marina, but after the news started making the rounds at school about the body being found, the boys came in with their dad to tell me they'd seen a small fishing boat circling the *Lucky Charm*."

"That's it? Just circling Russell's boat?"

Steve nodded. "And then leaving in the direction he'd come from—the south end. Based on the description of the boat and what happened earlier that night, I talked to Pete Lackey about it yesterday. He said he'd been sitting outside—*cooling off* as he put it—when Falco started his engines around one and headed back for the marina. But after ten or fifteen minutes, he noticed that Falco's boat didn't seem to be moving, so he decided to launch his fishing boat and check it out."

"And?" I asked, breathless with anticipation.

"And like the boys said, Pete circled the *Lucky Charm*, which by that time was adrift about a half mile from Cedars Cove. Only what they didn't know was that he was looking for Russell in the water because no one was on the boat."

"And you believed him when he said that?"

Folding his arms, Steve leveled his gaze at me. "It matched the boys' story, so what do you think?"

"*Fine.* I was just asking." Because if Pete Lackey didn't kill Russell, unless a rogue wave swept the guy overboard, I was out of ideas as to how a perfectly healthy man could have washed up on shore.

"My turn to ask a question. No one from your office contacted me about this becoming a coroner's case, so I assume Frankie accepted Zuniga's findings?"

"For now, but the cause of death will remain *Undetermined* until toxicology comes back."

"Then that's that."

Didn't mean that it was right, I thought as I sipped my chocolate martini.

"And where Russell Falco is concerned, your job is done, Deputy," Steve stated, narrowing his eyes as they locked onto mine.

"Uh-huh. Is your job done?"

"You know how it works. No coroner's case, no investigation."

"Don't you think this is weird though?"

"It's weird. I'll give you that."

It was too weird. "A guy gets in his boat to head back to the marina—and what—fifteen minutes later, he's dead in the water?"

Steve arched an eyebrow.

"No pun intended," I added.

"According to our witnesses, yeah."

"And both these boys and Pete Lackey see this boat drifting in the bay like some sort of ghost ship and nobody reports it?"

"Nobody wanted to get into trouble."

Which explained the fiction the Lackeys had been spinning yesterday but little else. "What do you think happened?"

Sucking down half his drink, Steve shrugged.

That narrowed it down. "Engine trouble?"

"Both engines started right up at the dock when I tried 'em, so no."

Then why would Russell have turned them off? "A little crabbing as long as he was in the area?" He wouldn't have been the first person in these parts to quietly drop a crab trap out of season.

"The water would have been too deep that far out."

"He had to have a reason to stop there."

"It could have been any one of many reasons," Steve said, focusing on his iced tea glass as if he wished it contained the answer.

That didn't mean he was being one hundred percent forthcoming, but I'd seen nothing to suggest that anything he'd told me tonight had been a lie. "This is really weird."

"I think we've established that by now."

"Okay, then level with me. Given all that, in your professional opinion do you think that Russell Falco had some sort of accident that night and just...drowned?"

Steve pulled out his cell phone and read a text message. "I have to get back to work."

"You didn't answer me."

Pushing away from the table, he stood directly in front of me. "I haven't seen any evidence to suggest this was anything other than an accident. Is that a good enough answer for you?"

He couldn't have made it more clear and, as a bonus, he was telling the truth.

Dang.

Thoughts of Steve, Pete and Joyce Lackey, and those kids on that boat kept me tossing and turning most of the night. Of course, the andouille sausage calzone that I had chased down with a second chocolate martini probably helped to fuel my insomnia, not to mention the churning funk in my gut tag-teaming with my cramps.

After dragging myself into the upstairs bathroom for a steamy shower, I dressed in my yoga pants and a deep purple knit tunic that made me look like a giant eggplant, but at least it didn't hurt me anywhere but in the pride department.

"No more andouille sausage, no more chocolate martinis, no more pizza, no more cookies," I muttered while

I searched my tote bag for my roll of antacids. "You can do it." If I ever wanted to trade in my stretchy yoga pants for a pair of skinny jeans, I had to make some changes, starting today.

Unfurling the wrapper on the antacid roll I found in the bottom of my tote, I groaned when I discovered nothing but paper.

No problem. I headed for the kitchen, where my grandmother used to treat my tummy aches with a half teaspoon of baking soda dissolved in water and gently chide me for my foolish choices.

Obviously not that much had changed in the last thirty years.

I opened the kitchen cupboard and reached for the golden box of baking soda and took the cure. As long as I was self-medicating, I grabbed the last two bottles of my mother's stash of French sparkling water from the refrigerator, downed one on the spot and drank the other one on the way to Duke's to see if one of my favorite fishermen could help me solve a mystery.

Alice squinted at me through her wire-rimmed trifocals when I stepped through the back door. "You look like death warmed over."

"I feel fine," I said, squelching a belch. Pulling a white canvas apron from a hook, I joined my great-aunt at her butcher block table to help roll out pie crust dough. "I just didn't put as much makeup on this morning." At least that much was true.

She pursed her lips. "Sure. Like you're the only one around here who can tell when someone's lying."

Carrying one of his glaze pans to the sink by the

doughnut fryer, Duke scowled. "What's going on with you? This is two days in a row you're in here at this hour."

I aimed my best smile at him. "I like it here."

He shook his head. "You're like a stray cat. We need to stop feeding you."

Since the notion of facing anything the least bit greasy made this cat want to cough up more than a hairball, I wouldn't fight him on that point. "Fine. I'm not here to eat. I just need to talk to you for a few minutes."

Exchanging glances with his wife, Duke pulled up a stool between Alice and me. "Okay, but make it snappy. I have things to do."

Alice swatted him, dusting his chest in white flour. "We *all* have things to do. Right now, your thing is to sit there and behave." She reached across the table and patted my hand. "Go ahead, honey, how can we help?"

Duke gave me the hurry up sign while Alice wasn't looking.

"There's a work thing that I'm trying to figure out," I said with a nod, my promise to him that I'd make this as quick as I could.

He reached for his coffee cup. "Shoot."

I didn't want to supply Gossip Central with any new information about the night Russell Falco died, so I knew I needed to proceed with caution. "You've done your fair share of fishing out on Merritt Bay."

Alice cocked her head. "This is about fishing?"

In a roundabout way. "Sort of. It's about boating."

"That leaves me out of it," she said, flattening another ball of dough with her rolling pin.

Duke waggled his bushy silver eyebrows at me. "You, young lady, have come to the right place."

"That's what I thought." I scooted my wooden stool a little closer to him so that I could paint him a picture in the layer of flour coating the table. "Here's the scenario: It's nighttime, and a guy is alone on his motorboat and is heading back to the marina after being out on Merritt Bay for a couple of hours of fishing." I drew a line in the white dust with my index finger while using a strip of dough to serve as my marina. "Halfway there he turns off his engine and drifts for a while."

"Why would he want to do that?" Duke asked.

"That's what I want to know."

He frowned at my flour dust scene. "It's dark, right?"

"Right."

"Shouldn't be much to see. A mechanical problem would be my guess. If he smelled or heard something he might stop to take a look at the engine—"

"The engine's running fine."

"Then, heck, I don't know. Maybe he dropped something and was shining a flashlight in the water to look for it."

"Maybe." Since Russell's cell phone was missing it would be impossible to prove that he didn't drop it into the water.

"What if Russell wasn't out there alone?" Alice asked, leaning on her rolling pin.

"Uh…" I had a sinking feeling my hypothetical jig was up.

She met my gaze. "That's who we're talking about, right?"

I nodded. "But everything else in this conversation is strictly speculation."

"Fine, then put this into your speculation pipe and smoke it," Alice said. "There's no reason Russell couldn't have met up with another boater and he shut his engine off to talk for a few minutes."

I turned to my great-uncle. "What do you think?"

"We could practically hear his twin diesels from here." Duke pushed off his stool. "So if he wanted to carry on a conversation with somebody, that's as good a reason as any."

And certainly better than anything that I'd come up with because it opened up another possibility—the person responsible for Russell Falco's death could have been on that other boat.

After picking up a replacement roll of antacids at Clark's Pharmacy on my way to the office, I turned left on 3rd to see if Steve's cruiser occupied its usual spot in the police station parking lot. Fortunately for me it did. Even more fortunately, I'd arrived with reinforcements.

"Hey, Wanda," I said to the chief's secretary, poking her head out from behind her computer monitor when the door chime announced my arrival.

"Mornin', Char." Her watchful eyes zeroed in on the white bakery bag and to-go cup in my hands like they had the dozen times over the summer that I had made deliveries for Duke. Luckily, Wanda didn't have x-ray vision or she would have seen me carrying two hard-boiled eggs—the diet breakfast I'd planned to have at my desk.

I raised the bag and cup to the video camera mounted in the corner. "Special delivery for Detective Sixkiller. Buzz me in?"

Wanda hit the button next to her desk that released the security door separating John Q. Public from the restricted area of the fourteen-person police force. "I don't see how that boy's cholesterol isn't up to the moon with all the junk food you bring him."

"Tell me about it." I headed down a narrow hallway, hoping he'd never tip her off that not one of these deliveries had been his idea.

"Knock, knock," I said, rapping on Steve's open door. "Since I missed you at breakfast, I thought you might be hungry."

Looking over his computer monitor, his eyes narrowed as they raked over me. "What happened to you after I left last night? You look like that chocolatini thing kicked you to the curb."

And then teamed up with the calzone to land several kidney punches.

I turned up the wattage of my smile, which probably would have been a more effective look if I'd applied some lipstick before I left the house. "I'm perfectly hunky dory."

"Sure you are." He reached for the bag. "What've you got?"

"Breakfast."

Steve opened the bag. "This has to be the worst bribe I've ever seen."

I snatched back the bag and plopped down in the

chair opposite him. "Okay, so it's my breakfast."

He popped the top of my coffee cup and took a sip. "And to what do I owe the pleasure of this very bad bribe?"

"I'd like to continue the conversation we were having last night."

"Yeah? I think I've already said everything I want to on that subject."

Truer words had probably never been spoken, but I still needed Steve to talk. "It would be helpful though if I could have the names of the teenagers who were joyriding in their dad's boat early Saturday morning."

He set the to-go cup in front of me and then leaned back in his chair. "Why?"

"I want to talk to them, find out what else they might have seen that night."

"I've already taken their statements."

"May I have a copy?"

"Nope."

"Why not?"

"Because you've done your job and it's time to stop playing junior investigator."

"I'll have you know that an important part of my job is to interview witnesses on behalf of the County Coroner so that she can make informed decisions as to the cause of death." She hadn't exactly told me that in so many words, but I thought it sounded good. "And if I think there are still some unanswered questions about what happened that night—"

"If there are, they won't be asked by you."

"You know what? You're being a real jerk about this."

His lips stretched into a lopsided grin. "Jerk? We're not talking about sharing toys here."

Springing up from my chair, I grabbed the paper sack and the to-go cup. "I know! We're talking about you not being willing to work with me on this case."

Steve crossed his office in three long strides and shut the door. "Let's get something straight," he said, looming over me. "We aren't partners. There's not even a case!"

"Obviously! But those kids could have seen another boat that night—a boat that hightailed it out of there before Pete Lackey came along."

Steve's mouth twitched a split second before he clamped it shut, and I knew that I'd just hit a bulls-eye.

"Ha!" I pointed at his mouth, creating a mini coffee tsunami that sloshed over my wrist. "I'm right, aren't I? They saw something."

"No." He took the cup from me and passed me a tissue from the box behind his desk. "And stop dripping on my carpet."

"What do you mean, *no*?" I asked, mopping up as he drank my coffee.

"I already asked. They didn't see any other boats in the area."

"What about their father back at the marina? He might have—"

"Nothing there either. The boys pulled into the slip. He chewed them out there at the dock like you'd expect, then he escorted their asses home. End of story."

"Doesn't mean that another boat couldn't have come and gone a few minutes before the boys came along. I don't think there was much of a moon that night. And being kids, with beer I assume...?"

I got a grunt accompanied by a little nod, which I interpreted to mean that they were being typical teenage boys with access to Dad's mini-fridge. "So they probably weren't paying a lot of attention until they spotted Russell Falco's running lights."

"Well, Deputy, that's not bad deductive reasoning."

I didn't bother admitting that I'd had a little help from Alice and Duke. "Gee, that almost sounded like a compliment."

"Yeah, well, let's not get carried away here. I told you the truth last night when I said that we don't have any witnesses to suggest that this is anything other than an accident."

"But you don't believe that it's an accident any more than I do."

"I believe what the evidence tells me," he said, his lips inches away from mine.

"Uh-huh. I believe what I see, too, but sometimes that doesn't tell the whole story."

Smiling, he opened the door. "Have a nice day. And thanks for the coffee."

I arrived at work ten minutes later to Patsy crooking her finger at me.

"We have a little emergency," she said with a wolfish gleam in her gray eyes.

I had a bad feeling that my *nice day* was about to be sliced, diced, and fricasseed, especially after I followed her swaying hips to the copy room.

She then left me alone with a box full of manila folders bulging like overstuffed strudel and a copier bigger than Duke's two industrial ovens, along with instructions to make two copies of everything.

Four hours later, that copier was putting out heat like one of those ovens, making me feel like a well-roasted eggplant. With both of us in need of a cooling-off period, I drove to my grandmother's house for lunch and a thirty-minute power nap.

"What good timing!" my mother exclaimed when I stepped through the back door. "Never mind, Mama. Charmaine can take me."

Standing in front of the refrigerator as if she wanted to crawl inside the stainless steel box to avoid this conversation, my grandmother rolled her eyes. "Lucky you."

Since the stories about Marietta totaling two of my grandparents' cars got retold at every family wedding and funeral, she knew better than to ask for the keys to Gram's Honda. But that meant I'd frequently receive the dubious honor of providing her my chauffeuring services.

"Do you want me to drop you somewhere on my way back to the office?" I asked her.

Marietta's unnaturally white teeth clenched into a tense smile. "Not exactly and if we're going to get there on time, we should leave in the next five minutes." Dropping the smile, she squinted, scrutinizing me from head to toe. "Plenty of time for you to freshen up. Honestly, sugah, you don't look so good."

Like she was telling me something I didn't know. "I'm as fresh as I'm going to get today."

"Okay." Her tone dripped with disapproval. "Then

let's go."

"I haven't had lunch yet." Something my growling stomach had been insisting upon the last couple of hours and had no intention of being denied.

"Want me to make you a sandwich, honey?" Gram asked.

"There's no time for that, Mama. I'll buy her drive-through." The gold bangles at Marietta's wrist clattered as she skittered to my car as fast as her five-inch stilettos would carry her.

I turned to my grandmother. "What's this about?"

She shrugged. "I know as much about it as you do."

Great. I followed my mother out the door. "Why the big hurry?"

"I have a meeting in Port Townsend."

I didn't like the sound of that. Ever since she'd slipped off the B-list, Marietta Moreau didn't have meetings unless divorce attorneys were present.

Sliding behind the wheel of my Jaguar, I watched as she checked her lipstick in the passenger side mirror. "What kind of meeting?"

"A *business* meeting." She flicked her left wrist, the clanging bangles setting my teeth on edge. "Come on, let's go."

"Anyone else joining you at this meeting?" I asked as I pulled out of the driveway.

"No."

"What about your agent and your business manager? Do they know about this?"

"My business manager! I should've fired his ass years ago, before..."

"Before what?"

She shook her head, her jawline set like tempered steel. "I made a mistake not letting your grandmother drive me. There wouldn't have been such a third degree."

She and I both knew that was a lie. Ben Santiago had nothing on Gram when it came to cross-examination.

"So where in Port Townsend is this meeting being held?" I was pretty familiar with the gallery and restaurant district of downtown, but the outlying areas not so much.

"The Grotto. It's near the waterfront from what I was told."

"I know it." I had interviewed for a job there when I first moved back to Port Merritt. Nice place but spendy. Whoever had arranged this meeting would be dropping some big bucks for lunch.

After a few moments of silence, I noticed my mother fidgeting with her engagement ring.

Crap. She looked as nervous as the first time I accompanied her to an audition.

"Do you want me to go in with you?" Marietta appeared to need an ally and I'd at least get an overpriced salad out of the deal.

She patted me on the thigh. "That's sweet of you to offer, but Lance is expecting just me."

"Lance Greenwood, that artist?"

"Of course. What other Lance do I know around here?"

"What does he want?" And it had better not be any more of her money.

"All he mentioned when I ran into him yesterday was an opportunity that might be mutually beneficial. That's worth a listen, don't you think? Plus I'll get a free lunch."

As my grandfather used to tell me, there was no such thing as a free lunch.

Chapter Fifteen

"About time you got home," my grandmother grumbled as I schlepped in two bags of groceries from my car.

Was I that late? I glanced at the clock on my way to the refrigerator. Nope, since it was only five fifty-two I had a feeling that I wasn't the source of Gram's irritation.

"We needed a few things." At the top of my list was my mother's seltzer water that was in my best interest to replace before she noticed it was missing. The bottle of aspirin I'd picked up for my copy machine-sized headache ran a close second.

"Did you buy more water?" Marietta asked from the living room.

Busted. "Yep."

"Her and her fancy water." Gram took a mallet to the skirt steak on the cutting board in front of her like she was playing Whack-a-Mole. "What's needed most around here is for everyone to exercise a little common sense!"

Marietta stood at the kitchen door, her green eyes firing daggers at her mother. "Hand me one of those waters if you would please, Chahmaine."

Knowing it would be prudent for me to do my best

Switzerland impression during this kitchen range war, I passed her a bottle. "I take it your meeting with Lance Greenwood went well?"

She sat at the kitchen table and took a sip. "It went very well, thank you." She aimed a frosty glare at Gram. "Despite what some people think."

"There is nothing good about a man you've known for less than a week asking for money," Gram said, taking another whack at our dinner. "Although, heaven knows you've had plenty of experience in that department."

Oh, Gram. Low blow.

"He's not asking for a handout, Mama! It's an investment opportunity."

I took the seat next to Marietta. "What exactly are we talking about?"

She brightened. "Lance is putting a small investment group together to buy the Benoit Art Gallery here in town and expand it into a performing arts center and—"

"And by small investment group," Gram chimed in, "she means he's trolling the local waters for whales to back this grand scheme of his."

My mother was more of a minnow than a whale, but since that wasn't the impression she'd left Lance with last Saturday, I wasn't surprised he'd put her on his short list of potential investors.

"Mama, really! You don't need to make him sound so mercenary."

"I can only call it as I see it," Gram said. "He's clearly someone with big ideas—in this case, a big expensive one—and there's nothing wrong with that as long as it doesn't cost *you* anything."

Especially given her poor investment track record.

"Sounds very ambitious." And much like the restaurant he chose to reel in his whales, very spendy.

"Maybe a little ambitious but nothing ventured, nothing gained." Marietta averted her gaze and inspected a lacquered nail. "Plus it could be a wonderful opportunity since both Lance and I are in the process of putting down roots in the community."

Stated with all the conviction she could infuse into each word, but the way my mother was chewing on her lower lip told me Gram and I weren't the ones she was trying to convince.

"But you can't afford to do this," I said, gently stating the obvious before Gram came over with her meat mallet to beat this expensive pipedream out of her daughter. "Can you?"

Marietta shrugged. "Probably not, but I told Lance that I'd think about it."

"More importantly." Gram whacked the skirt steak like she wanted to get my mother's undivided attention. "What did you tell Barry when he came to pick you up?"

Marietta focused on her water bottle. "That I'd had a successful afternoon of shopping, which I did after lunch, so—"

"Mary Jo!" Gram dropped the mallet on the counter. "He's the one that you'd be putting down these roots with and you still haven't told him about your financial situation?"

My mother's eyes widened, her cheeks ablaze. "Mama, we are *not* discussing that right now!"

"I already know," I admitted. "And Gram was right to

tell me."

Her gold bangles clanging, Marietta folded her arms under her double Ds and glared at her mother. "Is anyone else around here privy to what was supposed to have been a private conversation?"

Gram's expression softened. "No, but Barry should be. If you really want a future with him, you have to be totally honest with one another."

My mother's eyes glistened with tears. "I know."

"Not that I'm suggesting that he's marrying you for your money, but if you want this one to last, it's only fair that he knows the truth," Gram said.

Marietta took a swipe at the teardrop cutting through the layers of powder on her cheek and looked down at her fingers in horror. "Blast! I'm ruining my makeup and Barry's coming to take me to dinner any minute."

Shaking her head, Gram heaved a sigh as my mother dashed upstairs. "I hope I'm not beating the stuffing out of this piece of meat just for my benefit."

"I don't have other plans." At least not yet.

I went to the front window to see if Steve's Crown Victoria was in his driveway and it was. "Since you have enough for three, want me to ask Steve to join us?"

It would give me a good excuse to talk to him, maybe even get a hug—something that had been in short supply the last couple of days during my crampy hiatus from his bedroom.

Gram locked onto my gaze. "The same advice I gave your mother goes for you, you know."

"Huh?"

"You know what I mean. As in being open and honest."

Obviously Gram didn't understand the sex buddy rules after years of just being buddy-buddy, and I wasn't about to explain them to her.

She waved me toward the door. "That's all I have to say on the subject."

And when Steve came over it had better stay that way.

"Hey," I said to Steve when he opened his front door.

The laugh lines edging his eyes crinkled as he looked me over. "I don't see a bag in your hand. What, no bribe? And they've been so effective, too."

"Very funny. Keep it up and I won't set a place for you for dinner."

"I've got a meeting, so I'll have to pass," he said, shutting the door behind me. "But you can keep me company for a few minutes until I have to leave."

I followed him into his sunny yellow kitchen where the chicken-themed wallpaper never failed to remind me of his mother's love of French country decor and the cookies she would dole out to us from her red and white ceramic rooster.

He pulled a bottle of water from his refrigerator. "Want one?"

I still felt dehydrated from last night's overindulgence, so I sat at his kitchen table and took him up on his offer. "What kind of meeting?"

"PTA. The safety committee at Merritt Elementary is launching a new campaign and asked me to say a few words."

Not a shocker that a predominantly female committee would invite a speaker who was easy on the eyes to attract attendees to the Parent-Teacher meeting.

"Makes sense. It's a new school year and I'm sure they want to start it off right." And all the better that he was wearing a Port Merritt PD polo that showed off his tanned biceps.

Steve swallowed half his bottle in a few big gulps and nodded. "With a focus on accident prevention on and off school grounds."

Off school grounds? Around here that typically meant youth sports and water safety.

"You could talk about the recent drowning," I said, watching his reaction.

"I could, but I won't." He leaned against his kitchen counter. "And I really don't want that to be all we talk about."

Message received loud and clear. "Okay, if you'd like a change of subject, want to hear about the latest fiasco my mother is getting involved in?"

His brows drew together. "Now what?"

"Lance Greenwood wants her to invest in a performing arts center venture that he's trying to get off the ground."

"Where?"

"Here in Port Merritt."

"Sounds expensive."

"Yeah, and she can't afford that right now."

Steve held my gaze for several silent seconds. "I know her movie career isn't what it used to be, but what aren't you telling me?"

"She's having some financial difficulties." I debated about repeating what I had heard on the way to Port

Townsend. "I think her business manager steered her toward some bad investments. Don't let on that you know anything about it though. She's already not happy that Gram told me."

"The last thing I need is for your mother to be on my case." He grinned. "I already have enough trouble from her daughter."

"But I'm a good kind of trouble, right?"

He crossed the kitchen and pulled me into his arms. "Most of the time."

I whacked him on the back of the head.

"Ow! I said most."

"Thanks a lot." Resting my head against his chest, I breathed in his clean scent. "After your meeting you should come over for dessert."

"Chow Mein, I'd rather have you over at my house."

Whoa! That wasn't the kind of dessert I had in mind. "I'm a little indisposed right now."

He pushed me back to arm's length. "Huh?"

"You know." I gave him a look, hoping I wouldn't have to spell it out.

"Oh." His eyes darkened as they held mine. "I'm sure there's something else we could do."

"Play cards? Tiddlywinks?"

"Strip tiddlywinks? You're on."

"That is *not* how we used to play that game."

He planted a kiss on my lips. "It is now."

Chapter Sixteen

"My money's on Russell taking a tumble into the drink after he was poisoned," Lucille said as she ladled oatmeal into a cereal bowl, filling Stanley's usual Friday morning breakfast order. "The stuff's probably pretty easy to buy around here."

"Very easy." Not that I was completely diving feet first into the next phase of Lucille's *Fatal Attraction* theory, but if someone on another boat didn't cause Russell's death, the notion of him needing to turn off his engines so he could run to the railing and hurl wasn't inconceivable.

"Easy to use, too." I glanced at the utility closet near the rear door, where my great-uncle Duke stored a box of rat poison. Problems of a rodential nature were commonplace everywhere there was food or farming—and we had both in plentiful supply in Chimacam County. "Definitely could incapacitate someone."

Standing at the grill, Duke reached for an egg and arched a furry eyebrow. "Don't give her any ideas."

"It's way too late for that, old man," Lucille said with an evil grin as she squeaked past him.

He blew out a breath. "Swell."

I patted his beefy shoulder. "Just remember, what doesn't kill you makes you stronger."

"With that lunatic I should be strong as an ox. I swear she's obsessed."

I didn't want to admit that Lucille wasn't the only one.

Duke cracked the egg on the grill. "We need to get that funeral over and done with. That Falco boy is all anybody's talkin' about."

"The funeral's tomorrow afternoon. You going?"

"Nah, covering for Hector. He was friends with the family back in his deckhand days." Duke flipped two bubbling pancakes and then pointed at me with his spatula. "I should tell him to keep an eye on you and Luce. Make sure you two reprobates don't get into any trouble."

The bell hanging over Duke's Main Street entrance jingled, and I looked through the window over the grill to see that it had signaled Steve's arrival. "I'm sure that won't be necessary." Especially since I had a cop who seemed to have elected himself to that job. "Really, it's a funeral service. What kind of trouble could we possibly get into?"

He plated the pancakes. "Does a bear poop in the woods? Order up!"

"Nice vote of confidence." I filled another cereal bowl with oatmeal and pasted a smile on my face as I carried my breakfast to the counter and slid onto the stool next to Steve. "Good morning!"

"Is it a good morning? Let's see..." Leaning in he took me by the chin.

I'd been up since around four which had given me plenty of time to exfoliate my skin and apply liberal quantities of Marietta's makeup to clog it back up again, plus I'd straightened my hair, so I thought I had a chance of holding up to close inspection—something my ego needed after yesterday.

"Looks good to me," he said softly, his breath warm on my face, igniting a bonfire under my libido that he promptly extinguished when he tweaked my nose like I was his kid sister. "Could be even better if you'd get more than three hours of sleep a night."

"Oh yeah? Take that up with the woman playing Goldilocks in my bed."

"I hear there's a pretty nice bed in the house across the street from you. You might want to try it sometime instead of running home at the stroke of midnight like you've still got a curfew."

This conversation was careening down a dangerous path. With Lucille and her radar ears heading our way it would become a very public path if I didn't clue him in and pronto. "Oh, good. Lucille's coming with coffee."

He winked. "You could even get lucky..."

I clenched my teeth. "Keep it up if you want that coffee on your lap."

"And get a good night's sleep for a change."

Lucille plopped two white porcelain cups in front of us. "Who can talk about sleep at a time like this?"

I forced a smile at Steve. "Yeah!"

"Did you tell him about our theory?" she asked while she filled our cups with steaming, dark as coal tar java.

He reached for a creamer. "*We* have a theory?"

I passed him another creamer from the bowl in front of me. He was going to need it. "I'm sure he doesn't want to hear it." Very sure.

"I do," Stanley said with a spoonful of oatmeal inches from his mouth.

Steve smiled, stirring his coffee. "You heard the man. What have you got?"

Setting down the carafe, Lucille leaned on her elbows and lowered her volume to a stage whisper. "Two words—*Fatal Attraction*."

Stanley wrinkled his nose, his thick glasses bobbing up and down. "I don't get it. Somebody wanna translate?"

While Steve gave his breakfast order to Lucille, I provided an abbreviated version of the movie to Stanley, who'd never seen it.

"Okay, let me get this straight," he said. "Glenda Close—"

"Glenn," Steve and I corrected him in unison.

Stanley waved a liver-spotted hand at us. "Whatever her name is—she bumps off the family pet as a warning to the guy she had the affair with."

"Exactly." Lucille's eyes widened. "She's showing him that he messed with the wrong woman—the same message delivered by the one who slashed Russell Falco's tires."

Stanley pushed his glasses up the bridge of his nose. "So the moral of the story is that hell hath no fury like a woman scorned."

"You got it," she said. "Which is why it's so obvious that someone he two-timed bumped him off."

Steve sipped his coffee. "Uh-huh."

"Think about it." Lucille pointed at me. "You said he never called the cops about the damage to his truck."

Stone-faced, Steve shot me a sideways glance.

I swallowed the lump of oatmeal in my throat. "I may have mentioned it." Even though I was probably supposed to have kept that little tidbit to myself.

Lucille reached behind her for the carafe of decaf. "Instead, Russell confronts her—maybe looks her up Friday night after work. He doesn't want any more trouble. He just wants to talk. She makes them tea," she said, refilling Stanley's cup. "A special blend that has a little something extra in it. He tells her that he can't stay and she gives him a thermos of tea for later that night. Then on his way home, Russell is a little chilled in the cool night air and remembers about the tea. Pretty soon he starts feeling woozy and..." Lucille slapped her hand to the counter. "Bam! He hits his head as he falls off his boat, and Fred Wixey finds him the next morning."

"That's quite the detailed theory the two of you came up with," Steve deadpanned.

Yeah, quite. "Her version is a little more detailed than mine."

"Order up!" Duke barked.

Beaming, Lucille ignored my great-uncle, who was boring a hole into the back of her head with his glare. "I know. Pretty good, huh?"

"Very imaginative." Steve pointed at the plate of bacon and eggs getting cold on the counter in front of Duke. "If you're done, may I eat now?"

Lucille puckered. "Sure, don't take this seriously." She squeaked back with the plate and spun it in front of him like a blackjack dealer. "I'm sure Russell didn't take his ex-girlfriend very seriously and look what happened to him."

Steve bit into a strip of bacon. "I always give everything you tell me all the consideration it deserves."

"Yeah, right," she grumbled, topping off our coffee cups. "Then consider this—you'd better be at that funeral tomorrow."

Steve reached for another creamer. "Why's that?"

"She'll be there."

Stanley frowned. "Who? Our Glenda?"

Lucille nodded. "Someone that crazy about him won't be able to resist seeing him one last time."

Pushing aside my empty oatmeal bowl, I watched as Lucille squeaked away to make the rounds with the coffee pot. "She might have a point."

Steve shook his head as he reached for his cup. "You need to stop eating here. She's rubbing off on you."

"No, really. If there's a chance that Russell's death wasn't an accident, his killer could be there tomorrow."

"Uh-huh. Are you going?"

Was he kidding? I wouldn't miss it. "Yep."

"Then I'm going."

Awwww. I couldn't help but smile. "You don't have to go with me, but I'm glad that you are."

"It's not a date. It's more like security."

I dropped the smile. "I don't need a security detail."

"Between you and your co-conspiracy theorist I'm sure there will be plenty of other women there who will."

✳

Nine hours later, I was on my way home from the courthouse when I got stuck at the stoplight at 2nd Street and saw a blue and white truck turn right on Main. Ordinarily, I wouldn't give the truck traffic in town a second glance, but this one had a leaky faucet on the side panel and Pete Lackey at the wheel.

Pete may have moved off my suspect list, but that didn't mean he didn't have valuable information he could provide, particularly now that I knew he'd been out on the water the early morning of Russell Falco's death. All I had to do was win his trust so he'd open up to me.

Might be easier said than done since the last time I saw him he slammed a door in my face, but like my mother said, nothing ventured, nothing gained. At least my venture wouldn't cost me anything but time.

Once I got a green light I stayed back several car lengths so it wouldn't be too obvious that I was following him. Pete didn't turn on 5th to head to his shop nor did he take the left on Morton Road. Fine by me. Joyce's presence would only add stress to an already stressful situation for her husband, and none of us needed that.

After he turned onto 42nd Street, I knew exactly where he'd be heading, so I gave him a couple of minutes before I pulled up in front of his mother's house.

He scowled as I walked up the driveway. "I swear every time I drive through town you're following me."

Oops. "Sorry, I saw your truck as I was heading home and thought this might be a good time to follow up on a couple of things."

He turned his back on me and headed for the front

door. "I'm busy."

"I'm sure you are, but I really need to speak with you about when you went out on your boat that night."

Slowly exhaling as if I'd punched through the defensive bubble wrap he'd been surrounding himself with, Pete swung the door open. "Come on. Let's get this over with."

Not exactly a gracious welcome, but I was happy to take what I could get.

I followed Pete into what appeared to be a newly remodeled kitchen with granite countertops and a few manufacturer's labels still affixed to the oak cabinets. "Wow, this is nice. Did you do all this yourself?" Because if Pete was this kind of quality craftsman, why on earth would Joyce hire Russell for her odd jobs?

Except, of course, to have a hunky guy in her house.

"I hung the cabinets, but I traded labor with a couple of my buddies for everything else in here." He pointed to a wooden chair at a battered maple table that looked older than the two of us put together. From the sixties decor I saw in the adjacent family room, I assumed it was a leftover from his mom.

"Let's get to why you're here," he said.

"Fine. In a debriefing with the police I learned you were out on your fishing boat early Saturday morning." Not that Steve would call the few crumbs of information he fed me a debriefing, but I was trusting that I was the only one in the room who possessed an accurate BS meter.

Pete slumped into the chair across from me. "Yeah."

"Would you please tell me what you saw once you

launched your boat? Lights, other boats on the water, anything that caught your eye."

He frowned, his finger tracing a scratch in the table top. "I saw Falco's running lights, but instead of disappearing around the bend to the marina, I kept seeing them. That's what made me think he wasn't moving. I wanted to see him gone." He cringed. "That didn't come out right. I didn't mean—"

"Don't worry about it." Especially since it had been the most honest emotion I'd ever gotten out of the guy.

"I just wanted him to get back to the marina and out of my sight."

"Okay, as you got closer to the *Lucky Charm* did you see any other boats in the area? Any other running lights? Anything in the distance?"

"I saw a thirty-two...maybe a thirty-four-foot cruiser heading for the marina around the same time I came alongside Falco's boat. Didn't get a good look at the kid at the wheel, but he struck me as being pretty young."

Which was as I'd expected. "Anything besides the cruiser?"

Pete shook his head.

"How about a few minutes before that? Do you remember seeing or hearing anything?"

After a few seconds of him staring at that scratch, I got another head shake. "No, nothing until I circled around toward shore and saw a few lights on, a couple of cars on the road. You know...what you'd expect at that hour."

"You headed toward shore?" That wasn't what Steve had told me. His disclosure of his interview with Pete definitely hadn't been a full one.

"Just to see if he was in the water and was maybe swimming for it."

"And did you see him in the water?"

Narrowing his eyes, Pete's jaw set like he wanted to punch a hole in the freshly painted wall. "If I had, don't you think I would have said something about it?"

I politely smiled. "Of course." Again, honest emotion, but I was more inclined to believe Steve's read of Pete Lackey—a man who'd had a very bad night and hadn't wanted to get into trouble with the law.

"Thank you for your time," I said, getting up from my seat. "You've been very helpful." Mainly in confirming that Steve had told me the truth about the boys not having any additional information. Other than that I'd gleaned little that I didn't already know. In fact, after tailing Pete Lackey like the bad junior detective Steve thought me to be, I almost felt like I should apologize for wasting his time twice in the same week.

And I might have if Pete hadn't been so rude. It certainly would have saved us both a lot of grief if he'd been honest with me in the first place.

At least I'd had the opportunity to see how he'd been spending his evenings.

Peeking into a pantry on my way to the door I saw a thing of functional beauty with white wire rollouts that would dwarf Joyce's new pride and joy at their Morton Road house. "Your wife would love this pantry."

"Maybe." He surveyed the kitchen like a field general who'd only recently come to realize that he was facing a losing battle.

Following his gaze it struck me how beautifully the robin's egg blue walls coordinated with the blue tones in the granite, how much workspace the center island and countertops would afford someone who loved to cook, how the top of the line appliances gleamed under the recessed lighting. This kitchen had definitely been reinvented with Joyce in mind.

"If you don't mind me saying so, Mr. Lackey, you should tell her what you've been doing." He probably should have told her months ago. "From what she said when I interviewed her, she has no idea."

"I wanted to surprise her with it for our anniversary."

"You can still surprise her. Maybe when things settle down you can talk to her, tell her…"

He rolled his eyes, a sardonic smile pulling at his lips. "I'm not good at that stuff. Never have been. Besides, she's barely speaking to me. Hasn't since…"

I sure wasn't the right person to dispense relationship advice, but he looked so lost, I felt obligated to at least point him in the right direction. "Go home, Mr. Lackey. Joyce needs to know that you still care because you obviously do." Whether he could say it in words or not. "And once your wife has one look at what you've done here, she'll see it as clearly as I can." At least I hoped she would.

"Yeah, soon," Pete said, looking unconvinced. He grabbed the leather tool belt hanging on a hook in the pantry. "I have a few things I need to get done first."

He sounded just like my ex during the last year of our marriage. Funny how I'd given him a pass every time he invented an excuse to spend his evening at the restaurant instead of with me. I'd seen the lies, the lame excuses, and still I believed in us—that we were simply going through what my grandmother always referred to as a *rough patch* whenever Marietta separated from one of her husbands.

As usual, I should have believed my eyes, whether I'd wanted to or not.

After the door shut behind me, I was headed for my car when I saw Arnold Brubaker waving me over.

"Hi, Mr. Brubaker," I said, walking toward him.

Leaning on his cane with one hand and holding pruning shears in the other, he smiled, ignoring his bulldog barking at us from the sofa in front of his picture window. "You're back." He narrowed his beady eyes at my car. "Your mother wouldn't happen to be with you, would she?"

"Sorry, no. I just needed to speak with Mr. Lackey. My mom...uh...fell in love with his house the other day, so I wanted to make an inquiry about it."

His eyes widened, making him look a little less mole-like. "Ah, so she's thinking of moving back to town?"

She'd been entertaining lots of cockamamie ideas the past few weeks, none of which I wanted to discuss with this member of her local fan club. "She doesn't have any definite plans at the moment."

"Well, give her my regards." He leaned over and snipped several foot-long gerbera daisies. "And tell her these are from Arnold."

"I'll do that," I said with a glance toward the window where his dog was protesting my every move.

He snipped a dark pink daisy. "And this one's for you.

Goes with your outfit." He winked. "I've got an eye for fashion."

Arnold was also a black socks with sandals guy, but he had to be at least eighty so I figured he'd earned the right to define fashion however he pleased.

"Thank you. These are lovely. I'll go home and put them in water." I was tired and hungry, and with his dog's incessant barking, I wanted to do that as soon as possible.

Arnold slipped the handle of his sheers through a belt loop. "I need to get a move on, too. My boy in there is overdue for his walk. Creatures of habit us old dudes. We like our routines."

I had no doubt of that, just as I was certain there wasn't a thing that went on in this neighborhood that escaped his notice.

Driving down Bay Vista, I rounded the turn and looked out to the sparkling waters of Merritt Bay—a bay with a shoreline dotted with houses, some of which Pete Lackey had described as having their lights on. If even one of those houses was populated with an observant oldster like Arnold Brubaker I might find myself an excellent witness to what really happened the early morning of Russell Falco's death.

Chapter Seventeen

"Where do you want to sit?" Steve asked as we stood in the foyer at Tolliver's Funeral Home.

We'd arrived at two forty-five, fifteen minutes before Russell Falco's service was supposed to start, and almost every chair in the one hundred twenty seat chapel had been filled. Fortunately, Lucille was supposed to have saved us a couple of seats.

I scanned the crowd and spotted Joyce Lackey sitting in the back row between two other tearful middle-aged women. From the sniffling going on in the room, Russell's *friends* were well-represented. "Do you see Lucille?"

"You mean the crazy woman in the biker jacket waving at us?"

I peeked around Steve. "Where'd she get the jacket?"

"You're asking me? Come on," he said, leading the way down the aisle to the fifth row from the front, where Hector and Lucille were sitting.

Hector smiled at me as he stepped out from the aisle seat to give us access to the two blue chairs he bookended with Lucille. "You look nice, *mi querida*."

I could have looked better in the black wool pantsuit

I'd squeezed myself into if I'd lost more than a couple of pounds since wearing it to a funeral last month.

He winked, the old flirt, lightening the somber mood that Mrs. Fleming was fueling with her dirge on the organ. "Smell good, too."

"Thanks, but that's not me." I wasn't wearing any perfume. As I stepped by him I picked up a distinctively familiar musky scent and looked back to see Beverly Carver easing herself into a seat next to her daughter, Heather, two rows from us.

Not that it should have surprised me in the slightest, Steve stood in the aisle by Mrs. Carver's side, chatting with her and her daughter.

Lucille gave me a left elbow jab the instant I sat down. "Maybe that old flame isn't quite out between him and Heather."

"He's just being friendly." Steve was quite adept at playing *Good Cop* everywhere he went and seemed particularly skilled around former girlfriends. As long as he didn't make a move to frisk her, I didn't care. Much.

I turned to Lucille to get a better look at the black leather biker jacket with the winged shoulder patches that she was wearing over a charcoal gray dress. "What's with the jacket?"

She tugged on the collar, striking a pose like an aging fashion model. "Isn't it great?"

No. With her sensible shoes and platinum bob, there was no way Lucille could pull off the biker moll look. Instead she looked like a grandma who wasn't born to ride.

"My nephew let me borrow it," she said. "It's a little

stinky, but I thought it was fitting for Russell seeing that he used to be so into bikes."

Whatever. "Nice touch."

Lucille beamed. "I thought so. That way I'll fit right in with the boys from the club that are gonna provide Russell an escort to the cemetery." She waved back at the six burly guys in black leather filling the row in front of Joyce. "I plan on keeping tabs on everyone who goes there to say one last goodbye. Mark my words—one of them offed the dude."

I didn't have Lucille's confidence, but who was I to say anything to discourage her? Especially if she could provide another set of eyes and ears on the events of the afternoon.

Steve sat down between me and Hector and whispered, "So what's up with the jacket?"

"You don't want to know." I planted a smile on my face. "How's Heather?"

He patted my knee. "Fine."

"I bet."

I stared across the aisle at Heather, envying her perfect upswept, blond-streaked hairdo, her slender hips, the healthy glow in her sun-kissed skin that didn't freckle, and regretted that I hadn't worn control top pantyhose to keep from feeling like an overstuffed sausage.

"You're staring," Steve said.

I noticed that I wasn't the only one when I shifted my gaze to Kelsey, sitting in the middle of the row behind Heather. But Kelsey's focus was on Beverly, looking as if she wanted to take her high heel and pound the older woman like an ant at a picnic.

She knows.

That's why Kelsey's words didn't ring true when she told me about who Russell was leaving her to see last Friday. She knew it was Beverly Carver.

"I'm just interested in who's here," I said. "It's quite a turnout."

"Sure."

A hush came over the crowd as Reverend Fleming stepped to the podium positioned behind Russell's gleaming oak casket.

After a few words of welcome, the reverend aimed a beatific smile at Mitzi Walther in the front row. "What words of comfort can one offer when a young man is taken from us too soon?"

That launched a new round of sniffling and nose blowing from most of the women in the standing-room-only chapel.

I glanced over at Kelsey sitting statue still as she watched Beverly dab her eyes with a tissue. I wasn't close enough to get a good read on Kelsey, but from the steel in her gaze I knew she wouldn't be joining the sniffling chorus. Given how emotional she'd become in her shop on Wednesday, this wasn't what I'd expected to see from her today. Then again, I hadn't expected her to know about Beverly's relationship with Russell either.

Almost an hour later, Reverend Fleming announced to the crowd that we'd close with one of Russell's favorite songs.

As Mrs. Fleming played Aerosmith's *I Don't Want to Miss a Thing*, a stoic Mitzi and the Falco brothers filed out of the chapel followed by the cousins and close friends occupying the next two rows.

Appropriate song choice, I thought, as Beverly Carver and Heather fell into step seconds later. As they passed, Heather shot an enticing smile at Steve that promised a good time to follow, while of course snubbing me.

"Whoa," I muttered, watching Kelsey file into the center aisle with murder in her eyes as she watched Beverly.

Steve stood. "It's nothing."

"I wasn't referring to your ex. Did you see the way Kelsey was looking at Mrs. Carver?"

I followed Steve into the center aisle where he took me by the elbow. With a squeeze he whispered, "Leave it alone."

Yep, he definitely saw it.

I looked back at Lucille still in her seat. "You staying?"

She waved a pen and notebook at me. "I'll keep watch in here until it's time to head out to the cemetery. You stake out the foyer and watch people as they leave."

Sounded like a plan. If there was even the remotest chance that a killer had attended today's service and needed to have one last goodbye with Russell, I wanted eyes on anything that looked *off*. But I also didn't want to lose sight of Kelsey.

Groaning, Steve steered me toward the exit, where I had a clear view of the receiving line forming in the narrow foyer, and at the front of that rapidly growing queue stood Joyce Lackey and directly behind her, Beverly Carver.

Uh-oh.

I pulled free of Steve's grasp and headed in their

direction.

"The back of the line starts here," he stated, sounding like he was taking his self-appointed security role seriously.

Pretending that I'd forgotten to sign the guest book, I lingered in the area like Lucille doing the daily dish with her Gray Lady pals.

"I'm so…so terribly sorry for your loss," I heard Joyce say as she choked back tears.

Mitzi Walther extended her hand as if she were an automaton. "Thank you, dear. And you are…?"

"Joyce Lackey. Russell had been doing such beautiful work at my house and—"

"You're the one!" Mitzi's gaze drew so sharp she looked like she could slice the woman in front of her into bite-sized pieces. "Russ said you were trouble and now my boy's dead. You expect me to think that you didn't have a hand in all this?"

"Mom," Andy said gently, standing by his mother's side while Nate stared down at his feet as if he'd rather be anywhere than here.

"But I didn't," Joyce sputtered. "I wouldn't do anything…"

I could only see a fraction of her face, but I believed her.

Lucille might be on the right track with her *Fatal Attraction* theory, but Joyce wasn't our femme fatale. Besides, I never could get past the idea of her sacrificing one of her precious carving knives on Russell's tires.

"How dare you show your face here!" Mitzi pointed at the front door. "Get out!"

With a gasp, Joyce started shaking with sobs, looking as desolate as when I first saw her outside the police station. "I'm s-sorry."

If ever someone needed an emotional rescue it was Joyce. With the hope that I'd find a volunteer shoulder for her to cry on, I searched the line for Steve. Instead I found Kelsey's watchful eyes locked on Joyce and saw a flicker of a smirk that disappeared a split second before her gaze landed on me. Immediately it dulled as if she'd borrowed the carefully constructed mask I used to see on Marietta whenever I asked her questions about my father.

What the heck?

As I stood there feeling as conspicuous as a potted palm in the middle of the room while my brain raced to make sense out of what I had just observed, Joyce ricocheted off of me like a bumper car.

"I'm... so... s-sorry," she stammered between shallow bites of oxygen.

Steve took her arm before she crumpled to the floor. "Joyce, allow me to see you home." He gave me a sideways glance. "We're done here."

Fine. I couldn't imagine any other outbursts in the foyer. Not unless Heather decided to get into a grudge match with me, and with everything I'd witnessed in the last hour, that wouldn't surprise me a bit.

I followed Steve and Joyce out the door and down the funeral home steps, rain falling in a steady mist from the blanket of gray clouds that had been hovering overhead most of the morning.

"Hey! Wait up!"

Turning, I saw Lucille waving a piece of paper at me from the top of the steps. No point in both of us standing out in the rain, so I climbed the stairs, figuring that she had seen something in the chapel she wanted to report.

"The boys and me are gonna take off soon." She looked up at the gloomy skies. "Dang, I'm gonna get wet. And I thought this jacket was already stinky."

It was. "Anyone do anything that caught your eye in the chapel?"

She looked at the sheet of paper in her hand. "Fourteen gals laid flowers on his casket. Nine came up and said their goodbyes without flowers, and one... she just gave him a piece of her mind."

My ears perked up. "Could you make out what she said?"

"Honey, anyone in the building should have been able to hear her loud and clear."

"And?"

Lucille gave her head a shake. "She was a pisser. Wouldn't want her mad at me, that's for sure. Anyway, it sounded like she used to be head over heels for the guy. Even went somewhere and got a boob job for him, then she comes home to find out that he's left her for"—she checked her notes—"some chickadee named Chelsea, or as she put it, 'Effing Chelsea!' Then, after she dropped a couple more F-bombs, she showed him what he'd missed." Lucille demonstrated by pulling open her leather jacket by the lapels and sending some of her nephew's stink in my direction.

"She flashed a casket?"

"Nice rack, too." Lucille handed me the piece of paper

with a list of over twenty names. "Not that I think she's our girl. Not this one's style, but I made a column for her anyway." She pointed. "There she is, under Flasher."

A flasher in the chapel and Mitzi Walther reaching her flashpoint in the foyer, while Kelsey looked like she had murder on her mind. This afternoon was getting stranger by the minute.

"That should keep you busy," Lucille said.

"Yeah, I'll get right on it." Not.

"Good. I'll let you know if anything goes down at the cemetery, but right now I gotta get back in there and pay my respects before it's time to roll."

As Lucille headed back inside, I turned to see Steve at the base of the steps.

"I'm driving Joyce home." He handed me his keys. "You drive the truck."

Cool. "You've never let me drive your truck before. This day has just been one surprise after another." I looked up to the sky. "Are we having a full moon or something?"

He reclaimed his keys. "On second thought, I'll drive her in my truck. You can follow us in her car."

Me and my big mouth.

Twenty minutes after we arrived back at Steve's house, I was standing in front of my bedroom closet after trading my sausage suit for a black henley and a comfy pair of blue jeans when I received his text.

Got a call. Don't know when I'll be back. Sorry about dinner.

So much for the two T-bones we bought to grill on his barbeque. And since the steaks were in his refrigerator instead of downstairs in Gram's and my stomach was growling, I was even more sorry about the dinner I wouldn't be eating tonight.

"Oh, Chahmaine," Marietta said, standing in the doorway. She clutched her Kimono-style silk robe, her alabaster skin glowing from the shower I'd heard her taking while I was changing clothes. "I didn't realize you were in here."

"I was just hanging up my suit." Since it was still a little damp I pushed it to the end of the closet to put it in isolation like an infectious patient, away from the pristine designer wardrobe she'd brought with her. "I'm done."

I started for the door, but she didn't move to let me pass. Instead she looked down at my bare feet. "What are your plans for tonight? Staying in?"

"Maybe." Since Gram had headed over to Angela Doolittle's house for an evening of mahjong, I wanted to hear about my mother's plans before I committed myself to anything that sounded like interminable hours of mother/daughter bonding. "Are you getting ready for dinner with Barry?"

She sat on the bed. "I thought I was. Turns out his son is in town for the weekend. Barry wanted some alone time with him prior to telling him about our engagement."

He had a son? That was news to me. "Was he married before?"

"Years ago. Like me, he married too young—"

"Yeah, just like you and dear old Dad." The assistant

director who already had a wife and family stashed well away from where they had been filming in Paris.

She waved a manicured hand at me. "Okay, maybe not exactly like me, but the end result is the same." The look she gave me was as soft as warm butter. "He had a child that he loved very much, that he would have done anything for."

Anything? The woman who hadn't managed to squeeze in a visit home for even one of my school plays seemed intent on rewriting our family history tonight— all the more reason for me to get out of the house for a few hours.

"So they stayed together until Jason went off to college. That was quite a few years ago since he's now a teacher like his dad. Some high school north of Seattle, near where his mother lives." Marietta fluffed her damp hair. "I expect I'll meet him tomorrow."

I shot her a smile as I headed toward the door to make my escape. "I'm sure you will."

"You never really answered me. Do you have dinner plans for tonight? I was thinking about ordering a pizza."

Oh, sure. Dangle a pizza in front of me like a carrot on a stick. In my case, a really fattening carrot that should forever be on my banned food group list.

I stopped in my tracks, racking my brain for something she wouldn't do, such as traipsing around in the rain.

"Actually, I have some work I need to get done. You know, follow up on a lead I got today at the funeral." Not that I'd thought anything on that sheet of paper Lucille gave me qualified as a lead, but my mother didn't need to know that.

"At the courthouse?" She sat up straight. "I'd love to see where you work."

"No, I have some…canvassing to do. At least a couple of hours of going door-to-door in that." I pointed at my rain-splattered bedroom window to paint her a complete and very soggy picture.

"In the rain?"

"If I waited for perfect weather around here, I might not get anything done."

"What a wise daughter I have," she said, bounding up from the bed. "My hair is already wet and I haven't done my face, so what do I care about a little rain?"

What? Since when didn't she care?

She grabbed a pair of rhinestone-studded jeans from the closet. "Give me five minutes to get dressed and swish on some mascara, and I'll go with you."

Goody.

✳

I didn't want to risk the chance of my mother needing another potty break along the shore of Merritt Bay, so I had insisted that she hit the bathroom one more time while I sliced a couple of apples for us to snack on.

"You don't have to treat me like a child," she protested as she climbed into the passenger seat of my car. "I'm still capable of exercising some control over my bodily functions."

I handed her the plastic bag containing our apple slices. "Good, because I'm not planning on doing any breaking and entering tonight."

Marietta heaved a dramatic sigh.

Let the fun-filled evening of mother/daughter bonding begin.

As I took the turn on the corner of G and 5th, she opened the plastic bag and passed it to me. "Want one?"

I shook my head. I'd already fortified myself with one of the chocolate fudge macadamia cookies that Gram had baked in her quest to beat Alice, Joyce, and Beverly out of a blue ribbon. It was so not on my diet, and the fat cells in my ass needed more butter like I needed to walk barefoot on hot coals to make my headache feel better, but if Marietta and I both intended to get through the next few hours alive, I needed a fricking cookie. Okay, two.

"Where to first?" she asked, nibbling on an apple slice.

"I thought we'd start at the marina and work our way south." Since it was almost five-thirty, the early bird special at Duke's would wrap up in a few minutes, sending many of the Merritt Bay shoreline residents, who had ventured out on this rainy Saturday, back home to spend their evening in front of their television sets. Better yet, spend it admiring the bay view from their picture windows, where I hoped someone would tell me they had spent their early morning one week ago.

"What are we looking for at the marina?"

"A witness to something that I think might have happened last week."

"Hmmm." Marietta zipped up the bag of apples and tossed it onto the back seat. A second later she started singing, "Can I get a witness..." She snapped her fingers, swaying to some beat only she could hear. "Can I get a witness...yeah, yeah, yeah..."

I looked over at her as I turned onto Main. "What the heck are you doing?"

"Singing Grand Funk Railroad's *Some Kind of Wonderful*. It's a classic."

"Doesn't mean that we need a sing-along."

"Don't be such a grump. Your grandfather used to sing along with that song every time it came on the radio."

"Did not." The only station I'd ever heard him listen to was news radio.

"Hey, he even liked Grand Funk well enough to take me to their concert."

"No way," I said, pulling into the marina parking lot. "When was this?"

"Early seventies. I couldn't drive yet, so he took me. I remember that we made a day of it in Seattle. We got off the ferry and went to the Public Market, then headed up to the Seattle Center and took in the Exhibition Hall before the concert."

I couldn't imagine Gramps having that much energy. He certainly didn't when I was a teenager.

When I parked the car, Marietta patted me on the thigh. "We should do that."

"Go to a concert?" The only place she'd ever wanted to go with me before was to one of her movie premieres.

"Make a day of it in Seattle. Just the two of us."

"Uh...sure. It would be fun." And it was never going to happen.

Someone was getting carried away with all this bonding crapola, I thought, climbing out of the car. But my mother seemed to be having a good time and I didn't relish the idea of going door-to-door by myself, so I cut her some slack.

With the wind gusts from the bay pelting us with drizzle, I zipped up my hooded raincoat and handed Marietta my umbrella. I pointed toward the marina office to our right. "I'm going to see if I can get a list of the live-aboards to save us a little time."

Unfortunately, as we soon found out, the office closed at noon on Saturdays.

"Fine." I knew from experience with Russell's boat that Dock A was used for short-term moorage. Since the cabin cruiser and sailboat currently tied up to that dock weren't there last Saturday morning, I could start one row over.

"I'm gonna see if anyone's home on Dock B," I said, leading the way with Marietta right behind me.

I heard the heavy thunk, thunk, thunk of her heels as we walked down the steps to the dock and I looked over my shoulder. "Are you wearing boots?"

"What's the matter with my boots? All right, maybe they're a little noisy, but I didn't think we were going to try to sneak up on anybody."

"It's not about the noise and they're perfectly nice. Just—"

"You said we'd be canvassing the shoreline and I thought it might get muddy with all the rain."

It wasn't like I'd be taking her on a hike on the water's edge. "Be sure to watch your step. The dock might be slick from all this rain."

"Oh, my," my mother said without a trace of her fake accent as she tiptoed tentatively down the dock. "I see what you mean."

Criminy. If she broke a hip I'd never get my bed back. "Hold my hand," I said, extending it to her.

She gripped it like I'd offered her a lifeline.

I saw movement on a sailboat tied up in front of another one that was cinched up tight with a faded blue tarp. "Stay here. I'm going to ask this guy a couple of questions and I'll be right back. Okay?"

Hunkered under the umbrella, Marietta nodded.

Leaning over the railing, I rapped on the sailboat's side window. "Hello?"

Kyle Cardinale, the hunk of a doctor I'd met at the hospital last month opened the door and my heart did a little flutter—the same ridiculous reaction I'd had to my ex the first time I laid eyes on him.

Thankfully, I'd parked my mother out of visual range. The last thing I needed was for her to get a load of the swarthy Italian with the chiseled lips smiling up at me.

"Charmaine? What are you doing here?" he asked.

I needed to be careful with my answer in case it got back to Steve or Frankie. "I'm looking into an incident that happened not far from here."

Not bad. Certainly plenty vague and since Kyle already knew I worked for the Coroner, it should have been believable.

His smile vanished. "The drowning."

"Yes," I admitted as water dripped from my hood.

"Want to come in and get out of the rain?" He thumbed toward his galley. "I was just making a pot of coffee."

Just as I opened my mouth to reply, I heard heavy footfalls behind me.

"Oh, we'd love to!" Marietta said, extending her hand to him.

Chapter Eighteen

In my hierarchy of needs, watching Kyle Cardinale turn into *fan boy* and regale my mother with a litany of his favorite moments from her old TV show ranked just behind extending an invitation to Heather to join Steve and me for dinner.

Since Kyle had been working at the hospital early last Saturday morning and could provide me with little more than a caffeine recharge and some yummy eye candy, it was time for this mini-fan convention to come to an end.

"Thanks for the coffee, Kyle." I turned to my mother. "We should be going."

"So soon?" he said, on the edge of his seat, his dark eyes fixed on Marietta like he wanted to eat her up with a spoon. "I was hoping I could tempt you to tell me about working with Aldo Vinchetti. According to my father, he's a second cousin."

I stifled a groan. I didn't have time to play the Italian version of *Six Degrees of Separation*.

She smiled with enough wattage to illuminate the cabin of his liveaboard sailboat. "What a small world! Oh, the stories I could tell you about that man." She slanted her gaze my way. "Assuming we can intrude on Dr. Cardinale's hospitality for a few more minutes."

She could tell him as many stories about her glory days as he wanted to hear so long as I didn't have to listen to them for the umpteenth time. "Tell you what. I'm going to see who else is around who might have seen something last week, and then I'll meet you back here."

Marietta handed me the umbrella. "Take your time."

Right. I looked at Kyle. "I won't be long."

"We'll be just fine," he said with an earnestness that should have been reassuring, but it plucked at my heartstrings.

Jeez Louise! What was it with me and Italian men? I had a most inconvenient soft spot for them—much in the same way my dieting resolve turned to mush around butter. I knew it was very, very bad for me, but what I could do with it was so sinfully good.

Since no other boats were occupied on Dock B, I made my way over to C, where I spoke to a couple who had taken their Bayliner out Friday afternoon and anchored in Millen's Harbor, a sheltered area across the bay that many recreational boaters used for day trips and weekend getaways. They had been too far away to see Russell's boat, so I thanked them for their time and moved on.

I had barely cleared their line tied to the forward mooring cleat when I noticed a dreamcatcher hanging inside the rear cabin of the forty-foot cruiser occupying the slip in front of the Bayliner. Watching the cobalt blue feathers suspended from the hoop sway as waves gently rocked the boat, I remembered seeing a similar one on the *Lucky Charm.*

I turned back to the man on the Bayliner. "Do you know who owns…" I read the name painted in block letters on the stern. "*Boneweaver*?"

He thought for a moment. "Darned if I can remember his name. I know he's a doctor. Operated on my brother's hip last year."

It was probably a coincidence that two men with boats at this marina would have similar taste in Native American handicrafts, but I wanted a name in case this doctor had any connection to Russell Falco.

After making my way up and down each of the docks and finding no one amongst the eight people I spoke with that had seen the *Lucky Charm* early Saturday morning, I returned to collect my mother.

As I stood on his rear deck under my umbrella, Kyle opened his door. "That didn't take long," he said with a welcoming smile.

"I think the weather kept a lot of people home today. I did want to follow up with one boat owner though." I pointed at the cruiser with the dreamcatcher. "Do you happen to know who owns *Boneweaver*?"

Leaning toward me, Kyle looked over at the cruiser. "Sure. Dave Donovan, probably one of the better orthopedic guys in town."

Kelsey's father? Maybe. Seemed to me I remembered her telling me back in high school that her dad was a doctor.

"But I don't think he'd be able to help you," Kyle said, ducking back under cover. "I heard from one of the nurses that he was vacationing in Hawaii."

I shook the rain drops from my umbrella and followed him inside where my mother sat expectantly, her eyes focused on me. I motioned with my thumb that story time with Dr. Cardinale was a wrap. "Must be nice."

He chuckled. "Yeah, makes me think I should have gone into orthopedics instead of internal medicine. You might check with his daughter though. At least I assume that was his daughter who took the boat out last Friday. You know...the one who works at that artsy gift shop across from Hot Shots."

"Kelsey?" Marietta asked, meeting my gaze.

He shrugged. "Maybe. Cute, thirty-ish, wears a lot of silver jewelry."

My breath caught in my throat. There was no maybe about it. He'd just described Kelsey Donovan. "Do you remember what time it was Friday?"

Kyle raked his fingers through his spiky dark hair, giving him a roguishly appealing just-rolled-out-of-bed look. "Probably around eight-thirty. I remember being a little envious that she was going to enjoy an evening on the water while I was getting ready to go to work."

"Was she alone?"

"I only saw her for a minute." He nodded. "But yeah, I didn't see anyone with her."

"Any idea when she came back to the marina?" I tried to make the question sound casual, but from the way Marietta was staring intently at me I knew it was wasted effort.

"All I know is that the boat was back by the time I got home Saturday morning at a little after ten." A frown creased his brow. "You don't think that she—"

"I'm just gathering background information for Frankie," I said, trying to inject a palatable level of disinterest. "Thanks. You've been very helpful." I turned to Marietta. "We need to go." Immediately.

"It's been a pleasure meeting you, Dr. Cardinale. I so appreciated this delightful respite from the rain."

He took her hand in his. "Kyle, please, and the pleasure was all mine. I know my dad is going to get a big kick when I tell him your Aldo stories."

Whatever. I put up my hood and handed my mother the umbrella. "I'm sure he will." *Let's go.*

As I reached for the door handle Kyle's fingers grazed mine. "Maybe we can do this again sometime," he said with a lingering smile that betrayed his carnal interest.

Whoa. My imagination was already spinning like a hamster on a wheel from everything he'd told me about Kelsey taking out her father's boat. I didn't need this olive-skinned Adonis to tease my overheated brain with anything else to obsess about—probably not ever and definitely not tonight.

"Mmmm…" Marietta smiled knowingly at me. "Maybe we can."

I stepped up onto the dock first and offered her my hand. "Don't make anything out of that," I whispered after Kyle closed his door.

"Sugar, I don't need to. There's obviously a little spark between the two of you."

I had sputtered down this sparky road with Kyle Cardinale once before only to find him hesitant to create any real heat with me. "It's nothing." And it was going to stay that way now that I was with Steve. At least, kind of with Steve, in a semi-committed sex buddy, non-serious relationship way.

"It certainly didn't look like nothing."

"We're not talking about this anymore."

Holding my mother's hand on the wet, slippery wood, we thunk, thunk, thunked our way back down Dock C toward the *Boneweaver*.

"Where are we going?" she asked. "I thought we were done at the marina."

"Almost. I want to take a picture of that boat before we leave."

"You don't think Kelsey could possibly have anything to do with that poor boy's death, do you?"

"I don't know." But I wasn't going home before trying to find the answer to that question.

After the drive from the marina past the Cedars Cove boat launch on Bayshore Road, Marietta flashed a brittle smile at me. "I have a little problem."

Great. "What's the problem?"

"I need to go to the bathroom."

"We talked about how we weren't going to have this particular problem tonight."

She shrugged. "I know, but I had three cups of coffee."

"He had a bathroom on his sailboat."

"I didn't need to go then."

My fingers tightened around the steering wheel. "Do you want me to go back to the boat launch? There might be some facilities back there."

"No, I can hold it for a little while."

I'd heard that before. "You're sure?"

Looking resolute, she nodded.

After another quarter mile, I pulled over, ten feet from the entrance to a steep driveway for a house with an unobstructed view of the bay—possibly one of the houses Pete Lackey had said had its lights on early last Saturday.

"Okay, there's only about an hour until sunset, and I don't want to be going door-to-door in the dark, so I'll make this fast." Grabbing my tote and umbrella from the back seat, I gave my mother what I hoped was a reassuring smile. "Sit tight and I'll be right back."

Almost ten minutes later, I headed back to my car after having knocked on three doors.

The first didn't answer.

The middle-aged man with the scruffy beard at the second house had been disappointed that I wasn't delivering the pizza he ordered. When he added that he'd been out of town last weekend I shared in his disappointment.

My experience at the third house had at least been cordial since the elderly couple living there knew me from Duke's, but once Mrs. Houghton described her evening ritual of closing their front curtain after the sun went down, I knew they wouldn't be able to help me. Especially once the Houghtons started teasing one another about who fell asleep in front of their television first.

Squinting through the drizzle at where my mother should have been sitting waiting for me, I saw an empty passenger seat. "What about sit tight don't you understand?"

I'd expected that to be a rhetorical question to the

gray skies above, but a reedy voice answered from the hillside, and it was calling my name.

I looked up and saw Fred Wixey standing on a narrow foot trail that ran the length of the scrub-covered hill. "Hi, Mr. Wix...uh...Fred."

He motioned for me to join him. "If you're looking for your mom, she's up here."

Since he was the one who'd found her, I hoped it wasn't behind a bush.

Hiking up the slope, loose pebbles kicking out from under my sneakers, I tried to not pant like a dog by the time I reached the crest of the hill.

"Good thing me and Barney were on our evening constitutional," Mr. Wixey said, leading the way to his back gate. "I don't think Mary Jo could have sat tight too much longer if you catch my drift."

I caught it all right.

He opened his back door where Barney, the fox terrier, had been pacing, barking his intruder alert. "That's enough, boy." He winked at me. "Don't be trying to scare off all my lady friends."

I heard a toilet flush and knew his other lady friend would soon be making an appearance.

Mr. Wixey pointed at the barstool I had sat on last Saturday. "Might as well take a load off."

I didn't want to give my mother the impression that this rest stop detour could provide her with another trip down memory lane with one of the locals. "I'll stand. Been sitting all day."

"Want some tea? I was just gonna fix me a cup."

"Thank you, Fred, but we can't stay," Marietta said,

meeting my gaze as she stepped into the kitchen. "Charmaine has some work she needs to get back to." *Sorry*, she mouthed to me.

Filling up his kettle at the kitchen sink, he shot me a glance. "Since you're back in my neck of the woods, you must still be working on the Falco kid's drowning."

"Just to wrap up loose ends," I said, inching closer to the door to send him the message that I didn't have the time to stay and chat. "Need to find out if any of your neighbors with a water view saw anything that might be helpful to our investigation."

Mr. Wixey set the kettle on to boil and then folded his arms as he leaned back against the stove with Barney curling into a ball near his feet. "Like what?"

"Like if they happened to look out and see any boats in the area." Which he clearly couldn't have done. The only thing Fred Wixey had a view of was his neighbor's backyard.

"Ah. Like that one that hung around Cedars Cove for a few hours."

I pulled out the barstool he'd pointed to moments ago and motioned for Marietta to have a seat.

"I thought we were leaving," she whispered.

"Not now we're not." And not before Mr. Wixey told me everything he could about this boat.

Sitting next to Marietta with my notebook in front of me and pen in hand, I smiled at our host. "So you saw a boat hanging around Cedars Cove late Friday night?"

He nodded like that should have been yesterday's news.

"Would you mind telling me everything you remember about that?"

He loudly exhaled. "Here we go again."

"Sorry," I said under my breath. Obviously answering questions wasn't his favorite thing.

"Barney hadn't done his usual business earlier and it was a nice night, so we set out around nine-thirty to go for a little walk. Up on the trail, where I was waiting for you, there's a pretty good vantage spot of the cove. Anyway, that's when I saw the boat's running lights. Thought he was having trouble setting his anchor at first, the way he kept going back and forth."

"What do you mean back and forth?" I asked.

"He'd nose out past the point and then put her in reverse a minute later and move back ten or fifteen feet." Mr. Wixey waved his hands in unison as if he were conducting an orchestra. "Back and forth over and over again. I don't know what he was trying to do, but this went on for a good ten minutes."

Ten minutes. "But you said that he hung around for hours."

The kettle whistled and Mr. Wixey picked it up. "You sure I can't offer you ladies some tea?" He arched his eyebrows, a tease of a smile at his lips. "Or ice cream if you prefer."

"Ooooh," Marietta cooed. "That would be—"

"No, nothing, thank you." I didn't want anything else distracting Fred Wixey from the story I wanted him to tell me, since having my mother in the kitchen was probably distracting enough, and that was before she started pouting about the ice cream. "As you were saying..."

"Let's see...where was I?" He poured the steaming water into an insulated plastic mug and dropped a tea bag into it. "Oh yeah, so a couple hours later, I let Barney out one last time before bedtime and I got curious about whether that boat was still there, so I went back over to check. It wasn't as easy to make out because the running lights were off, but there was a light flickering in the cabin, so I figured the guy was in there watching TV or something. Then the strangest thing happened."

"What?" Marietta and I both asked as he took a sip of tea.

"He did the same darned thing he did earlier. Nosed his boat out past the point, stayed there for a minute and then backed her up again."

My mother leaned toward me. "Could he have been looking for something in the water?" She tapped my notebook like I should write that down.

Someone on the water would be my guess.

Mr. Wixey shrugged a thin shoulder. "Don't know. I guess I stood there for another five, ten minutes, trying to see what he was up to, but then that light in his cabin went out, so I figured he was done for the night."

I checked the notes I'd made to guess at the time. "So this was between eleven-thirty and eleven-forty?"

"Maybe a little later," Mr. Wixey said between sips. "The *Tonight Show* was on." He looked at my mother. "You ever do that show?"

"Years ago with Johnny Carson." She sighed contentedly. "Charming man."

Mr. Wixey nodded. "Hasn't been the same since."

Now wasn't the time for fond remembrances of television hosts gone by. I wanted to hear more about this boat. "Okay, so it might have been closer to eleven forty-five. Anything else that you saw or heard?"

"I came in and watched the rest of the show, then Barney and me went to bed."

That sounded like the end of his story unless he could give me more specifics. "Back to the boat you saw, can you describe it?"

He slurped his tea. "Not really. At this distance and with my old eyeballs I'm doin' good just to see that there was a boat down there."

Fine. "From what you observed, did it look big, like it would have been moored at a marina?"

"Probably."

I pulled out my cell phone and leaned across the counter to show him the picture I'd taken at the marina a half hour earlier. "Maybe a boat like this one?"

Setting down his cup, he squinted at the picture of Dr. Donovan's boat. "Similar shape, so yeah, could've been that one. Wouldn't swear to it though."

Holy moly! That meant it could have been Kelsey on that boat.

My hand started shaking as I held the cell phone. *Breathe.*

I dropped the phone back into my tote. "Anything else that you can think of that I should know?"

He shook his head. "You already know the rest. I got up the next morning, the boat was gone, then a couple hours later, Barney found Russell near the boat launch."

"Yes, we talked about where you and Barney discovered the body, but this is the first I'm hearing about the boat. So you're saying it was gone when you got up in the morning?" I asked, poised with my pen to capture his exact words in my notebook.

Mr. Wixey frowned for a second, accentuating the marionette-like folds under his cheeks. "I coulda sworn that I mentioned that the boat must've taken off pretty early. Oh, I remember. It was Steve."

I stared at him. "What do you mean 'it was Steve?'"

"Steve was in the neighborhood a couple of days ago and asked me about what I saw that night, and I told him about that boat."

I painted a tight-lipped smile onto my face. "Really."

Mr. Wixey pointed a bony finger at me. "Just like I told you last Saturday, this is another example of government bureaucracy. Left hand and right hand not knowing what they're doing."

Of course not. As per usual with the man I'd been sleeping with. He'd open his mouth to kiss me senseless, but when it came to information-sharing he clamped it tight like he had an iron jaw.

"Well, sorry to ask you to rehash everything with me," I said, putting away my notebook, "but we've certainly appreciated your time."

"And the use of your facilities." Marietta slid off the barstool and extended her hand. "Lovely to see you again, Fred."

"Come back anytime." He grinned mischievously. "Maybe next time without the chaperone. You still like chocolate mint?"

She beamed. "You remember!"

"I never forget a favorite flavor," he said, tapping his

temple. "You're sure you two don't have time for a quick scoop?"

Marietta turned to me. "We don't, do we?"

What the heck. Steve probably wouldn't be home for hours, and after what Fred Wixey had told me about the boat he'd seen, the only person I had questions for was Kelsey, and that would have to wait until tomorrow.

I nodded. "We can make some time."

"Okay then." Mr. Wixey rubbed his hands together. "Two ice creams coming right up. Strawberry again, Charmaine, or would you like to branch out and try the chocolate mint?"

His serving sizes ran on the small side, and I wasn't in a little scoop mood tonight. "Could I have a scoop of each?"

"Ooooh, mixing flavors. Watch out, Mary Jo, your girl's livin' dangerously."

Not yet I wasn't, but I had a feeling I soon would be.

While Fred Wixey went to his freezer for the ice cream I texted Steve. *Can u make some time for me tonight?*

About a minute later, I received his response. *Sure. Will call when I get back.*

A few seconds passed and I received another text. *Should I pick up ice cream on my way home?*

Heck no!

Chapter Nineteen

"You didn't answer so I picked up some Neapolitan," Steve said, following me into his kitchen after I pushed past him at the front door. "Strawberry for you. Chocolate for me. That way everybody's happy."

I planted my hands on my hips. "Do I look happy?"

"Okay, fine, you can have some of my chocolate."

"I knew you knew more than what you were telling me that night at Eddie's! But there you sat, handing me your 'No coroner's case, no investigation' line."

Steve blew out a breath as he made his way to the refrigerator. "I told you everything you needed to know and then some."

"You just neglected to mention the boat that Fred Wixey saw hanging around the point at Cedars Cove."

"Like I said..." He pulled out two bottles of beer and headed for the living room. "Everything you needed to know."

"Yeah, right," I said, hot on his heels.

Setting the bottles on a pair of soapstone coasters, he sank into the brown leather sofa and extended his arm across the top of the seat next to him like an invitation to get cozy.

Not a chance.

I needed to see his face, so I grabbed a bottle and perched on the overstuffed chair across from him.

I pointed my bottle at him. "You don't believe Russell Falco's death was an accident any more than I do."

Without wavering, Steve met my gaze. "We've talked about this."

"I'm not done talking about it."

He reached for his beer. "Shocker."

"I'm sure Fred Wixey told you the same basic story he told me." Given the editorial comments poured on like sugar sprinkles by an annoyed Mr. Wixey to the story I'd asked him to dish out twice, quite sure. "That boat was there for hours, like it was lying in wait for Russell to return to the marina."

Steve sat, studying the label on his bottle. "Fred didn't describe it quite that way to me but—"

"But it's pretty obvious that someone was there, waiting for Russell to come back from seeing Beverly Carver, and I think I know who that someone was."

His gaze locked onto mine.

"Kelsey Donovan," I said, watching for a reaction.

A flicker of amusement registered at his lips. "Kelsey."

"I know. It sounds ridiculous, but wait until you hear this." I took a sip of beer and then set the bottle down on the end table next to me. "Kyle Cardinale saw her take her father's boat out earlier Friday night."

Steve's jaw tightened, his eyes hard as obsidian. "You've been busy on this non-coroner's case."

I could feel my cheeks burning from the intensity of his stare. "I just happened to be at the marina, and when Kyle mentioned that Dr. Donovan also moored his boat there—"

"And I bet he just happened to mention it."

"Sort of. Anyway, that's when he told me that Kelsey took off in her dad's boat around eight forty-five. Based on what she told me about Russell needing to leave around eight because he had a date, I think she decided to follow him and find out who he was seeing."

Steve shook his head, the tic above his jawline warning me to choose my next words carefully.

"Come on, people do some crazy things when they're in love, so it makes some sense." In a temporary insanity kind of way.

"Very little of what I'm hearing is making sense."

I ignored the wisecrack. "Oh, and I took a picture of Dr. Donovan's boat." Pulling out my cell phone, I sat next to Steve to show him. "When Mr. Wixey saw this picture he said it looked like the same boat."

"Know why he said that?"

Was that a trick question? "I just told you. Because it looked like the boat he saw."

"It was dark and the only reason he could tell there was a boat down there was because of the navigation lights. All he could make out was the general shape of a boat."

"A boat like this," I said, shaking my phone in front of his nose. "And Kelsey was on the bay that night—"

"And there's a witness who saw something— something that looked strange—but with Fred Wixey's eyesight, we don't have much more than that."

"But..."

Steve's arm curled around my shoulder. "Really, that's all we've got—a boat, and it could have been any one of a hundred boats that were on the bay last weekend."

I stared at the picture on my phone. "Have you talked to Kelsey recently?" Because I sure was itching to.

"Not since I interviewed her on Monday."

I leaned into Steve's warmth. "Are you going to schedule another interview with her?"

"Since she neglected to mention taking out her dad's boat, yes."

"I'd like to be there."

"I'm sure you would."

I sighed. "Will you at least fill me in on what she has to say?"

With a finger under my chin he turned me to face him. "What do you think?"

"I think it's unlikely."

He gently kissed me. "Smart girl."

Frustrating boy, but I didn't need his help to pay a visit to Kelsey on my own.

He drained his beer bottle and pushed out of his seat. "And don't even think about seeing Kelsey for more of that background information you keep saying you need."

"I...I wasn't."

"You're such a bad liar."

"Am not."

"Then are you going to pay her a visit tomorrow?"

"Hadn't planned to," I said, pocketing my phone.

"Are you telling me the truth?"

"Yes."

"You promise?"

I threw up my hands. "Yes!"

"Okay, then. I'll trust you on that promise."

Dang. So much for my Sunday plans, but I hadn't made any promises for Monday.

※

I woke up at half past four to the sound of sobbing.

As if I hadn't already been sufficiently motivated to kick off the covers and find out what was going on, a metal bracket in the Crippler poked me in the butt to launch me out of my not-so-comfortable bed.

"You don't have to push! I'm up already," I grumbled, pulling on a pair of sweatpants to wear with my rumpled *Sleepless in Seattle* sleep shirt.

Padding into the kitchen in my bare feet, I saw Gram in her pink robe standing at the coffeemaker, and my mother with her head in her hands at the kitchen table, next to a box of tissues.

Any Marietta sighting before ten in the morning typically wasn't a good sign. The fact that she was dressed in the rhinestone-studded jeans she'd worn last night made this an even worse one.

"Good morning," I said, testing the waters.

Surrounded by a semi-circle of wadded white tissues, she reached into the box and blew her nose. "What's good about it?"

My grandmother rolled her eyes as I pulled my favorite mug from the cupboard.

"Did something happen that I should know about?" I hoped against hope that she'd follow Steve's lead and this would be something on the *Char doesn't need to know about this* list.

Gram pursed her mouth. "I'll let your mother tell you."

Swell.

I stared longingly at the coffeemaker that had yet to spit out enough caffeine to gird my loins for the drama waiting for me at the kitchen table.

Just as I was considering grinding a few beans between my molars, Gram pulled my mug from my clutches and set it on the counter. "I'll bring it over when the coffee's ready."

When my feet didn't move, Gram gave me a little push, just like she used to when I was a teenager and Marietta wanted me to come running to her open arms the instant she stepped into the house.

"Sheesh, everybody's so pushy this morning," I muttered on my way to the table.

Sweeping the used tissues littering the tabletop behind Arnold Brubaker's colorful bouquet of gerbera daisies, I took the seat to her right. "Since you haven't changed since last night I assume you just got home?"

Marietta nodded, wiping the tears from her puffy eyes, her cheeks dappled with ghoulish color like an extra from one of her old zombie flicks.

I grabbed a tissue from the box and wiped away the smoky streak of eyeliner and shadow smeared at her temple. "Are you wearing waterproof mascara?"

When in doubt the cosmetic line she repped had been

my go-to safe subject for the last couple of years. Whatever was going on had taken its toll on Marietta Moreau's famous face, but since her long, feathery eyelashes looked relatively unruffled, I figured this could give us both a welcome distraction.

"When you said…we'd be out in the rain," she managed to get out between sniffs, "I thought…I should test-drive…the mascara that was just added to the line."

"Well, it looks like really good stuff." I grabbed another tissue to clean the gunk from her cheeks before she ran into the nearest bathroom and started screaming at the sight of her reflection. It was bad enough the three of us were up before the birds. We didn't have to make it worse by waking up the rest of the neighborhood.

Her face crumpled like the white tissue balled in her fist, her frame shaking as she slumped over the table. "I just didn't realize that I'd be adding more waterworks to the test."

Evidently my distraction had run its course.

I passed her another tissue. "Mom, did something happen between you and Barry?"

"Not exactly." Shaking her head, she blew her nose again. "I don't know…sort of."

I saw a murky soup of raw emotion that didn't jive with, "I don't know."

"Take a breath and tell me what happened."

I could only hope that she had finally leveled with him about the financial pickle she was in.

Squaring her shoulders, my mother breathed in and out, signaling for another tissue. "Barry told me that Jason doesn't approve of me."

Sheesh. That's what all the drama was about? Since when did Marietta require the approval of family members? She had certainly never solicited mine before any of her weddings.

Passing her the tissue box, I tried to remember what she'd told me last night about Jason Ferris and my caffeine-deprived mind couldn't fill in the blank. "When did you meet him?"

She wiped her nose. "I haven't yet. And maybe Barry didn't use those exact words, but that's what he meant."

"Okay, well, maybe Jason's a little concerned about his dad getting involved with—"

I ran through the likely scenarios in my mind.

One, Jason Ferris didn't want his dad to gain any notoriety as Marietta Moreau's husband number four. Since I wasn't all that keen about that notion, I viewed this as a strong possibility made even stronger when coupled with the knowledge that none of her marriages had lasted more than three years. What would this relationship do to his local reputation, his standing at the high school, especially once it started to unravel?

Two, Jason didn't want to see his dad attach himself to a celebrity—even though her star status no longer had much of a sheen—and move away to California. If Jason Ferris ever found out why there would soon be no house in California for his dad to move to, that would be the least of his concerns.

Three, Jason didn't want his dad to be in love with anyone other than the former Mrs. Barry Ferris. How old was this guy? Twenty-six? Twenty-seven? Certainly old enough to be able to handle the idea of Dad moving on with his life without Mom.

I opted to place my bet on scenario number one, the clear front runner.

"—with someone new," I said, burying my true feelings just like I always did when the subject came to her relationship with my high school biology teacher.

"I'm sure that's part of it, and at some point I hope I have the opportunity to tell him that I'd never dream of trying to replace his mother." She started tearing up again. "But Barry asked me to tone down the makeup and jewelry."

Using the moisture from her latest shower of tears, I wiped the apple of her cheek clean of the gray and pink streaks. "I'm sure he just wants you to make a good first impression." Unfortunately, he didn't do a very good job of communicating it.

"H-he also asked me to lose the accent." Marietta grasped my wrist. "Don't you see? He's trying to change me." Almost choking on her words, she swallowed. "He's ashamed of me."

"I'm sure that's not true." More likely he wanted his son to meet the woman he loved—the real woman, not the public persona she enjoyed projecting. Only he didn't know how to say it. But he'd better learn fast.

Gram set two steaming mugs of coffee in front of us. "He loves you, Mary Jo. Barry just wants Jason to love you, too."

I waved toward my grandmother like she was the grand prize in a game show. "See? Gram agrees with me."

Marietta blinked, staring at me as I took a sip of coffee.

I took that as my cue to give up. I obviously wasn't getting through to her.

Gram squeezed her daughter's shoulder. "As my mother used to tell me, the darkest hour is just before the dawn. Lucky for us, the sun will be coming up soon and it's supposed to clear up and be a beautiful day. You and the Ferris boys will have a lovely lunch, I'll bake the winning cookies for this year's county fair, and Char will..." She looked across the table at me. "What are you doing today, dear? Did you want to come with me when I head over to the fairgrounds?"

Gram tended to be a nervous driver, and I knew she'd be even more nervous today since she had a deadline to get her entries ready. "Sure. What time do we need to be there?"

"The Exhibit Hall office closes at five," she said. "We should leave here before four to be on the safe side."

Marietta brightened. "That will work out perfectly."

Since the caffeine hadn't kicked in yet I wasn't following her. "Perfectly for what?"

"For the two of us." She pointed at me. "You're coming to lunch with Barry, Jason, and me."

Oh, no. No, no, no. "That's not—"

"It's a brilliant idea. I don't know why I hadn't thought of it before. You can do that lie detector thing you do and then I'll know exactly where I stand with the man. No second guessing."

This wasn't the first time my mother had tried to trot me out in front of a boyfriend like I was a trick pony. "I don't—"

"I know. You've told me a million times before. Trust me, I don't expect you to be foolproof. It would just be nice if you could help me avoid playing the fool in this situation." She took my hand. "Could you do that for your mom this one last time?"

"Fine. When's lunch?"

"Barry will be here to pick me—excuse me—*us* up at eleven forty-five. What time is it now?"

Gram looked at the clock over the stove. "Four fifty-two."

My mother pushed to her feet and headed for the stairs. "I need to get to bed! Be a dear and wake me up at ten, okay?"

Gram gave me the *look*, making it crystal clear which one of us was the dear in charge of the wake-up call.

Criminy! "Fine!"

The upstairs bathroom door clicked shut. Seconds later, I heard my mother scream, "Oh, my God!"

"What now?" Gram asked as the dog next door started barking.

"My guess is that she's in front of the bathroom mirror."

"Poor thing. Hope she gets some sleep. Are you going back to bed?"

Go back to the Crippler? Fat chance. Since the sun wouldn't paint the sky in shades of pink and violet for another hour, this was the perfect opportunity to do something more important.

I went into the study to pull on a pair of heavy socks and hiking boots, then I grabbed Gramps' binoculars and headed to the hall closet for my stadium jacket.

When I emptied the contents of my cup into an insu-lated travel mug, Gram frowned at me. "Where do you think you're going?"

"For a walk." A long walk.

"But it's dark out."

Which was exactly why I needed to leave as soon as possible.

Minutes later, I turned off Bayshore Road and parked the Jag near a beater pickup at the long stretch of peb-bles and weeds used by the anglers who frequented the Cedars Cove boat launch. The half moon, low in the sky as it peeked through wisps of clouds, did little to illuminate my path but my ten-inch aluminum flashlight was up to the task, plus it could double as a club if I ran into any trouble.

As I set off to the point marking the southern entrance to Cedars Cove I heard nothing but gentle waves lapping against the shore, the crunch of my hiking boots on the rocky trail, a barking dog, and the motorized whine from a fishing boat—probably the one launched from the twelve-foot trailer hooked to the beater truck.

After a short hike up the rocky outcrop dotted with dozens of the scrubby pine trees that bordered the inlet, I stepped out on the point that Eddie, floating in an in-flatable raft with Steve, had dared Rox and me to jump from back when we were teenagers. Since I still bore a scar on my shin as a badge of courage and had no desire to create any new memories of skin sacrificed to the jag-ged edges lurking below the surface, I gingerly stepped to the center of the stony slab that formed the point's tip.

From sunrise to sunset, this outcrop afforded a breathtaking vista of the snow-capped Olympic Mountains looming in the distance like ancient guardians. In the predawn darkness, however, I could barely make out the rocks under my feet let alone a mountain range hunkering in the inky southwestern sky. But that was okay. I was interested in only one thing: Could I see the southern shore of the bay from here?

Turning off my flashlight, I set it down on a flat edge of the slab supporting me and pulled on the strap of my grandfather's old bird-watching binoculars slung around my shoulder. I looked through the binoculars, aiming them at what I thought should be the shoreline in front of the Lackeys' house and saw nothing but an out of focus house light.

I dialed in the focus, the cool breeze ruffling my bed head hair. Still nothing distinctive. I couldn't see an outline of the dock next door to Beverly Carver's house. Really, I couldn't make out much of anything that didn't have a light attached to it.

If Kelsey had followed Russell that Friday night in her father's boat, my money would be on her trailing him close enough to know exactly where he had anchored. And if she knew that, she could wait in the cove behind me and watch for his running lights, and then once she had seen them... Heck, I didn't have a clue what she'd do after that. Try to talk to Russell? Confront him about Beverly Carver?

Hearing the sound of a boat motor rumble to life, I swung around to watch two men in ball caps take off in an aluminum fishing boat. Once again, that was about all I could see.

"You're not thinking about jumping again, are you?" said a deep voice behind me.

Scrambling backwards with loose rocks skittering at my feet, my hands flew into the air, my heart pounding in my throat as I gasped for air.

A pair of strong arms wrapped around my waist, stopping my backwards momentum, but that did nothing to keep the binoculars from giving me a stiff upper cut.

"Whoa, girl," Steve said, steadying me. "You okay?"

My arms heavy with adrenaline, I pounded his solid chest with my fists. "Are you crazy? What are you trying to do?"

He glanced down at the binoculars swaying from my neck. "I should be asking you that."

I straightened. "I couldn't sleep so I thought I'd come out here and watch the sunrise."

"That won't happen for over an hour."

"I'm early."

"Uh-huh."

"And what are you doing here?" I smacked him in the chest again, not waiting for his answer since it was so obvious. "You followed me, didn't you?"

"Hey!" He took me by the wrists and pulled me close. "I was on a jog and saw your car in the parking area."

"Sure." I looked down at his white T-shirt, dark sweatpants, and running shoes. Okay, so maybe he had been jogging.

"And I'm starting to get cold. Want to go get a coffee?"

Oh sure, twist my arm by appealing to my caffeine

addiction.

He smiled. "Of course, if you'd rather stick to your lame story and wait for that sunrise…"

"It was a perfectly good story," I said, pulling a hand free so that I could retrieve my flashlight. "I just had a little timing problem, that's all."

Steve took the flashlight to lead the way back to the trail. "You going to tell me what you were really doing?"

"I was just looking. Whoever Mr. Wixey saw down there wouldn't have been able to see much other than lights coming in this direction."

Steve said nothing in response and kept walking.

I picked up my pace to keep up with him. "The person would have had to know it was Russell Falco's boat coming this way."

"Are you fishing, Chow Mein?"

Sort of. "I was wondering what you thought about that."

He chuckled. "It's a little early for fishing. Cold, too, so move your ass and let's get off this rock."

I heaved a sigh.

As usual, Steve was being less than helpful, but one fact seemed obvious whether he wanted to agree with me or not. As much as I didn't want to believe it, Kelsey Donovan was involved with Russell's death.

Almost five minutes later, we piled into my car and I fired up the heater. "Where do you want to go for coffee?"

Steve fastened his seatbelt. "I was thinking about my place. If you play your cards right, I'll even make you breakfast."

"Now you're talking." Maybe my morning was looking

up. I needed to use a bathroom pretty soon even though, moments earlier, I'd felt like he'd scared the piss right out of me.

The second that thought hit my brain I realized why I was feeling a growing sense of urgency – because I'd skipped that little morning ritual earlier, when I bounded out of bed and headed straight for the kitchen. And by skipping that morning ritual, I had also skipped a few others, including anything that had to do with looking into a mirror.

Oh, crap.

Raking my hair with my fingers, I peeked at my reflection in the rearview mirror and saw raccoon eyes staring back and a mark on my chin where the binoculars must have hit me.

Crap, crap, crap! Minute by minute this morning, I was turning into Marietta.

"Don't worry about it," Steve said as if he could read my mind. "I've seen you look worse."

Chapter Twenty

"Whew," my grandmother said, collapsing into a kitchen chair after we returned home from the Chimacam County fairgrounds. "I need a nap."

Sounded good to me. After a three-hour, stress-filled lunch with Marietta, Barry Ferris, and his son, followed by another hour with Gram fretting about sprinkling too much cinnamon on what she hoped would be her blue ribbon pumpkin cheesecake snickerdoodles, I wasn't just ready for a nap. I needed a drink.

Depositing my tote on the kitchen table, I headed for the wine cupboard and found an old bottle of burgundy. It wasn't my favorite, but it was here and I was here—a good enough pairing.

I held up the bottle. "Would a little wine help you sleep?"

Gram gave me a nod. "Wouldn't hurt. And what's this 'little' stuff? Make it a double."

My kind of girl.

"Oh, goody, you're home," Marietta sang out as she bounded into the kitchen. "Because I have big news!"

She grabbed the bottle of burgundy and put it back in

the cupboard. "I also have something better than this because..." She pulled a magnum of Dom Perignon from the refrigerator, her eyes sparkling as if they'd been infused with the champagne's bubbles. "We're celebrating!"

After the heated glares Barry Ferris aimed across the table at me when I asked him question after question from the list my mother had passed me like a note before class, I couldn't imagine that we had anything to celebrate.

Gram's gaze shifted between me and my mother. "What are we celebrating, dear?"

"Right after lunch, I received a call from my agent... with a movie offer!" Marietta squealed, raising the bottle like she'd just won an Oscar.

"Well, that's wonderful, Mary Jo."

"Wonderful?" With a smile that lit up her face, she hugged the bottle of champagne to her bosom. "Oh, Mama, this is freakin' fantastic. This is big, huge—the biggest role of my life in a major motion picture!"

"And they just happened to think of you?" It wasn't like Marietta Moreau had been a blip on any casting director's radar for years. There had to be more to this story, like her agent having some pictures of the guy with a goat.

Pursing her glossy red mouth, she shoved the bottle at me with a little more force than necessary. "Be a dear and open this for me, and allow me to finish my story if you would please."

I forced a smile. "Sorry."

Marietta glided across the kitchen floor in her stilettos, joy oozing from every pore. "They happened to think of me because Jody Haver announced she was pregnant a week before filming was supposed to start and they needed a replacement *tout de suite*."

I remembered Marietta bitching about losing a few plum roles to Jody Haver, a younger, auburn-haired body double, back in the 90s, so the reason that this opportunity suddenly dropped in my mother's lap was starting to make some sense. Plus it wasn't like she had other commitments and couldn't start right away.

Still, I couldn't discount the goat theory.

"Ooooh, she was good in that western—what was it called?" Gram said, looking at me like I could help her play *Name That Movie*. "You know, that one with what's his name."

That narrowed it down. "Can't help you, Gram."

"Well, she's not gonna be good in *Loving Lucian* because the role of his mother is now all mine!" Jumping up and down like a bouncy cheerleader, she clapped. "And so is her salary."

Since I had been peeling the foil from the champagne cork and not looking at my mother's face, I couldn't be sure that she'd lied about getting the same money as Jody Haver. But I strongly suspected the production company would want to save some dough on her replacement, especially since Marietta wouldn't have the same box office cachet. "Did your agent tell you that you're getting her same salary?"

She sniffed, jutting her chin. "Not in so many words, but the advance is very good money."

Gram leaned forward in her chair. "What kind of money are we talking about?"

My mother grinned. "Let me put it this way—I already called my real estate agent to take my house off the market, at least until after the wedding. There's no reason to rush into any big decisions, and I certainly don't have any time to think about moving right now."

Then this was truly good news—a turn of events that would allow her to keep her home, possibly revitalize her career, and get her out of my bed. And I'd happily toast to all three, especially if it meant that she wouldn't be rushing into that wedding.

Gripping the champagne bottle, I opened it with a soft pop and quickly filled three wine flutes. "Mom, Gram," I said, handing them each a glass. "I think this calls for a toast."

Lifting her glass, Gram winked at her daughter. "Here's looking at you, kid."

"To me and Lucian! I don't know who you are yet, but I love you!" Marietta announced with a giggle. "Now drink up and get dressed for dinner because we're going out."

"Out?" My grandmother's shoulders slumped. "When?"

"Barry made reservations at the Grotto for seven."

I glanced at the clock. Since it wasn't yet five o'clock, Gram and I had plenty of time to have another glass of wine, and given the fact the Barry wouldn't be overly thrilled to see me again so soon, I had a feeling I was going to need one.

Gram took a sip of champagne. "What does he think about you leaving to make this movie, Mary Jo?"

She stared down as if she had a sudden fascination

with the bubbles in her glass. "We haven't really talked about it. We'll do that later tonight, when we're alone. Then tomorrow, I want to drive by the gallery property that Lance showed me and talk to Barry about that, too."

Cripes, now that she was feeling flush, that investment deal seemed to be back on the table.

With concern etched in her eyes, Gram met my gaze. "Surely there's no rush with the investment that artist was proposing. Wouldn't that be a bit like counting your chickens before they hatch?"

"Mama, you don't understand how these things work. If the investment group comes together and this thing moves as quickly as Lance suggested it might, I'll need someone there to represent me."

My mother was doing me a favor by naming Barry— the fiancé she now had complete confidence in—instead of me to that honor, but that didn't give me any warm fuzzy feelings about her handing over a chunk of her advance money to Lance Greenwood.

Marietta knocked back the last bit of bubbly in her glass. "But this isn't the time to talk business. We need to celebrate!"

She held out her empty wine flute for a refill. "Barry made the reservation for five in case his son wanted to join us, but he had to catch the four-thirty ferry, so tell Steve to come join the party." She leaned into me as I filled her glass. "Truth be told, I'd rather spend my time with Stevie any day."

Me, too, but I couldn't guarantee he'd feel the same way.

❄

Almost four hours later, since Steve kept signaling me by tapping his watch under our table's white tablecloth, I was quite sure that he didn't feel the same way.

While Marietta savored her crème brulee, insisting that Gram take a bite, I took the opportunity to pull out my cell phone and selected Steve's name from the top of my contact list.

"Excuse me for a moment," he said, pulling his chirping phone from his jacket pocket.

The second he made a show of leaving the table to answer the call I hit *End* and politely declined my mother's offer to try her dessert. The only thing I wanted to top off this evening was a short trek to the nearest exit.

Moments later, Steve returned to the table. "Sorry, but I have to go."

Not quite the "*we* have to go" line I was expecting to hear since we had driven over together in his pickup. If he wanted any future rescues from my mother, he had better think about returning the favor and soon.

"Oh…what a shame," Gram and Marietta said like a chorus.

Going counterclockwise around the table he shook Barry's hand. "Always a pleasure."

Stepping between Barry and my mother, Steve squeezed her shoulder. "Congratulations again and thank you for allowing me to join in the celebration."

She patted his hand. "It wouldn't have been the same without you." She smiled across the table at me. "After all, you're almost part of the family."

Also a line I hadn't been expecting to hear and one that had me cringing at the insinuation that a ring would soon be back on my finger.

Moving to Gram, Steve kissed her cheek. "See ya, beautiful."

While she tittered, he shot me a lopsided smile. "I feel badly about asking you to cut your evening short, so if you'd rather stay—"

"No!" I slowly eased back my chair so that I wouldn't appear as eager as I had just sounded. "After all the champagne and wine with dinner, I'm ready to head home."

Feeling like a traitor with the way Gram was scowling at me, I said my goodbyes, and Steve and I headed for the Grotto's lobby.

"Thanks for helping me get out of there," he said, his palm warm against the small of my back. "I don't know how much more I could take of your mother's giggling."

"I know. She's giddy about being cast in this movie and all the wine only made her giddier."

"She mentioned that this would allow her to take advantage of other opportunities. Was she referring to that investment deal you told me about?"

"Yeah, now that she'll have money at her disposal I'm even more nervous about her getting sucked into that."

Steve turned to me as he held the Grotto's heavy wooden door open. "What do you know about the pitch that Greenwood gave her?"

"Not much other than the fact that it sounds expensive."

"Hmmm..."

"What's that supposed to mean?" I asked, trying to read him in the shadows of the parking lot.

"Nothing."

"You're lying."

He took my hand. "Hopefully, she'll ask someone to study the plans for this performing arts center before she writes him a check."

Since my mother seemed to want to seal this deal prior to flying back to Los Angeles later in the week, I knew that would be an unlikely possibility at best. "Yeah, but she tends to be a little more impetuous than that."

"Must be a trait that runs in the family."

"Bastard."

"Such language. Keep it up and you won't get any dessert."

My heart danced a little jig at his implication. "You have dessert waiting for us at your house?" I asked, feigning innocence.

He squeezed my hand. "Not yet, but she should be there in about thirty minutes."

Yum.

✳

"Well, what do you think?" Aunt Alice asked the next morning, hovering over me as I sat at her butcher block table and crunched a cinnamony-sweet snickerdoodle.

I thought that she was going to give my grandmother some serious competition for that blue ribbon. "Sweet, chewy perfection. Really buttery, too. What can I tell you? It tastes like a winner to me."

She smiled with satisfaction. "We'll see if the judges agree with you."

"Gram mentioned that the judging will start at nine."

Alice arched her eyebrows. "Did she also happen to mention what divisions she entered?"

"Oh no. Don't you drag me into the middle of your bake-off. It's bad enough that all these cookies I've been taste-testing are going straight to my hips, so until those ribbons get awarded, my lips are sealed."

"You're no fun."

Exactly what my mother had said five hours earlier, after we polished off the bottle of champagne and I told her I had to go to bed. It was either that or open up another bottle of wine and listen to more of her big plans for the performing arts center carrot Lance Greenwood had dangled in front of her nose. And then she would have had to shoot me.

"I'm lots of fun." I just didn't feel like it at the moment because I needed to think of a good reason for Marietta not to bite on that carrot. First things first, I needed a caffeine recharge to get my brain in gear.

On my way to the coffee station, I said hello to Stanley, who had his nose buried in Sunday's classified section.

Since Lucille was busy with another customer, I poured fresh decaf into his empty cup while he perused the want ads. "You looking for a job, Stanley?"

He snorted with laughter as I expected he would. "Don't have the time. Gotta keep this barstool warm."

"What are you looking for then?" I knew Stanley was a former aerospace engineer and a woodcarver, but other than the fact that he was a widower, I knew very little about what he did with his time when he wasn't here at his post.

He turned the page of the newspaper. "Just lookin'. You never know what you might find that you need."

Maybe so, but I doubted I could find the answers I needed in the classifieds. However, the salty guy taking breakfast orders at the grill had never been shy about dispensing his opinion about money matters and could probably point me in the right direction.

I swung open the kitchen door. "Would you scramble me a couple of eggs?"

"You got it." Duke pointed his spatula at me. "You want some bacon with that, don't you?"

Heck, yes. But if I ever wanted to stop wearing my stretchy yoga pants to work I needed to put an end to my cookies and bacon diet. "Nope, just the eggs, thanks."

Standing next to him I breathed in the aroma of sizzling bacon and cursed my thunder thighs.

Duke glanced at me. "Something on your mind? Besides the bacon?"

"Yeah, something I heard regarding the Benoit Gallery. Are you familiar with it?"

He cracked two eggs on the grill. "Sure, I buy all my fine art there."

Right. Duke's so-called fine art hanging in the cafe consisted of a half dozen vintage soft drink signs, two art deco telephones, several antique coffee tins and posters, and the singing big mouth bass mounted next to Aunt Alice's eighty gallon fish tank.

"Have you heard any scuttlebutt about it?"

"I know the old man died a while back, and his son's been trying to unload it for almost a year," he said, scrambling my eggs.

"Tucker," Stanley chimed in. "The younger Benoit is Tucker, and it's been listed with Mirabelle Realty for seven months."

Duke looked at Stanley through the cutout window. "How would you know that? You moonlighting over at Mirabelle when you've had your fill of my decaf?"

With a glance over his horn-rims, the white-haired ninety-year-old straightened his newspaper. "I read."

"I stand corrected," Duke said. "Seven months."

Still, seven months was a long time, and in a small retirement community like Port Merritt I doubted that Tucker Benoit's real estate agent had received many inquiries about it.

"The old furniture store next door probably isn't helping the place sell." Duke slid my eggs onto a plate and handed it to me. "It's been empty for years and is gonna need some major renovation."

"Same goes for that warehouse across the street," Stanley added. "Been empty since the store closed."

If the key to success in the real estate game was location, it sounded like selling Benoit's Gallery could present a serious challenge. Unless, of course, there were an investment group with some big plans to renovate the area.

Maybe I'd go over there during my lunch hour and check it out. Maybe right after I paid a visit to Kelsey.

Two hours later, I was deep in thought and on my knees in front of a filing cabinet when I noticed a pair of black oxfords by my side. I looked up to see Ben Santiago smiling down at me.

"Praying or filing?" the Deputy Criminal Prosecuting Attorney asked, his hooded eyes crinkling at the corners with amusement.

Straightening so that we were almost eye to eye with the aid of my two-inch wedge heels, I knew I'd better act like I hadn't already heard that line from a couple of his junior staffers. "Just tidying up the never-ending paper trail you guys are so good at creating."

"And don't think for a minute that we don't appreciate it."

Sure. Ben hadn't wandered back into the bowels of the third floor to blow me kisses. "May I help you with something?"

"I hope so. Will you let me steal you away for a half hour?"

Was he kidding? "Gladly."

"We've got a fraud case coming to trial in a couple of weeks," he said as we walked down the hall. "I thought it was a pretty strong case, but there's something about it that isn't passing the sniff test."

His sniffer was almost as good as mine. If he thought something didn't jive, he was probably right.

Ben slowed as we approached the conference room. "Brett will be taking the plaintiff's deposition in a couple of minutes, but I'd like you to sit in to get your read on it."

"No problem." But I doubted that the junior assistant prosecuting attorney, who hadn't acknowledged my existence in the department until we ran out of coffee, would be quite as agreeable to have my company.

When Brett Kearney entered the room three minutes

later, he leveled a gaze at me that felt like a warning shot. The message couldn't have been clearer—*I don't want to hear anything out of you.*

Stifling a sigh, I pasted a smile on my face and turned my focus to the willowy brunette taking the seat across the conference table from me.

Standing to my right, Brett waved his pen at me. "Ms. Tomlin, this is my...colleague, Charlene...uh..."

Good grief, he didn't know my name? I extended my hand. "Charmaine Digby."

"How do you do," she said, her upper lip slightly puckered like she had a perpetual sour taste in her mouth.

Since Junior wasn't offering her anything to drink, I figured he wanted me to handle the hostess duties. "May I get you a cup of coffee or water, Ms. Tomlin?"

She folded her hands on the tabletop. "No, nothing."

"I'll take a water," Junior said, thumbing through several pages of notes.

I felt like telling him that he could reach the pitcher of water at the opposite end of the table more easily than I could, but I held my tongue and poured him a glass.

Looking up from his notes he smiled deferentially at Ms. Tomlin and proceeded with some opening remarks as if he were already trying the case.

Occasionally she'd nod, but mainly she quietly sat, folded and puckered, looking as if Brett were taxing her patience.

He was certainly taxing mine.

After another minute of him clarifying who was who in the case, I'd learned that Cecilia Tomlin had an elderly mother with Alzheimer's, who had been duped into signing over some valuable commercial real estate holdings to Cecilia's ex-husband.

"My mother thought she was signing some documents necessary to sell the buildings—that this was about his sales commission of all things," Ms. Tomlin said through clenched teeth. "She trusted Derek. Forgot that I had divorced the lying bastard three years ago."

True. Plenty of anger wrapped around the truth but nothing there that didn't pass my sniff test.

Brett reached for a file folder and started flipping pages. "And the buildings are located..."

She exhaled, exercising her mounting frustration with enough volume for a fire-breathing dragon. "On 1st Street. The Mayhew building and a warehouse."

"Is that the building where Mayhew Furniture used to be?" I asked.

Brett tapped his pen and shot me a sideways glance of irritation.

Excuse me for making a point of clarification.

Ignoring him, she met my gaze. "My mom bought the store from her father, Carter Mayhew, back in the sixties. Then after the mill closed and business slowed to a trickle, she had to shut it down."

"I see." Brett pulled out a photo of the old furniture store from the folder and laid it next to the stack of papers in front of him. "And the most recent assessed value of the property is?"

"With the warehouse across the street the combined value is over half a million dollars. Could be a lot more with some improvements."

Wow. No wonder this had become a criminal case.

I leaned closer to Junior so that I could see the photo and noticed a partial sign on the newer-looking building next door. "What about this building with the wood shingles?" I put my finger next to the sign in the photo. "Is that also your mother's?"

Cecilia Tomlin gave the picture a cool glance. "No, that's a gallery that's owned by Tucker Benoit."

Whoa! Part of the property Lance Greenwood had proposed for the performing arts center had been obtained in a fraudulent land-grab?

Her lips tightened. "If he hadn't listed his property with Mirabelle Realty I might not have heard about the deal Derek and his cousin were up to."

Again, true, but buried beneath the anger I sensed something else smoldering. I wanted to dig deeper and uncover whatever it was she was holding back, but I also needed to know if these two men were somehow connected to Lance Greenwood.

I turned to Brett. "You already know about this cousin, right?" Because if he did, I wanted to read everything he had on the guy.

He rifled through his papers again. "The listing agent, right?"

"Kip Tomlin. Handles commercial real estate for Mirabelle. I told you this last time," Cecilia said, her cheeks flushed as she raised her voice. "I always knew something was shady about him. Always trying to impress Derek with his big deals."

That sounded more like twenty-twenty hindsight, but with what her ex-husband did to her mother, I figured

Cecilia Tomlin was entitled to bend the truth.

"And how exactly did you hear about this deal as you put it?" Brett asked.

"Kip's wife was bragging to her hairdresser about all the money they'd be coming into if they could land the right buyers for the three properties." Her lips curled in satisfaction. "And we share the same hairdresser."

I sensed there was more to it than that. "That's it? You only found out about this because your hairdresser told you about it?"

"Yes."

No, she was a smart woman, so there was definitely more to this story. Maybe that was what Ben had sensed when he first met this woman.

"Seems that Derek planned to cut Kip in for a generous portion of the proceeds," she added, inspecting her manicured nails.

What a guy. "Giving him all the more reason to find the right buyer." Or group of buyers.

Cecilia Tomlin's gaze hardened. "Exactly."

"Your mother's properties laid vacant for a number of years." Thanks to Duke and Stanley, I could sound like I knew what I was talking about. "As a salesman paid on commission, Kip certainly would have approached her about them on occasion."

She blinked. "He did, and she was always adamant about not selling. My mother thought the real estate market would improve and she'd get a better price. At least she did before she started having memory problems and was diagnosed last year."

Junior glared at me. "It doesn't matter. She didn't sell

it to him. Moving on..."

I raised a finger. "Not just yet." He needed to give me a minute to get to what she had yet to reveal about this deal between her ex and his cousin. "Ms. Tomlin, do you have Power of Attorney so that you can handle your mother's finances?"

A crease formed between her dark brows. "Yes, but I don't understand what that has to do—"

"You said that she was diagnosed last year. When exactly did you officially take over your mother's affairs?"

"It took a while to make it official, but January of this year."

"And when did your ex-husband get your mom to sign over her property to him?"

Sucking in her lower lip, she stared at me for several seconds as if I'd asked her a multiple choice question and she couldn't decide upon the correct answer, or perhaps more accurately, the most advantageous answer for this case.

I pointed at the stack of papers in front of Junior. "It's a matter of record, isn't it?" *Please have the answer in there somewhere.*

She heaved a sigh as Brett looked through his notes. "He visited my mother a few days before Christmas. Brought her a tin of peanut brittle to sweeten the deal, the unscrupulous swine."

"Interesting timing, don't you think?" I sure did.

I received a frosty stare from the other side of the table.

Brett was staring at me, too, and I didn't care. "It was probably just a couple of weeks before you could have signed with Kip to sell the property legally."

Cecilia Tomlin folded her arms against her thin frame. "I hadn't yet made that decision."

Sure you hadn't.

By now even Junior should have picked up on the more accurate version of the truth. "Since Kip is one of the most successful commercial real estate agents in town and he'd expressed interest in the properties, I imagine you would have mentioned that you'd soon be able to act on your mother's behalf."

She pressed her thin lips together, wearing the same expression as my ex whenever I told him we needed to talk.

And just like my ex she didn't respond aside from looking like she wanted to grind me under her heel. "And from what you said, he probably would have bragged to his cousin about it, don't you think?"

Staring down at the table top, Cecilia Tomlin slowly blew out a breath. "That property has belonged to my family since 1922. Derek had no right to steal it out from under me. I want him prosecuted. I want both of those bastards prosecuted to the fullest extent of the law."

I had absolutely no doubt of that.

"It's a strong case. Not only of fraud but of elder abuse," Brett assured her. "If everything goes as we expect it will, your mother will get her properties back."

And then, if the price were right, Cecilia could turn around and sell the Mayhew building to Lance Greenwood's investment group, so this case changed nothing except for the players pocketing the cash. Still, the timing of his business proposal to my mother seemed more and more fishy. In fact, now that I knew that this case was coming to trial in two weeks, it stunk more than three-day-old salmon.

She shifted her gaze to Brett. "Are we finished?"

After he asked her a few more questions, he escorted her down the hall and I hightailed it back to my desk to see if I could find any connection between the Tomlin boys and Lance Greenwood.

Entering their last names along with *real estate* into my internet search, I retrieved over thirty-six million results.

"Give me a break," I muttered under my breath.

I changed my search to *Tomlin, Lance Greenwood* and *artist* to see if that would create a more manageable list. It did, but I still had over four thousand results to crawl through.

Since I didn't know exactly what I was looking for, I scanned the headings on the first page. After wading through results that included a Lance Greenwood from Tomlin, New Jersey, as well as one in his fifties who went to Tomlin Middle School in Florida, I eventually landed on a Seattle newspaper story from last year in which Lance Greenwood and Derek Tomlin were quoted.

Bingo!

After waiting an interminable length of time for the advertising pop-ups to finish loading, I paged down to read the first paragraph of the news story.

"Holy smokes!"

Chapter Twenty-One

I pulled out my cell phone and selected Steve's number. Since it immediately went to voice mail I figured he had forwarded his phone. "Call me," I said as I grabbed my tote and dashed down the hall. "Better yet, meet me at Kelsey's shop as soon as you can."

Seconds later, bright sunshine warmed my skin as I ran toward my car, the absolute last thing I needed since I was already sweating.

Fumbling with my phone, I tried to call my mother. Again, it went straight to voice mail. "Why won't anybody answer their phone?" I shouted, waiting for the end of her southern-fried invitation to leave her a message. "Call me as soon as you get this. And if you planned to see Lance today, don't do it until you talk to me first. Okay?" *Please, Mom.*

Firing up the Jag, I peeled down the hill toward Main Street and took the left on 4th so that I could park in the first available space behind Hot Shots.

By the time I crossed the street and the Feathered Nest's buzzer announced my arrival, I was sucking down oxygen as if I'd sprinted the six blocks to get there.

I did a sweep of the two rooms and saw only Kelsey behind the counter and a couple of tourists browsing the jewelry aisle. By Kelsey's curt nod I could see she wasn't any more pleased to see me than last time. Probably because she assumed that I wanted to ask the same questions about her father's boat that Steve had asked. Fair assumption. Until I stumbled upon that news story, she would have been absolutely right.

"I need to talk to you," I whispered to her when the two women wandered over to the far wall displaying several dreamcatchers similar to what I had seen on the *Lucky Charm* and Kelsey's father's boat.

"Char, I have customers," she said, glancing in their direction.

"I know. I'm sorry but it can't wait."

She scowled at me. "If you're here to ask me more questions about Friday night, I suggest you talk to Steve. I already told him everything and I'm not going to go through that embarrassment twice today."

"No, there's something I need to tell you. Better yet, show you."

"Oh, miss," one of the ladies said, waving Kelsey over.

Kelsey painted a warm smile on her face. "Be right there." Turning back to me, she lowered her voice. "Not now."

I saw that she had a laptop on the counter next to her cash register. "I'm going to use your computer a minute."

"Do whatever you want. I just don't want to hear a peep out of you while I have customers in the store. Do you understand?"

Marching toward the back wall, Kelsey didn't wait for

an answer, which was fine with me. I didn't want to tell her this story. She needed to read it for herself.

Her internet connection was slower than at the courthouse, but in less than a minute I had the news story up and ready for her. While I waited I called Steve. Once again I went straight to voice mail, but this time I told him to check out the news story I'd found and provided him the web address. "And get over to Kelsey's as soon as you can."

Kelsey glared at me from the other side of the room.

Sorry. I had to peep.

While I was willing the two ladies to hurry up and buy something, the buzzer sounded, announcing another customer's arrival to the Feathered Nest.

Crap! Lance Greenwood's smiling face was heading straight toward me.

My heart thudding like an alarm in my chest, I lowered the cover of Kelsey's laptop. "Howdy!" I said an octave higher than normal.

"What are you doing back there?" he asked with a glance at the laptop. "Aren't they keeping you busy enough at the county?"

I jutted my chin at him in an effort to exude more confidence than I felt. "Actually, I stopped by with the hope of whisking Kelsey away to lunch. I was just looking at the online menu when you walked in."

"Oh, really. What a coincidence. I'm here for the same exact reason. Maybe we could make it a threesome."

Despite his polite demeanor, his fake smile told me I was in no danger from him wanting to break bread with me.

He pointed at the laptop. "What did you find? Anything tasty?"

"Nothing I'd recommend. Since it's a gorgeous day I thought we might grab some sandwiches and eat by the water."

Lance's dark eyes narrowed. "Hmmm...we should be able to do better than that, don't you think?" He extended his hand toward the laptop. "May I?"

Just as beads of sweat broke out on my upper lip, my cell phone started ringing. With any luck I could use the call as a diversion. "Excuse me a minute."

I prayed the caller ID would display Steve's name, but I saw Marietta's instead. "Hi, Mom."

"I just got your message."

"Uh-huh." My mind raced, trying to come up with a good excuse to make tracks for the exit.

"What's this about not seeing Lance?" she asked, sounding all too loud and clear.

I could only hope that he hadn't heard her. "You and Gram want to go out to lunch?"

"What?"

"Okay, sounds good. I'll be there soon." I hit *End* and shrugged. "Well, it looks like my plans just changed."

He stepped around the counter. "But mine haven't so maybe I should take a look at that menu." Gripping me by the wrist he pulled me away from Kelsey's laptop. "Especially since your mother said nothing about lunch."

Uh-oh!

Keeping me at arm's length, Lance raised the cover and stared at the screen while my pulse pounded in my ears. He then calmly closed the internet browser and turned to me. "I'll take that phone."

A lot of good my cell phone had been doing me since Steve hadn't taken my last two calls. Still, I felt like I was losing my safety net when I dropped it into Lance's palm.

He slipped it into the front pocket of his jeans. "Let's step outside, shall we? And do it quietly or I swear I will do more than twist your wrist."

Not on his life, and if I wanted to continue breathing, definitely not on mine. "Ow! What are you doing? You're hurting me!" I shouted, doubling over as if I'd been punched in the gut. "Kelsey, help!"

She rushed to my side. "What's going on?" Wedging herself between me and my would-be assailant, she wrapped her arm around my shoulder. "Are you okay?"

"No. Call the police." Please.

She helped me to a stool behind the counter and then glared back at Lance. "Explain to me what's going on and right now, or I will call the police."

"It's all an act. I swear I barely touched her." With Lance staring at me with eyes as cold as death, he edged past Kelsey and me. "I've heard about you. Constantly badgering Kelsey with asinine questions, always trying to point the finger of blame at someone for the death of that handyman, and now you come up with this bit of theater." An evil smile crept over his lips. "And here I thought there was only one bad actress in your family."

"Is everything okay?" the younger of the two tourists asked, peeking around a display case near the dream-catchers.

I shook my head, but Lance was quick to step in front of me. "Sorry, our friend is off her meds and is being particularly disagreeable today. You'll have to excuse us, but we need to close for lunch a little early."

"*What?*" Kelsey demanded. "No, we—"

"Trust me, it's for the best." Lance directed the full force of his charm at the two ladies as he herded them toward the exit. "Thank you for stopping by."

Kelsey turned to me. "What the heck is going on?"

"We need to call the police," I whispered. Now, while Lance was playing the gracious host at the front door. I pointed at the cordless phone Kelsey kept by the cash register.

Giving me a quick nod, she passed it to me behind her back, and I punched in *nine-one-one*. Without saying a word I dropped the phone in my tote and kicked it to the back wall with my foot. I could only pray that I'd pushed it far enough away so that the murderer locking the door couldn't hear the operator asking me about my emergency.

Lance flipped the sign hanging in the window to *Closed* and looked back with a satisfied smile. "Alone at last." He dropped the smile when his gaze landed on me. "Well, almost alone."

"Hey, I know three's a crowd, so I'd be happy to leave." And run straight to the police station.

Easing his way toward us, he shook his head. "I don't think that's a good idea."

"Lance, I don't understand why you're doing all this, but you're scaring me," Kelsey said, her knuckles a ghostly white as she gripped the counter.

His expression softened with each step he took. "My dear, I simply want to talk to you without interruption."

"Are you going to tell her the story about your wife?" I asked with enough volume for the nine-one-one operator to hear. "I'm sure Kelsey would be eager to hear it."

"Were you not listening? I said *without interruption.*"

"Wife?" Kelsey asked. "You're married?"

"No, not any longer. Charmaine read about my wife's unfortunate accident and promptly leapt to a ridiculous conclusion, just like she always does."

Right. "Why don't you tell her about that accident?"

He sneered at me. "Why don't you just shut up?"

"Okay, if you insist, I'll tell her about how you and your wife were out on your boat last year and she mysteriously fell overboard and drowned."

Backing away as Lance stepped behind the counter, Kelsey sucked in a shaky breath. "Oh, my God!"

"No." He reached for her. "She's taking a very sad event in my life and twisting it to serve some vigilante agenda I will never understand."

She gazed at me wide-eyed, as if to plead for a reason to believe him.

"Think about it, Kelsey. His wife drowned in Puget Sound the same way Russell did here. What are the odds of that happening?"

Lance took her hand, wrapping it in his. "I love you. There isn't anything I wouldn't do for you."

Sadly, I found that to be very true. "Including killing the man she was in love with?"

He reached back and slapped me hard across the face. "I will not let you poison her against me!"

Kelsey shrieked, pulling away from him.

"Still have that boat?" I asked, my cheek burning as I

battled an onslaught of tears. "If I were you I would have kept it 'cause it sure looked like a beauty from the photo I saw. Looked a lot like your dad's boat, Kelsey."

"Bigger." Her lips trembling, she struggled to find her voice. "We...we went out on it two weeks ago."

"And didn't we have a wonderful time?" Lance wrapped his arms around her. "That was just a taste of the life we can have together."

Tears cascaded down Kelsey's cheeks. "No, I—"

"Sweetheart, I know you're upset." He drew her closer. "But surely you can see it as clearly as I can. We're meant to be together. I knew it from the first moment I stepped into this shop and saw your lovely face."

Criminy, where was Steve? "Very touching. Was this before or after you killed your wife?"

"I'm not dignifying that with a response," he said, wiping away Kelsey's tears.

"My guess would be before. Maybe you were on one of the weekend excursions on the Sound that your wife loved to take. Isn't that what your old buddy Derek told the police? That buying the boat was her idea so that she could have you all to herself a few days every month? Yep, his quote in that news story made it sound like you had lost your one true love. I guess he didn't know about the truer love you'd found here in Port Merritt."

He smiled at Kelsey. "Ignore her. She doesn't know what she's talking about it."

"Please." Kelsey's face crumpled like a wet newspaper as she looked up at him. "Let me go."

"My dear, you don't need to be afraid. This fiction she's concocting is ridiculous."

My phone rang in his pocket. "If it's so ridiculous, why did he take my phone?"

"What do you say we let it go to voice mail?" Lance asked with enough frost to turn me into a human popsicle.

Kelsey's gaze shifted from his pants pocket up to his piercing dark eyes. "You killed Russell."

"No." Lance's jaw tightened. "He had some sort of accident."

She flattened her palms against his chest and tried to push away from him. "That you caused!"

He shook his head, panic gleaming in his eyes. "No, it wasn't like that. You have to believe me."

No, she didn't. Kelsey had to see that he was lying, except she wasn't looking at him. Her eyes were focused on the front window, where a man in a ball cap was looking in.

"Andy!" she screamed. "Help!"

A second later, he pounded on the door. "Kelsey! Open the door!"

She contorted her body, straining against the arms locked around her. "I can't!"

Neither could I. Lance was blocking my path.

He covered her mouth with his palm. "Shhhh, my darling, please... If you'd just let me explain... OW!"

"Andy!" Kelsey yelled, her mouth bloody as she wriggled away from Lance and made a run for the door. Sticking out my foot, I tried to trip him, but he was too quick, and Kelsey only made it five feet before he wrapped his arm around her waist and pulled her tight.

"If you don't open this door right now, I'm going to

break it down!" Andy shouted.

"It's time for us to go, my dear." Blood oozing from where she bit his hand, Lance inched back with a squirming Kelsey in his grasp. "I'm sorry it has to be this way, but someday I hope you'll understand that everything I've done I did for us."

While Andy was using his shoulder as a battering ram, I looked for a weapon, something that I could use to keep Lance from dragging Kelsey to the rear exit in the storeroom.

Screaming, she tried to stomp on his toes. "Are you crazy? I'm not going anywhere with you!"

To make sure that didn't happen I picked up the wooden barstool I'd been sitting on. It was ten times the weight and much more unwieldy than the aluminum bat I used to swing on my high school softball team, but the rounded legs afforded me a good grip. And as my coach always said, "A good grip is key to a good swing."

My heart pounding as I crept toward Lance and Kelsey, I knew I'd have the opportunity for only one really good swing or he'd see to it that I got benched, permanently.

With sirens wailing in the distance, I squared up to my target and swung away at Lance Greenwood's back with all my might, knocking him to his knees.

Stumbling forward, Kelsey steadied herself on a display case and then limped to the door. Flinging it open, Andy rushed in and she fell into his arms.

"Are you okay?" he asked, holding her tight.

She nodded, clinging to Andy, her body shaking with sobs.

He looked at me. "How about you?"

I knew that the detective who had just burst through the doorway behind him wanted an immediate answer to the same question.

I locked gazes with Steve. "We're fine."

He sidestepped Andy and Kelsey, his revolver in his hand and his brow slick with sweat as if he'd run here. Motioning me away from the artist grimacing in pain at my feet, Steve did a visual sweep of the room. "Anybody else here?"

"Just us," I said, stepping aside. "And are we glad to *finally* see you."

Muttering an obscenity, Steve eyeballed the stool in my hands.

Okay, maybe I shouldn't have made it sound like he was deserving of a tardy slip, especially when I was so happy to see him and his gun.

He scowled down at Lance, who, other than rubbing what was sure to become a big, lumpy bruise on his back, had made no attempt to move. "I take it you did this?" Steve asked, slanting a quick look in my direction.

"I didn't hit clean-up in the batting order for nothing."

"You know you can put the stool down now, Babe Ruth."

"Oh." With shaky limbs from the adrenaline coursing through my veins, I maneuvered around the contents of an earring rack that had scattered throughout the aisle and set my *bat* down near the window.

"Does that mean that I may get up now?" Lance asked as if we'd been inconveniencing him.

"No! Spread-eagle on the floor, and keep your mouth

shut until I read you your rights," Steve barked, slapping a pair of handcuffs on Lance's wrists. He glanced back at Andy. "Take Kelsey across the street and wait for me there."

After they left he cupped my chin and frowned. "You've got a nasty welt on your cheek."

"Artistic temperament, I guess." Trying to avoid a lecture about putting myself in harm's way, I didn't want to make the smack to my face sound worse than it was.

The tic in Steve's jaw counting down to a major explosion told me something much worse than a lecture was on the immediate horizon. "He didn't hurt me." Much anyway.

"You should have waited for me."

"Who knew when you'd be showing up? Certainly not me because you didn't answer your phone!"

"I was busy."

"Not too busy to read that story I told you about, I hope."

"I didn't get to finish it because of a call I got from a nine-one-one operator."

"Hmmm...that's a pity. It's a killer story." I smiled, trying to diffuse the tension between us with my bad pun.

Lance groaned. "For God's sake, either shut her up or get her the heck away from me!"

"You shut up!" I said, wanting to grab the stool and take another whack at him. "And give me back my phone!"

Minutes later, red and blue lights flashed outside the Feathered Nest's windows as Lance was escorted out the door.

I turned to Steve. "Now what happens?"

"I'll need you and Kelsey to come to the station and give your statements, then I'll work with Port Townsend PD to do a search of Greenwood's boat. First things first though." Steve held his hand out to me. "Let's get out of here."

"Where're we going?" I asked as we headed out the door.

"I'm going to buy you a mocha latte. I think you could use one." He gently squeezed my hand. "Sorry to say it's going to be a long day for you."

Probably an even longer one for him. "In that case I'm having a scone with it, but if you think that will get you off the hook for the breakfast you still owe me, you've got another think coming."

"What breakfast?"

The man might ignore me occasionally, but he never forgot anything. "The breakfast date in Port Townsend we didn't get to have."

"Oh, *that* breakfast. I'll make that up to you later."

"Later like breakfast for dinner?" Yum. I was hungry already.

"Who said anything about eating?"

"Huh?" Oh. "That sounds good, too."

A shirtless Steve came to his door when I arrived with two Eddie's Place pizza boxes almost ten hours later. With a hint of a smile he tossed a hand towel over his shoulder. "Don't think I ordered any pizza." Leaning over the white boxes in my hands, he sniffed the air.

Steve's hair was damp and he smelled of menthol and lime, tempting me to linger near his freshly shaved neck as I walked past him. "Since when do you say no to pizza?"

"Rarely," he said, following me to his kitchen. "And I never say no to pizza girls, so make yourself at home."

After a quick side-trip to his laundry room for a white T-shirt, he grabbed two beers from the refrigerator while I popped one of the pizza boxes into his microwave oven.

I joined him at the table and slid two pizza slices onto a ceramic plate in front of him. "Bon appétit."

"Two slices? That's all there was in those boxes?"

"Hey, my mother and Barry ate almost the entire large supreme that I ordered for you. I was lucky to salvage these two slices."

"Your mother wanted to go out for pizza?" he asked with his mouth full. "I thought The Grotto was more her style."

"It is, but since Gram and Alice were the ones celebrating tonight, it was their choice."

Steve frowned. "Okay, I know I was a little distracted today, but what are we celebrating now?"

I opened up the other pizza box containing a half dozen each of their blue ribbon-winning cookies. "My grandmother and her sister each won a first place blue ribbon in different divisions, beating out—"

"Don't tell me—Joyce Lackey."

"Yep, must have been off her game."

He almost choked on his pizza. "And whose fault would that be after you hounded her and her husband most of the week?"

"Never mind that. Anyway, the girls were sorry you couldn't join us earlier, and since there wasn't much pizza left they wanted to make sure that you had plenty of dessert."

He gave me an evil grin.

"Those sweet old ladies were referring to the cookies!"

"Did I say anything?"

"You didn't have to, pal."

He ran his index finger over my cheek, tracing the red welt Lance Greenwood had left me with. "The swelling's gone down."

"It's nothing." With the knowledge that the man had killed two other people he deemed to be standing in the way of true love, I knew that I'd gotten off easy.

Steve's eyes darkened. "It's not nothing. You could've been—"

"I wasn't hurt and it will be gone by morning." And if it wasn't, I had my mother's makeup treasure trove at my disposal.

I sipped my beer and mentally replayed some of the events of the day. "So what happened after I left the station?"

"The usual. By the time his lawyer arrived from Seattle, Greenwood broke down, crying about losing Kelsey to someone like Russell Falco." Steve popped the last bite of pizza into his mouth. "The lawyer couldn't shut him up."

"That's great that he talked. Did he go into any detail about what exactly he did that night?"

"Enough to convince me that he struck Falco on the

head with enough force to knock him into the water after he didn't take the hint to stay away from Kelsey."

Okay, that solved the mystery of Russell's cell phone and shoes not being found on his boat. They had to have been on him when he went into the water, but Steve was losing me with that last part. "What hint?"

"Greenwood slashed Russell's tires."

"He probably saw Kelsey with Russell that Monday night, just like Andy." And then flew into a jealous rage, as I had suspected, only I'd been looking at Pete Lackey, the wrong jealous guy.

"Sounded to me like that's when things started escalating."

"Because he hadn't done everything he did, including killing his wife, to lose Kelsey to Russell."

A humorless smile flickered across Steve's lips. "You got it."

Wow. "The fact that he told you all this should make it easier to charge him, right?"

"It should. Ben will have to make that determination sometime tomorrow, before arraignment."

"But you can at least tell Mitzi that you have a suspect in custody, right?"

Steve nodded. "She'd already heard it from Andy, but I told her."

"Good." Not that the knowledge of an arrest could dull the pain, but maybe it would serve as a first step in the healing process for Mitzi and her family.

He leaned back in his chair and took a long pull from his bottle. "Your turn to talk. How'd you happen to find that news story?"

"Listened in on a deposition this morning. Turned out that one of Lance Greenwood's buddies defrauded an old lady out of some valuable property—right next door to the Benoit Gallery. So it was just a matter of time before that whole investment deal came crashing down like a house of cards, but with the plans my mother had been making for that performing arts center, I knew that I'd have to provide a convincing argument for her to walk away. Then I stumbled onto that news story."

"That's also called following a lead." Steve lifted his bottle in a salute. "Way to go, rookie."

I couldn't help but smile. "It was a good day." A little tough on my diet with another celebration dinner, and my mother wasn't happy to see her investment plans go up in smoke, but still—it was a good day.

I reached for the pizza box with the cookies. "Are you ready for dessert?"

Grinning, he took my hand. "Yes, I am."

THE END

ABOUT THE AUTHOR

Wendy Delaney writes fun-filled cozy mysteries and is the award-winning author of the Working Stiffs Mystery series. A long-time member of Mystery Writers of America, she's a Food Network addict and pastry chef wannabe. When she's not killing off story people she can be found on her treadmill, working off the calories from her latest culinary adventure.

Wendy lives in the Seattle area with the love of her life and is a proud grandma. For book news please visit her website at www.wendydelaney.com, email her at wendy@wendydelaney.com, and connect with her on Facebook at www.facebook.com/wendy.delaney.908.

Made in the USA
Middletown, DE
18 June 2020

97731637R00189